Staked

By Chelsea Lynn Charters

Ink Smith Publishing

www.ink-smith.com

Book cover designed by Jeff DuBay

Formatted by V.J.O. Gardner

Edited by Corinne Anderson & Eric Marsh

Printed in the U.S.A

The final approval for this literary material is granted by the author.

ISBN: 978-1-947578-05-0

Ink Smith Publishing
710 S. Myrtle Ave Suite 209
Monrovia, CA, 91016

This book is dedicated to Aaron, who has encouraged my writing since the day we met. Thank you for having faith in me, always supporting me, and for showing me what true love is.

Chapter One

It was a chilly night for vampire hunting. I set up camp on top of an abandoned apartment building in downtown Chicago, along with my partners, Bill Sects and Harvey Johnson. To observe the neighboring building closely, we arranged our equipment with precision—snipers in their correct positioning, while other various weapons were kept in duffle bags within arm's reach. Our team had been given an anonymous tip that the decrepit structure was actually a vampire coven, and I wanted it heavily surveilled in the event the tip turned out to be valid.

We were first-rate hunters, excellent at what we did. Never was there a time when my team and I couldn't handle our mission. Our leader, Leland, was considered the best vampire hunter in Chicago, and he had personally trained us in the art of vampire slaying. We operated covertly, under Leland's guidance, and the general public knew nothing of our existence. Leland claimed it was better that way. If the city knew of the dangerous creatures lurking in the shadows, chaos would most certainly ensue.

However, tonight could prove to be rather dangerous, as I had reason to believe that the infamous vampire Stoney was hiding out in the building nearby. No matter what happened, I would not allow him a chance to escape. There was a silver bullet loaded in my gun with his name on it, and I sought to fire it straight through his stone-cold heart.

I had been tracking him for years, never actually seizing the opportunity to execute him on account of Leland, who always chastised my hastiness. But he wasn't with us tonight—I had made sure of it. Although Stoney was no easy mark, nothing would've been able to cease my motivation in taking him out. I had waited long enough to have my showdown with him, and tonight I was going to put an end to my twenty-year vendetta.

Unfortunately, I had to keep my team in the dark. They had no idea that I planned to invade the vampire coven. I had only relayed the orders that Leland had given me, which was to investigate the area and report our findings. Although I felt guilty, I had no choice but to conceal the real reason for us being here tonight. They would have never agreed to follow me in the first place if they had been aware of my true plans. Although I was the strongest, I wasn't naïve enough to think to go after Stoney without back-up.

I stood gingerly on the edge of the rooftop, with one foot planted on the roof, while the other hung halfway off the ledge. A pair of night vision binoculars in my hands, I skimmed the building thoroughly in search for the vampires. Suddenly, I spotted movement in one of the windows, and a rush of exuberance swept over me. I didn't need to see his face. I had a gut feeling about who the shadowy figure belonged to. There was no doubt in my mind that I had found Stoney.

"I knew it!" My voice shook with excitement, and I turned around to face my partners with a triumphant smile on my face. "He's in there! Stoney is hiding out next door."

Harvey frowned at me before replying. "Did you see him, Lina? Or are you jumping to conclusions again?"

With a roll of my eyes, I retreated from the ledge and trudged over toward my duffle bag. I removed a shotgun, two pistols, silver stakes, and all the ammunition I could carry from within the bag. After thrusting the small guns into the holsters around my thighs, I slung the shotgun strap over my head and down my back. I ignored Harvey's confused expression and slid the stakes into the empty slots on the inside of my black Kevlar vest, then strapped it securely.

"I thought this was a surveillance mission, Lina?" Harvey shouted as he rushed toward me. "What do you think you're doing?"

"What does it look like?"

He stiffened at my reply. "Come on, Lina. You're not that stupid."

I ignored his insult. "What did you think all these guns were for then?"

"A precaution, of course."

"You must have known something was up when I loaded all this weaponry."

He glanced over his shoulder at Bill, who was watching us with a grave expression on his face. "Bill, did you know about this?"

Bill shook his head. "No. Like you, I thought this was a survey and report back type of deal. I didn't know Leland gave us permission to infiltrate."

"That's because he didn't," I responded.

"You lied to us?" Harvey asked, glaring at me.

"I had to."

"Because of him?"

"Yes," I whispered, and glanced over at the warehouse, my heart racing with adrenaline at the thought of cornering the one vampire who had taken everything from me. I smiled as I tried to imagine the satisfaction I was going to experience once I shoved a stake through Stoney's cold, dead heart.

"Lina, it's too dangerous."

I glanced back at my team, their looks of disapproval not affecting me in the least. "I'm sorry to disappoint you boys, but I'm going."

"Lina, please don't do this."

"I have to, Johnson. I wouldn't expect you to understand why."

Harvey's hardened expression softened at my response. "I know why you're doing this, Lina, but you can't just barge in there. This isn't a weak, newborn vamp you're taking on. I mean, this is Stoney ..."

"And?"

"And we don't hunt vampire overlords without Leland." He sighed. "I don't know why I have to remind you that Stoney is the fiercest vampire in Chicago. You're tough, Lina, but not that tough," he muttered.

"I can handle Stoney," I replied, my tone firm.

"Can you? I know acting without thinking is how you usually operate, but—"

"Stop!" I interrupted him, holding up my hand. "I'm taking that asshole out tonight, Johnson. I've been waiting years for this moment, and now that Leland's not here, holding me back, I'm going to have my revenge!"

"Do you think your parents would want you risking your life like this?" Harvey asked. "You escaped Stoney once. You might not be so lucky this time."

I ignored Harvey's piercing stare and looked away, my gaze returning to the neighboring building. As I stood there, staring at the crumbling exterior of the vampire nest, I considered my options. I understood where Harvey was coming from—why he was concerned. I was nervous about facing Stoney myself, but I knew that if I let the opportunity pass me by, I may never get the chance to face him again.

"I'm sorry, Harvey, but I've already made up my mind."

Harvey sighed at my admission and threw up his hands. "Fine. If I can't change your mind, then I'm going with you."

"No," I told him. "I'm going alone. I need you to stay here and out of sight. You'll be a better help to me if you just keep watch." He appeared to be insulted, so I added, "I'm sorry, but I can't afford to worry about your safety while I'm in there. I need to be focused."

"I can take care of myself," Harvey began.

"I know you can, but this isn't your fight."

"Lina, it's a vampire coven, you can't go in there alone." His grey eyes flashed with worry. "I know that you hate Stoney—we all do—but you can't be reckless. Honestly, do I have to remind you what happened the last time you threw caution to the wind?"

I narrowed my brows at him. "He murdered my parents, Johnson. It's about time he paid for their deaths."

"Lina, please think this through. You can't—"

"I'm not having this discussion with you again! I'm going in that building, whether you like it or not."

Harvey glanced at Bill, and then back at me, his mouth curving into a frown. "Aren't you going to say anything, Bill?"

Bill shook his head. "Nope."

"She's going to get herself killed in there!" Harvey crossed his arms over his chest with a huff. "Not to mention, she'll be putting our lives in danger!"

"She'll be fine," Bill remarked.

"Jesus Christ, Bill! Can't you offer her any useful advice for once?"

Bill looked to Harvey and scratched his blonde head. He then turned to glance at me, and after giving me a long, stern look, he finally replied, "There's nothing I can say that will change her mind, Harvey. You know that. Lina's in charge, we have to follow her command."

I grinned at Bill, relieved that at least one of my teammates was on my side. However, I was a little surprised. Out of the three of us, Bill was the one who usually followed Leland's rules to a T.

"I knew I could count on you, Bill."

Harvey scowled at me. He was not amused. "You're such a stubborn bitch."

"I know."

"Leland won't like this, Lina. You need to think this decision through!"

5

"He doesn't have to know, Johnson. Besides, you know the penalty if you rat me out."

"Oh, come on! Don't start pulling rank on me when you're directly disobeying orders, Lina."

"But I am the captain of this team, Johnson. And it's like Bill said. You are to do as I say, and if you don't, and you rat me out to Leland, you know damn well that I can make your life a living hell."

Harvey sighed and rolled his eyes, but said nothing in return.

"I'm glad you see things my way. Now, keep your mouth shut and your eyes open. That's an order."

With a frown, he shoved his hands in his jacket pockets and replied, "It's too cold to deal with this shit."

"Oh, suck it up, you big baby." I blew Harvey a smug kiss and hurried towards the rooftop door, ignoring his final pleas as I went.

Once I passed through the door, I ran in the direction of the stairwell, pleased to see that there wasn't anyone hanging out in the hall. I figured there wouldn't be—it was an abandoned building after all. Usually the sight of me caused most civilians anxiety, on account of the weapons and combat gear I carried. It wasn't like I could hide my guns in my pockets, and I needed all the weapons I could carry if I was going to face Stoney. I quickly descended the empty stairwell, and prayed no civilians crossed my path tonight. My concern was focused solely on finding the vampire who murdered my parents. Instigating a commotion right now was the last thing on my to-do list.

The cold wind slapped my face as soon as I emerged from the side door of the apartment building, and I now walked towards the neighboring building, the one rumored to be the coven. I ignored the slight shiver that crept up my back, but I kept one hand near my right thigh, where one of my pistols was harnessed. Better to be safe than sorry.

I skulked closer towards the decaying structure, my eye out for anyone or anything suspicious. The alley was deathly quiet, which seemed unusual, but I ignored the alarms going off in my head and carried on. I couldn't stop now—not with Stoney only a few feet away. Once I realized the coast was clear, I carried on towards the entrance of the vampires' nest, keeping my stride brisk.

I tried to remain calm as I reached out to tug on the door handle, but as my fingertips grazed the metal piece, I overheard movement. Twisting my torso, I pulled my gun out and aimed it towards the dimly lit street. I narrowed my eyes when I found no one in the vicinity, but my grip was still firm on the gun. I knew better. Suddenly, a low growl sounded off behind me and I wasted no time. Jumping around, I pointed the barrel in the direction of the noise. Scowling at the sight of a raggedy-looking dog cowering before me, I sighed and kept on moving.

"Stupid mutt! Get lost!" I whispered, my voice hoarse, and waved it off. I watched it limber towards a fallen trashcan near the side of the building with a frown, and it was then that I noticed a cracked window just above the garbage can. After glancing back at the door, I decided against entering that way; the window would be much more covert.

As soon as I was about to make my move towards the window, my earpiece buzzed with Harvey's annoying voice. "Lina, what's going on? Are you inside yet?"

I reached for the radio and replied, "Not yet." I took a careful look around, making sure my voice hadn't alerted anyone. No one had emerged from the shadows and I breathed a quiet sigh of relief.

"Okay, well just be careful."

"I will."

"Bill and I have the third and fourth story windows covered. If you need anything else, Lina—"

"What I need right now, Harvey, is for you to shut up and let me get inside before one of those bloodsuckers finds me out here."

Harvey grumbled obscenities in my ear, but I ignored them all. I refused to give him the satisfaction. Instead, I holstered my gun and climbed atop the trash can, careful as to not make too much noise. I opened the window wider, which gave me enough room to hoist my body inside the dark building, and I landed on the dusty floor in a perfect crouched position.

Once I rose to my feet, I peered about the dim room, now finding myself inside a small abandoned office. The damp smell of the old building made me gag, but I was distracted by another scent that was lingering in the air. It was faint but distinct, and I stiffened when I realized it was blood. I reached for my gun quickly, and switched on the flashlight attachment, eager to expose every corner of the small room with light. However, I found no local threat. Taking a deep breath to steady my nerves, I crept towards the closed door and placed my ear gently against it.

There was not a sound to be heard. It was quiet on the other end of the door, and so I carried on, reaching for the rusty door handle. I opened the old door slowly, and it creaked and shook, but I kept my cool and waited with my gun raised. After hunting vampires for five years, I knew to always have my guard up. It was the only way to stay alive. However, to my surprise, nothing jumped out at me, and I waited another quiet moment before continuing on.

After ten minutes of wandering around inside the deteriorating office building, I was getting anxious. I hadn't spotted one vampire yet, and this was supposed to be their newest hiding spot. Leland had been tipped off from a reliable source, and so he had reason to believe that the tip was valid. If this was Stoney's coven, where were all the vampires? Something wasn't right here.

"Stoney, where are you?" I whispered to the darkness.

Then, a loud thumping noise sounded off from the room to my left. I froze and twisted my head to stare into a dark and open doorway. This was it, the moment I had been waiting for. I wasn't sure what I would encounter in the dark room, but if it was a vampire, I was going to enjoy killing it. I took a short breath and a rush of exhilaration surged through my body at the thought of Stoney waiting for me inside.

I advanced towards the doorway with a vigilant stride, my gun aimed at the black abyss. Once I crossed the threshold, the foul scent of blood filled my nostrils and I had to bite down onto my tongue to keep from gagging. Someone had died here, and due to the strong odor, it had been awhile since their blood was spilled. After a minute or so, I adapted to the harsh smell and moved on to inspect my surroundings.

The light from my gun traced empty walls, but when I directed it to the floor, it fell upon a miniature pale face. I studied the face closely, realizing it belonged to a small child. My throat burned with anger and I bent down towards the fallen corpse. His hazel eyes were opened wide and glazed over: he had passed and was not of the undead. When I touched the cold, ashen cheek of the dead boy, I had to fight back tears. Only a true monster was capable of ripping the life from a child, and I vowed to tear apart every vampire I found within the coven. No one would be safe from my stake. In my eyes, they were all responsible for the young boy's death.

There was slight movement from behind me and I gripped my gun and spun around, flashing the light in the direction of the noise. I almost dropped my weapon in surprise. There, sitting up against the wall, was a young woman. I stared into her pleading eyes and wondered what to do. I wasn't expecting to find a wounded civilian tonight. The woman's long brown waves were matted with blood, as was her white nightgown. She had a small gash on her right cheek, but the large hole in her neck, near her left shoulder was my main concern. Blood poured down the woman's

9

chest, and I knew she had been a fresh hunt. A small tremor of rage shook me at the thought of the woman being kept alive to suffer.

"Help ... me," the woman struggled to say, as she reached her hand out.

I walked over towards her, glancing out into the empty hallway as I went. I bent down to face the woman and asked, "Can you move?"

The woman shook her head and grimaced. "No. My neck—it hurts so much."

"I know it hurts," I replied with a sigh. There was no way I was going to be able to get out of the coven with the civilian successfully, and by the looks of her wound, the woman wouldn't last long if I moved her.

"Please help me. Those things, they—did this to me. They bit my neck and left me here, but they said they would be back soon."

"Shush now, it's all right," I assured her. I reached for my radio and whispered, "Harvey, I've got a civilian inside. She's badly injured."

I waited for his reply. After a minute or so, his voice blared into my ear.

"Someone's alive in there? Shit." There was a long pause on his end before he asked, "What do you need from us?"

"I don't know," I said with a sigh.

I glanced back at the woman and pondered my options, which weren't numerous. We could leave the same way I entered, but we'd have to be extra careful not to cause too much noise. It was suicide to get between a vampire and his kill. Their power nearly doubled when you tried to tear them away from their blood source. There were many obstacles I would have to face in order to retreat with the civilian out of the warehouse alive. It wasn't going to be easy. However, as I gazed over at the woman's pale, terror-stricken face, I knew it was worth a try. I couldn't just leave her to die. I would never forgive myself.

"Harvey, I'm getting her out of here. I'll radio you for back-up once we retreat from the west side of the building."

"Copy that."

Turning to face the ailing woman again, I removed a knife from my vest and bent down quickly to cut a strip of fabric from the hem of her gown. After presenting it to her, I said, "I'm going to tie this around your neck to stop the bleeding." I paused before doing so and added, "You might want to brace yourself. This is going to hurt."

The woman said nothing, only closed her eyes when I wrapped the fabric around her neck. I shuddered when the woman's blood dripped onto my hand, but I ignored the burning desire to wipe it away and carried on. When the fabric covered most of the wound, I gripped it and pulled, tying it into a fierce knot against her throat.

The woman gasped and bit down on her lip. "The pain!" she howled.

Turning to face her, I whispered, "I need you to stay quiet, all right? If they find us, it's over. Do you understand?" I then used all of the strength I had to stand the ailing woman. "Lean into me," I told her. I opened my arm to her and waited for her to grab onto me.

The woman did as she was told, but not before she took a long look at the boy on the floor. Her eyes brimmed with tears and she brought a hand to cup her face. "My son," the woman cried, her voice breaking. She turned to bury her face into my shoulder and I remained still, unsure of how to react. After an awkward moment, I rubbed her back for comfort.

As I consoled the sobbing woman, my throat burned with anger and regret. If only our team had arrived earlier, maybe then I would have made it in time to save the child. However, I knew this was not the moment for mourning. We had to act fast if we wanted to stay alive.

"You need to remain strong." I told her, holding onto the woman's arm to restrain her from flinging herself on top of the boy. "There will be time for that later. We have to get you out of here first."

The woman nodded but said nothing when I proceeded to walk her out of the room. I gazed down the dimly lit hallway, searching for danger. Nothing jumped out at us, and I took that as a good sign. I figured the coven must've been empty. The vampires would not have let me roam around in their haven for as long as I had. Once they realized just who was inside their coven, their pride would not have allowed it.

I retraced my steps, eager to return to the window I had climbed through earlier. The civilian proved to be stronger than she looked; not once did she ask me to slow down. I thought it rather odd. In the position she was in, she should've been scarcely able to move. But I didn't overthink it. All I could afford to concentrate on was getting out of the building safely.

When we stumbled into the tiny office, I breathed a sigh of relief that we had made it this far without any trouble. I did not doubt that I would be able to handle any vampires if they presented themselves, but it never proved to be an easy feat when I had to protect a life at the same time. No matter if I came in contact with a bloodsucker, I would not fail the suffering woman. Her safety was just as important as my own.

After a close inspection of the room, and once I deemed the coast was clear, I walked towards the cracked window and leaned the woman against the adjoining wall.

"Why are we stopping?" the woman asked, her brown eyes full of fear. "Is something wrong?"

"No, don't worry. Everything is fine. I just need to call for backup."

"What for?"

"As a precautionary measure," I responded, and then I raised my radio up toward my mouth. "Harvey, I need you and Bill to keep a lookout for me on the ground floor. I'm retreating with the civilian."

I glanced out of the window, gazing up at the rooftop of the neighboring building. I frowned when I couldn't see the men, and worry crept up my back when Harvey didn't respond. Pressing the radio again, I whispered, "Harvey, are you there?"

My earpiece blared with my teammate's irritated voice. "Yeah, yeah. We heard you, Lina. We've got you covered."

"Thanks," I responded. Glancing back at the young woman, I motioned towards the window and said, "Come on. We're almost home free."

The woman approached the window but hesitated, now staring out at the empty street. "What if they're out there waiting for us?" she asked me, her voice shaky. "They told me they would never let me go."

"Don't worry." I placed a warm hand onto her shoulder. "My team and I will protect you."

"How can you protect me?" the woman replied, skepticism on her face. "You're just a woman, like me. Those things aren't … they're not—"

"Human? I know." I disregarded the woman's fears and guided her against the window. "You have to climb outside now. I know you're scared, but I need you to trust me. We don't have much time left before they return."

Her eyes widened with surprise as she stared back at me. "Aren't you afraid?" she inquired.

"No."

My voice was steady, confident, and I kept my expression firm. I knew the woman was afraid, but I couldn't afford to be. In my many years of experience in hunting vampires, fear only made you weak and stupid. I had seen my share of hunters succumb to their fear of the monsters that came out at night, and I had watched those same monsters rip the life source straight from their veins. If you wanted to stay alive, fear wasn't an emotion you were allowed to possess.

The young woman continued to watch me, and she must've realized I was serious, because she climbed out the window without another word. I waited until she had successfully crawled off the trash can before I lifted my leg over the windowsill. I paused for a moment and glanced over my shoulder, considering the idea of journeying deeper inside the building. But I knew Stoney was not here. He would've made his presence known shortly after I'd broken in. He hated me almost as much as I loathed him, and our confrontations always ended in a plethora of bruises, bloody cuts, and insults.

I rubbed at my tense neck and resisted the urge to scream. The disappointment in missing the opportunity to face my enemy was great, but after taking one last look around the dark and musty office room, I tucked away my regret and joined the civilian outside. The ailing woman was my mission now, and I could not leave her to her injuries. Staking Stoney would have to wait … for now.

Chapter Two

"Harvey, we're out."

I led the injured woman across the alley and back towards the apartment building. While we waited on my team to respond, I checked on the woman, who was now leaning up against the brick wall. I could tell by the vacant expression on her pale face that she didn't have much time left. She had lost a lot of blood, and only a transfusion could save her life. Thankfully, if we made it to a hospital, they would be able to take care of her wounds. The tough part would be getting there without any interference.

Static filled my ear as Harvey replied, "Bill sees you." He paused before asking, "What now?"

"I need to get this woman to a hospital as soon as possible. She needs a blood transfusion."

"How much time does she have left?"

I gave the woman a quick once-over, then cupped my mouth and whispered, "Not much. Maybe an hour or so at the most."

"Copy that," Harvey replied. "We'll meet you at the rendezvous point."

"Gotcha."

I searched the alley, my brows narrowing upon the realization that my motorcycle was missing, as were Harvey's and Bill's. I brought my radio up to my mouth. "Where are our bikes, Johnson?"

"What do you mean? The motorcycles are right where we parked them."

"No, they aren't," I responded with a snort. "They're not fucking out here!"

There was pause on his end before he muttered, "Oh shit."

I gazed up at the rooftop, where Harvey and Bill were camped out, and I exhaled from annoyance when Harvey peeked his head out over the ledge. He locked eyes with me first, before turning to look up and down the alley. When he noticed the bikes were missing, Harvey then reached for his radio to whisper, "It looks like they got to our vehicles."

"You've got to be fucking kidding me!" I retorted, now gritting my teeth. "You two had one job: survey and guard the surrounding area. I'm gone for less than thirty minutes, and you let the vampires hijack our motorcycles? What use are you two?"

"Hey!" Bill spoke up. "It was Harvey's fault. I told him to watch the alley after you went inside."

"Thanks a lot, Bill. Just throw me into the fire, why don't ya?"

"Well, you should have been paying more attention," Bill shot back.

"Okay, boys …" I interrupted, feeling a headache coming on. "Enough with the bickering. The bikes are gone—there's nothing we can do about it now. We're going to have to make it back on foot."

"That sucks," Harvey replied.

"Yeah, well, I don't like it either, Johnson, but I'm out of options. I can't use the bus or hail a cab because I don't want to get any other civilians involved in this. It's too dangerous. Besides, they'll ask too many questions." I took a deep breath to steady my nerves before adding, "There's not much time left for this woman and I'm definitely not going to spend it arguing with you two. I'm taking her to the hospital. I'll radio you when I get there."

I snapped the radio back onto my vest and reached for the woman. "Are you ready?"

"Where are you taking me?" the woman asked, her voice barely audible. "To a hospital, right?"

I nodded, but was confused as to how she hadn't overheard me telling Harvey I was taking her to the hospital. I figured the pain she was in was causing her to slip farther from reality. I draped her arm over my right shoulder carefully and allowed her to lean most of her weight against me. Once I felt her body relax, I checked her makeshift gauze, noticing that the blood had already soaked through it. The woman's time was ticking away. We needed to act fast.

Not wanting to bring anymore unnecessary attention to ourselves, I removed my black leather jacket and draped it around the woman's shoulders, hoping to conceal most of her blood soaked gown. Without another moment's hesitation, I rushed out of the alley and out into the open street. The woman and I scrambled down the empty sidewalk, and while I kept her on her feet, I made sure my eyes were trained for threats as well. For some reason, I had a strong feeling that we were being watched. I scanned the tops of the buildings in the surrounding area, searching for signs of danger. Thankfully, I found nothing out of the ordinary, but it did not put my mind at ease. Only when I caught sight of the main street did I finally breathe a sigh of relief.

The loud buzz of the busy street was like a safety net, and as soon as we stepped foot onto the main stretch of downtown, I knew we were finally safe. Vampires didn't like to attack their prey in the open, so for now we were out of harm's way. I reached for my radio again, eager to report my progress to the team.

"Harvey, we're good to go. Meet you in ten," I reported, and after I tucked the radio away, we continued on down the sidewalk.

By now, I figured we were home free, but when I overheard the faint sound of gunfire, I came to an abrupt standstill. The woman clung to me, frightened by the noise, and I soothed her fears the best I could. I glanced back at the empty street from where we had just emerged, searching for the rooftop of the building where my friends were camped. My stomach dropped when I saw nothing. I was too far away to get a visual.

With my free hand, I unlatched my radio and brought it to my lips. "Johnson, what's the situation?"

Unfortunately, Harvey did not reply. A few seconds passed by and there was still no response from him, causing me to fear the worst. Had the vampires overpowered Bill and Harvey? If they had, I knew they would not keep them alive, not even to use as bait. If a vampire got a hold of a hunter, they were rarely left breathing. Suddenly, heavy static emitted from the headset, and I grinned with relief when Harvey's voice buzzed in my ear again.

"Damn bloodsuckers," Harvey growled. "They just came out of nowhere!"

"Are you okay?" I asked.

"Yeah. They jumped us when we were trying to leave the rooftop, but I took them both down." I overhead Harvey mumble something to Bill before he added, "Mr. Sects wasn't much help though."

I breathed a sigh of relief that they were both unharmed, and I continued on walking down the sidewalk. "I'm glad you guys are all right." However, my reassurance was cut short when I came to the sudden realization that the vampires were on to us. "I guess that means they know I raided their coven."

"Yeah," he replied. "I told you going in there was a bad idea."

"Just keep your eyes out for them. I'm sure there are more coming after us."

"I know we're protecting mankind and everything, but fuck this career choice," Harvey exclaimed. "I should've taken that job at Lowe's when I had the chance."

"You would've hated working at Lowe's and you know it," I told him.

"How do you know?"

Staked

"Because you would have never had the opportunity to shoot anybody."

There was a pause on his end. "You're right ... but at least then I wouldn't be having horribly vivid nightmares of vampires ripping out my insides with their bare hands."

"Jesus, Harvey," I muttered, shaking my head. All of a sudden, the ailing woman slumped down against my left shoulder, her feet dragging along the pavement. I used all the strength in my left arm to prop her up, and she moaned from discomfort when I forced her to keep walking. I knew she was suffering, but I couldn't give her a chance to rest. We had to keep moving.

"Just hurry up and get down here!" I shouted into the radio, before snapping it back onto my vest.

"Roger that."

As we carried on, I guided the woman closer towards the bustling city street. Every step we took seemed to cause the woman more pain, and I was unsure what to do with her. We were miles from any hospital, and the only place closer, where I knew someone could perform a successful transfusion, was back at home base.

I stole a glance at the woman, frowning once I noticed how pale she'd become in the last few minutes. When her feet began to drag again, I was forced to wrap her right arm around my shoulders to keep her from collapsing onto the ground. From the sorry state she was in, I realized that she would not last much longer. Taking civilians back to our base was against protocol, but it was the only chance the woman had left at survival. I was confident that we would not make it to a hospital in time. She would bleed to death on the sidewalk.

"I'm bringing the civilian back to base," I informed my team as she and I staggered down the sidewalk. I ignored the heavy stares from the handful of citizens who passed by us on the sidewalk, but I envied their innocence and naivety. They had no

19

idea of the monsters lurking in the shadows. The boogeyman was real, and he had fangs.

"Lina, are you sure that's a good idea?" Harvey asked me. "Leland won't like it."

"I know," I admitted with a sigh. "But it's the only option we have left. She'll bleed out by the time we reach a hospital."

"Why didn't you just call an ambulance?"

"Oh, that's a great idea, Harvey! Let's endanger more innocent lives by bringing them into this dangerous fucking situation. I don't need to baby-sit anymore civilians!"

I glanced down at the woman, wondering if she had been listening in on my conversation with Harvey. However, I noticed that she appeared to be in a daze; her brown eyes were cloudy and aloof, and upon asking if she was feeling all right, she did not respond. The woman's condition had grown far worse in a matter of minutes.

"Okay, Lina," Harvey responded. "We're behind you one hundred percent. Bill and I, we—"

Harvey's voice cut off in mid-sentence, causing my shoulders to tense up. When he didn't speak, I began to worry, once again, that my team was in danger.

"Johnson?"

This time, there was no response. Only silence.

"Shit," I muttered, quickening my pace. The woman moaned and began pawing at her neck, but I forced her to keep moving her feet. We only had a few more blocks to go before we would make it back to the underground bunker—the secret vault where my team resided. Completely vampire proof, it was the safest place in all of Chicago. Leland would be waiting there, and that thought brought nothing but warmth to my heart. He would let no harm befall me, and I knew that he would do his best to save the dying woman.

As we hurried down the sidewalk, I scanned the surrounding rooftops, in search of any possible threats. I knew that

20

if the vampires had already gotten to Harvey and Bill, they were most certainly on my trail. Nevertheless, if they made an attempt against me, I would stop at nothing to fend them off. Fortunately, the rooftops were clear, and it seemed as if no vamps were following us at the moment.

I found this odd. My partners, although effective, were not matched in my combat skills. Even though they had killed a fair share of vampires, my headcount surpassed both Harvey's and Bill's put together. It was why the undead hated me, and why they always targeted me over my male counterparts. I didn't mind that vampires wanted me dead. Their hatred gave me sheer satisfaction. It meant that I was doing a good job—a damn good one at that.

"Jesus Christ!" a male voice blared through the headset, the shrill sound causing me to wince. "He's dead ... he's fucking dead."

I realized it was Bill who was speaking. "Sects, what happened?" I asked him, growing nervous from his recent statement. "Are you injured? Where's Johnson?"

"She got him, Lina," he replied. "She fucking took him!"

"Who took him, Bill?"

There was crying on his end, and my breathing turned heavy. No matter what Bill saw, I couldn't believe that Harvey was gone without proof. "I couldn't save you, Harvey," Bill said, and I realized he was still holding the button down on the radio. "I'm so sorry ..."

When he finally opened the line, I spoke again. "Bill, I know you're upset, but if you didn't see her kill him in front of you, there may be a chance that he's still alive. Now, I need you to focus and tell me who took Harvey, so I can try to find him."

There was a considerable pause on his end before he whispered, "Scarlett."

My brows narrowed with anger at the vampire's name. I knew Scarlett well. My team had come into contact with her once before. Scarlett was Stoney's right hand, and she was as powerful as she was beautiful, with long red hair that fell in waves and sharp red eyes. It was how she got the nickname. Just one stare from her, and it cut into you like a knife. Scarlett was a formidable foe and was not to be underestimated.

"Okay, Bill. Can you tell me which way they went?"

"Toward the sewers," he murmured. "I heard them remove the manhole cover out in the street."

I drew a deep breath and glanced down at the woman in my arms. I didn't know what to do. If I left the civilian on her own and went to search for Harvey, she would most certainly bleed out, or worst-case scenario, the vampires would reclaim her. Out of options, I realized I had no choice but to pray that my teammate was strong enough to fend off Scarlett. I unfortunately agreed with Bill in thinking Harvey was already done for. Just like her sire, Stoney, Scarlett took no prisoners.

Suddenly there was heavy static on the radio, mixed with ear-piercing screaming, and my heart stopped cold. "No! Please, don't—" It was the voice of Bill once again, and with one last scream, his line went dead.

"Sects?" I pressed the earpiece closer against my inner ear, hoping to hear him respond. "Bill, are you there?"

After a minute of unwavering silence, soft laughter came in through the headset, but it wasn't Bill's. I swallowed the lump in my throat as I listened to the female vampire giggle over the frequency. I knew whose voice I was listening to, and it made me see absolute red.

"Lina Holiday, we're coming for you," Scarlett whispered, trying her best to frighten me. "We killed your friends, and now we're going to kill you."

"I don't think so, Red," a familiar voice spoke up.

My crushed spirits lifted at the sound of Harvey's weak voice. "Harvey, you're alive?"

"Barely," he muttered. "But yeah, I guess you could say so. That vamp you sent to deal with me, Scarlett, wasn't much of a challenge. He didn't even check to make sure I was dead before taking off."

There was loud hissing on the third line, and I overheard Scarlett chastising one of her vampire lackeys. "Yes, well, he's a newborn and doesn't know the rules. But don't worry, hunter," she said with a snort. "Someone will be there to deal with you shortly."

"Why don't you come down to the sewers and deal with me yourself, Scarlett? Or are you too chicken-shit?"

The vampire laughed, but eventually agreed. "Why not? If you want something done right, you have to do it yourself."

"Good girl."

"Harvey, no," I pleaded over the radio. "You can't face her on your own. Let me deal with the bitch."

"You have a civilian with you, Lina. It's no good," he told me. "I'll be okay."

"I hear the doubt in your voice, hunter," Scarlett said, teasing him. "You're not a fool. You know you won't make it past me. As for you, Lina, I've already sent some hungry vamps to deal with you—and to collect our human. They'll be seeing you shortly."

"I look forward to it," I snapped.

"I suggest you two say your goodbyes now," the vampire laughed. "You won't be seeing each other again."

Although I didn't agree with Scarlett's assumption of our probable deaths, I figured it wouldn't be a bad idea to tell Harvey how much I valued his friendship. After all, I'd never had a chance to tell Bill before Scarlett killed him. Now that he was gone, I wished I had.

"I know you're going to give this fight with Scarlett your all, Harvey, but don't let her manipulate you. Stay focused, all right? I have faith in you, Johnson. You can beat her."

"Yes. Stay focused, Harvey," Scarlett chuckled. "Who are we kidding? You and I both know that you got a hard on the last time we came into contact. It's going to be so easy for me to break you."

"You hypnotized me! I had no control over it," Harvey replied.

"Right," she muttered, and then the loud splash of water blared through the headsets. "Well, sorry to cut this short, but I believe Mr. Johnson and I have some unfinished business to take care of." With a twisted laugh, she added, "Ta-ta, Lina," and the third line clicked off.

"Take her out, Harvey," I whispered, fighting back the tears in my eyes as the civilian and I crossed the next street. I was glad he wasn't able to see how distraught I was at the thought of his demise.

"Lina, before I die, there's something I have to tell you," he replied, his tone of voice worrying me. "Wait … I think I hear her coming."

"Harvey, you're not going to die! Just stay focused like I said and you'll be fine. Whatever it is that you have to tell me, you can tell me later, okay?"

He let out a weak laugh and said, "I may never get the chance to tell you again. You know that."

"Don't think that way, Johnson. You're going to be all right. We're both going to make it out of this alive."

"Either way, I think you should know the truth," he replied, and it was at that moment that I detected the faint sound of splashing water coming from his end. Scarlett was almost upon him now, and the sentimental state he was currently in was going to cloud his judgment and reaction time. I knew that Harvey had to concentrate in order to make it out of those sewers alive.

"Harvey, Scarlett's getting closer," I warned him. "I can hear her moving towards you."

"I know. I hear her too. Listen, Lina, I know this isn't great timing, but I need to tell you how I feel. I should have told you this a long time ago, but I—"

His voice was suddenly cut off by the violent sound of gunfire and splashing water. I overheard Harvey struggling with his foe, and the image of their scuffle was clear in my mind. Suddenly, there was more gunfire, followed by a deep scream, which caused me to gasp. The scream had sounded masculine, and I was certain it had come from Harvey. Before I had a chance to ask him if he was okay, the line dropped.

"Oh, Harvey," I whispered, finally allowing myself to cry as I mourned for my dead colleagues. I could hardly believe that the two men I had trained with—grown up with, were gone. I had lost my family all over again, and just like before, it was at the hands of vampires. At that moment, I vowed to avenge Harvey and Bill, by making the vampire responsible for their deaths, pay.

"Who is Harvey?" the woman asked, snapping me out of my gloomy thoughts.

"A friend of mine," I told her as I wiped away my tears. "But he's gone now."

"I'm sorry. Did those things kill him?"

I nodded. "Yes."

"Are they going to kill us too?" she asked, her voice shaking. "They're coming for us, aren't they?"

"No," I told her, trying my best to sound confident. "No one else is going to die tonight."

We successfully crossed another block, but I struggled to remain calm. I did not want the woman to see me distraught. Her already frazzled nerves couldn't handle to watch her rescuer break down. With a deep breath, I let go of my frail emotions and focused on the task at hand. We were only a short distance away from the base, but I was aware that getting past the vampires Scarlett sent our way was not going to be an easy feat. If they weren't already waiting for us near the entrance, they were close by.

The base was more like a vault than an actual building, and its entrance was located inside an abandoned factory on the outskirts of town. Our leader, Leland, had the bunker constructed in the early eighties, but he had made quite a few adjustments to the old structure over the years. One of the upgrades had been adding UV lights above the door, to keep vampires from breaking into our headquarters while we were out hunting. Two thousand watts of light that was motion activated, so no vampire could get past them without frying. I was grateful for them tonight because once we stepped inside the frame of the light we would be safe.

"Are we there yet?" the woman inquired, leaning her head against me carefully.

"Yes," I replied, as I led her inside the decaying building. "You're safe now."

We hurried through the abandoned factory, avoiding fallen walls and dangerous debris. Once the door to the vault came into view, I grinned, relishing in the bright glow of the UV lights. I towed the woman towards the metal door, and just as I made the attempt to unlock it, I heard the scuffling of feet from behind. I peeked over my shoulder, and there, standing in the shadows, were Scarlett's vampire groupies. There were about four vampires in total, and they were hanging back in the shadows, standing two feet from the edge of the light.

I had had a feeling that we were being stalked as soon as we made it inside the factory. I had waited for my vampire foes to make the first move, but when they hadn't, I realized this was a better outcome. Although I could've faced off with all four of them had it been necessary, I was overjoyed at the look of disappointment on their ugly faces. It went against Leland's strict idea of training, but I found that toying with the enemy was nearly as fun as killing them.

"Sorry, boys," I told them with a cheerful smile. "Looks like you'll have to dine elsewhere tonight."

"Bitch!" the largest vampire in the pack growled. He looked to be at least six feet tall and made of solid muscle. His long brown hair was pulled in to a loose braid and his thick shoulders heaved as he glared daggers at me.

26

"You hide behind that light in fear, hunter, because you know damn well that you're no match for us!"

The other vampires nodded in unison. "Yeah, some hunter you are!" another vamp said, with a snicker. "I've fought eighteen-year-old girls with more guts."

I smirked at the vampire's mediocre insults, but decided against responding. Now turning my back to them, I placed my palm against the fingerprint scanner, which was another upgrade of Leland's. When the screen flashed green and the metal door slid open, I entered the vault with the woman, ignoring the loud hissing objections from the vampires.

I took care in bringing the woman down the flight of stairs that led to the first floor of the underground bunker, and guided her towards a couch centered in the bleak cement foyer. After I sat her down and made sure she was comfortable, I reached for the speaker system on the wall behind me and buzzed the medical wing, where I knew Switch, our lead physician, would be.

I waited until his voice buzzed through the speaker. "Yes?"

"Switch, there's a woman in need of immediate medical attention in the foyer. She's bleeding out, and needs a transfusion as soon as possible."

There was a considerable pause on his end before he responded. "Lina, you know that it's against protocol to bring civilians to base."

"She's dying, Switch. We can argue about protocol later."

"All right. I'll be right there."

I turned to face the woman and said, "I have someone coming to take care of you. You don't have to worry anymore." After giving her a reassuring smile, I turned to walk back towards the staircase. I was eager to face the smart-mouthed vampires outside, but the woman slid off of the couch and latched on to my arm, preventing me from leaving.

"Please, don't go out there," she begged me. The woman was clutching at her neck with her free hand, and I noticed that more blood had begun to trickle down her ashen skin. "Don't leave me alone."

"You won't be alone. Switch—the doctor, will take good care of you," I assured her. "You'll be in good hands. He won't let anything happen to you."

"If you go outside, they'll kill you!" the woman replied, fear etched in her eyes. "They're monsters!"

I nodded, agreeing with her statement. "I know they are. That's why they must be stopped."

I flashed her a confident smile before marching towards the staircase, which led to the exit of the vault. I balled my hands into fists as I went. I was itching to tear the undead group apart. When the metal door finally slid open, I grinned and stepped back into the UV light. The vampires had begun walking away, but they froze in their tracks when they detected my presence. I laughed at the shocked expressions on the vampire's faces, including the large, boisterous one.

"What's with the surprised looks?" I asked them, still grinning. "Did you honestly think I was going to let you four get away?"

The large vamp growled, baring his fangs at me as he shouted, "You talk big, hunter, but until you step out of that UV light, your threats are meaningless!"

My brows narrowed at the vampire's protest, but my pulse was steady. The idea of retreating from the protection of the light overhead did not frighten me in the slightest. "Okay then."

I sauntered towards the group of bloodsuckers, and the thirst in their eyes did not bother me at all. When I neared the edge of the light, my pulse began to race, but it was not on account of fear. Quite the contrary. What was coursing through my veins now was due to pure exhilaration.

As soon as I retreated from the bright light and allowed darkness to wash over me, my body surged with adrenaline. I looked to each vampire, determining which would attack me first.

To my surprise, none made an attempt to strike. My eyes then fell on the loud-mouthed insolent vampire, curious as to why he seemed so hesitant to make the first move.

"Cold feet?" I asked the vampire with a smirk.

He growled, and ignored the muffled chuckles from his undead brethren. "I've never been more anxious to kill a human before," he told me, trying to sound menacing. "I will enjoy tearing out your heart, vampire hunter."

I laughed and took a step towards him, tilting my head back to stare up into his black, soulless eyes. "I was going to stake you first, but I feel your smart mouth has earned you a slow and agonizing death."

The vampire snickered at my threat. "Don't be absurd! You're the one who's going to suffer!"

"We'll see about that."

Then, before he had a chance to respond, I yanked both pistols out of their holsters. I aimed one barrel at the large vampire's chest, and the other at his group.

"Are you leeches ready to die?"

Just as I had predicted, one of the vampires in the group lunged for me, while the others spread out. I fired one silver bullet at the advancing vamp, and it struck him in the chest. He growled with pain and made an attempt to reach for me again, but he froze suddenly, his black eyes growing wide with fear.

I watched smoke rise out of the hole in his chest; it was the silver doing a fine job of burning him from the inside out. However, I noticed that the bullet had missed his heart, and I sprinted towards the vamp, removing one of the silver stakes fastened on the inside of my vest as I went. Then, as soon as I was upon him, I drove the stake straight through the vampire's heart. His entire body exploded in a matter of seconds, and he was now just a bloody mess beneath my boots.

There were two different tactics when it came to killing vampires. The most popular way was to cut off their head and let them shrivel up. It was less messy than my preferred technique, which involved staking them right through the heart. It caused the vampire to erupt from the inside out. It was quite disgusting.

His gruesome death didn't stop the other vampires from attacking though. Another rowdy vamp jumped me from behind, shoving me to the ground. I simply laughed, my adrenaline still pumping as I somersaulted backwards. There was nothing I loved more than a challenge, and facing a vampire who fought back was much more interesting than facing one who did not. With a huff, I rose to my feet just as my undead enemy tried to sink his fangs into my neck, but I gave him a head-butt before he had a chance to have a taste.

"Sorry, no free samples," I told him, and then delivered a violent kick to his stomach.

The vampire howled and stumbled backward, and I wasted no time. I ran towards him at full speed, the stake in my hand outstretched and ready. The vampire recoiled and made an effort to elude my attack, but I was too quick for him. As soon as he tried to escape, I leapt onto his backside and wrestled him to the ground.

We struggled for a few moments, until I came out on top. I kicked at the vampire's head with the heel of my boot, which was, unbeknownst to him, coated with silver. He hissed as I pressed the heel deep into his neck, and his pale skin turned black. The vampire was done for—he knew it too, and once I was through torturing the soulless creature, I staked him.

As soon as the vampire was nothing more than a pile of blood and goo, I turned around to search the dark factory for the leader of the group. I was disappointed to find that he had escaped during the commotion. However, there was still one vampire lingering in the shadows. He looked terrified to death—confused even. I had seen the same expression many times before. Vampires were so arrogant. They assumed that just because they were immortal, they would come out of every skirmish unscathed. Boy, were they dead wrong.

"Hey, you!" I called out to the vampire, and began to stroll in his direction.

The vampire backed away from me, desperately searching for a route of escape. His worried expression worsened when he realized he had nowhere to run. He held up his hands as if surrendering, but it was too late in the game to raise the white flag. Under different circumstances, I might have given the vampire a second chance at existence out of pity. But his friends had slaughtered my comrades, and he was going to pay for their deaths.

"There's nowhere for you to go," I told him, shaking my head as I drew closer. "Just accept your fate and die."

With an evil sneer, the vampire turned and ran in the opposite direction, ignoring my loud groan of disapproval. I lifted my pistol and took aim; my hands steady as I fired one single shot. The silver bullet struck the vampire in the sweet spot, straight through the heart, and I watched him fall to his knees. The vampire deteriorated in a matter of seconds, blood and guts now decorating the cement ground.

Even after slaying vampires for ten years, I still found the way they expired disgusting. Although I loved a good staking, their deaths were messy, and a bitch to clean up.

I holstered the gun, and without a second glance at the now permanently incapacitated vamp, I trudged back towards the entrance to the vault, eager to return to my wounded guest—and to wash the vampire guts off of my face.

Chapter Three

Once I returned to the vault, I noticed that Switch was in the process of moving the civilian onto a stretcher, no doubt intending to wheel her to the small hospice. I managed a smile at the sight of Switch's frazzled hairdo, and followed him back to the hospice, not yet making my presence known.

He rolled the woman towards a station that appeared to be set up with an IV and heart monitor. Once he noticed I had walked into the room, he motioned for me to assist him in lifting the woman. I obliged without a word, and the two of us raised her off of the stretcher and onto the crisp, white bed. I studied the woman's pale face, my heart dropping to the pit of my stomach when I noticed she wasn't conscious.

Switch checked the woman's vitals first, before placing his attention on her neck, where the bandages were coming loose. Blood was dried along most of the tender skin. With a sharp inhale he unraveled the rest of the bloody fabric strip from around the woman's throat. He grimaced when he caught sight of the torn and decaying flesh underneath.

"Jesus," he murmured, taken aback by the condition of her neck.

"It's bad, isn't it, Switch?"

"I'm afraid so," he agreed. "I'm surprised she even made it this far with such a terrible wound. I've seen civilians die in a matter of minutes from far less severe vampire bites."

"Her will to live is strong."

Switch reached for a damp white cloth and began washing the woman's neck, wiping away all traces of dried blood. Once he had thoroughly cleaned the area, he pulled a small metal table towards him, which contained a pair of scissors, more rags, needles, and thread. I watched quietly as he stitched her wound, and I was grateful that the woman was passed out and unable to feel the needle mending her flesh.

I glanced down at her ashen face, noticing how it was void of any expression. She reminded me of a corpse. "Is she going to make it?" I asked him, once he had finished stitching her up.

Switch used a fresh cloth to clean his hands, and then reached his hands up to rub his temples. For some reason, my question seemed to bother him. "Honestly, I don't know." His tone hardened as he added, "She's going to need a blood transfusion, just as you recommended."

"Which is why I had to bring her back here," I said, knowing where he was going with that remark. "If I had left her inside that coven, she would have died."

"So, in exchange for saving her life, you endanger everyone else's?" Switch muttered, shaking his head. "I saw that pack of vampires on the surveillance camera, Lina. What were you thinking bringing her here?"

"What would you have had me do? I couldn't just leave her to die, Switch."

"You could have taken her to a hospital."

"That was the plan, but our bikes were stolen, and I didn't want to involve any more innocent people in this mess."

"Your bikes were stolen?" Switch replied. "How did that happen?"

"How do you think?"

"Vampires?" he asked. Once I nodded, he muttered, "That's not good."

"I wasn't happy about bringing her here either, but now don't you see? I had no choice."

"Yes, well … this civilian's well-being is hardly our first priority. Once again, you did not follow protocol."

I glared at him. "Fuck protocol! You didn't see this poor woman's child lying in a pool of his own blood—his skin cold and pale. I had to save her, Switch. I couldn't leave her to the same horrible fate."

He fell silent at my curt admission, but after a moment, he replied, "People die, Lina. You know that, and I know that. In our line of work, death stalks us everywhere we go. You can't escape it … and you can't be expected to save everyone."

My face heated at Switch's cold words. "I would have rather died trying to protect this woman than to pass her by without a second glance. You don't work the field, Switch—you have no idea what goes on out there."

"You're right. I don't hunt vampires. I'm a healer—that's my line of work. However, I do know that you're a loose cannon, Lina, and the next time something like this happens, you might not make it back here alive."

"I really appreciate your vote of confidence, Switch."

Switch sighed and shook his head. "I only say this to you because I care. I don't want to see something like this happening to you," he said, motioning to the unconscious woman.

"I'll be fine," I snapped. "I always am."

He frowned at my stubborn reply. "Please put your priorities in order, Lina! Are civilian lives really worth yours or your teammates?"

I stiffened at the mention of Bill and Harvey. Switch had no idea that our friends perished, and I didn't want to have that conversation with him just yet. The pain was still too fresh. I scowled and turned my back on him, as my bottled emotions were on the verge of imploding. Before I had a chance to flee the room, he grabbed hold of my arm, holding me in place.

Still refusing to face him, I took a deep breath to steady my nerves. "Let go of me, Switch."

"Where are Sects and Johnson?" he inquired, ignoring my demand. "I haven't seen or heard from them since your return." When I said nothing, his grip on my arm tightened.

"Where?"

"I don't want to talk about this right now."

"God dammit, Lina! Where the hell are they?"

I finally turned back around, and once I faced him again, I knew that the guilt on my face was a dead giveaway. Switch didn't have to ask what the look meant. He dropped his hold on my arm and backed away, dragging his hands through his messy blonde hair.

"What happened?" he asked after a moment of silence had passed.

"It's all my fault," I replied, bowing my head. "Fucking Stoney and his vile lackeys!"

"Stoney?" Switch uttered the vampire's name. "You ran into Stoney tonight?"

"Not exactly," I sighed, and my cheeks flushed with shame. "We located one of his hideouts, and I went inside to investigate, hoping to draw him out."

Switch glared at me. "You've got to be kidding me, Lina! You went to face Stoney on your own—without any back-up, and without Leland?"

"I know it was stupid!" I shot back, my temper rising. "I just thought—"

"No! You weren't thinking!" he interrupted. "If you had been thinking, Lina, your team would still be alive, and there wouldn't be an unconscious woman lying in our hospice!"

I opened my mouth to argue, but I closed it when I realized he was right. I swallowed the lump in my throat and whispered, "I'm sorry, Switch. I really am. I didn't want any of this to happen."

"We don't have time for this right now," he responded, and waved his hand at me. "We've got to give this woman a blood transfusion before she dies, which I don't want to have happen in my infirmary. Also, we aren't even sure if she fed off of a vampire, which gives cause for concern. If she did, we have a possible vamp inside our base."

"I don't think she did …" I whispered, feeling foolish for never even considering the possibility.

"You don't know, therefore, it's possible. If this woman turns, Lina, you're going to take care of her."

I nodded. "Okay."

"Now, if you don't mind, I would prefer to work on her alone."

"I can help—"

"I've got a lot to do in here, and I don't need you getting in the way." Switch turned his back on me then, which was equivalent to a slap in the face. And it hurt just as much.

"I'll leave," I said, swallowing the lump that had formed in my throat. "But first I need to know where Leland is. I've got to tell him what happened …"

My voice faltered at the prospect of explaining Harvey and Bill's deaths to him. He was going to be so disappointed in me. I had failed my team, all on account of my personal vendetta against Stoney. As I stared down at my hands, I wondered how I was going to be able to live with the knowledge that I was solely responsible for my friends' deaths.

"He's not here. He left a few hours ago," he explained. "I don't know where he went."

The information was useless, and I turned away from Switch without a reply. I knew he didn't want to be around me after what I'd done, and I would happily grant him his isolation. I hurried towards the washroom, eager to feel the refreshing sensation of a hot shower. As soon as I reached the large bathroom, I stripped down and jumped into the shower stall, turning the hot water on full blast.

The water burned my skin, but I welcomed the harsh feeling. As I scrubbed at my body, I noticed that the water now swirling down the drain was bright red. The reality of my situation suddenly came crashing down on me, and I leaned my head against the cool white tile, closing my eyes and unable to breathe. Before I realized it had happened, my knees buckled out from under me and I fell down onto the slick shower floor. My emotions taking over me, I crouched down in the corner of the shower and began to sob.

I lifted my head and smoothed back my hair, squeezing my eyes shut as the steaming water beat down onto my face. The water had washed away all of the blood and grime covering my body, but I remained on the floor of the shower stall, unable to move. As the water flowed over my crouched form, I hoped that my guilt would eventually swirl down the drain as well, because if it remained, I wasn't sure how I was going to live with myself.

Chapter Four

All was quiet in the vault, and I roamed about the empty halls of my underground home with unshakeable restlessness. It was unusual for the vault to be so still and quiet. Every time I turned a corner, I expected to see Harvey and Bill causing some type of chaos, and Leland scolding them both with a deep frown on his face. I was used to Harvey's constant harassment and Bill's loud mouth, and as I looked about the empty base, I came to the harsh realization that life just wouldn't be the same without them. That thought broke my heart.

I avoided the infirmary as I wandered further, knowing that Switch did not want to see me at the moment. I didn't blame him. After I had cleaned up, it was nearly impossible to face my own reflection in the mirror. I acted tough and arrogant, but the love I possessed for my strange family was my one and only weakness knowing I had failed them was destroying me.

I proceeded to kill time as I waited for Leland to return. When I passed by his study, I got the odd sense that something was off, and I found myself coming to a halt in the open doorway. I stared into the dimly lit room, surprised to find that Leland had left his table lamp on. When I walked inside to switch it off, I noticed he had also left one of his journals open on his desk. Leland was a private man, and it wasn't like him to leave his private notes just lying about. Like usual, my curiosity got the best of me, and I sat down at his desk and began to read his erratic calligraphy, trying my best to decipher the scribbled words.

Leland's handwriting style was barely legible, but I managed to discern a few important lines. He mentioned an inevitable age, where vampires emerged from the shadows and became supreme rulers, living as gods amongst humans. I gasped when my eyes fell upon Stoney's name, and how he would lead this movement. It appeared that the vampire planned on bringing this change about soon, and would kill any who stood in his way. My stomach churned with fear as I read.

"Those who oppose the vampires will be slaughtered, as will their families. No body will be spared from his wrath. To strike fear in the hearts of the human race, until they have no choice but to succumb, is Stoney's ultimate goal."

Startled by this unsettling information, I backed away from the desk slowly, confused about Leland's forewarning. I wondered how he knew of Stoney's plan, and then pondered their next move. We had to stop the vampires before they tried to take ultimate control of the population, but without a team of hunters, we didn't stand a chance. I was one of the best vampire hunters in the area, next to Leland, but I was still just one woman. I couldn't be expected to take down an entire coven on my own.

There were other hunters in Chicago and in nearby cities that could be called upon for help, but I preferred to work with my team or on my own. While most hunters were skilled in the art of slaying vampires, some were reckless and naïve, and I found that I had a hard time cooperating with hunters I couldn't trust in combat. I had my careless moments—tonight was one of them, but I wasn't gullible when it came to killing vamps. At times I may have made it look easy, and I enjoyed taunting them a bit, but I knew how dangerous they were and I always took a fight with one seriously. However, if Leland's notes were true, I may not have a choice but to enlist the help of the other hunters.

Wanting to get to the bottom of this scary newfound information, I removed my cell phone from my back pocket and dialed Leland's number. The phone rang and rang, and when he didn't pick up, I hung up and tried again. When I got his voicemail for the second time, I left him an urgent message and then pocketed my phone. I wondered where he was and what he was doing; he always picked up his phone, especially when I was calling.

Without a second to waste, I rushed out of the study, eager to find my father and question him over everything I had just read. I wasn't sure where he had run off to, but I would check his usual spots, hopefully locating him before the sun rose. The sooner we put a plan together, the better chance we had at stopping Stoney and his undead army from complete world domination. My revenge for the vampire aside, I knew it was my duty to protect the human race. It was one of the many reasons I enjoyed being a hunter. I was defending others from the horrid creatures that went bump in the night, and living with the knowledge that I was saving lives was a fantastic motivation.

Slaying the undead was the least I could do for my fellow man. Not everyone was capable of defending themselves against vampires; my parents included. In the beginning, avenging their murders was the sole reason I agreed to allow Leland to train me as a hunter. He had taken me in at such a young age, before I had fully understood the severity of the situation, but it wasn't until I became a teenager that he began to mold me into the bold and vivacious killing machine that I was today.

Leland was like a second father to me. He became my sole guardian when my parents were killed, and he raised me on his own. When I was with Leland, I was always safe, and although he never said the words, I knew that I was loved. I looked up to him, and I would always be grateful to him for taking me under his wing.

Of course, I still possessed memories of my biological father, but they were more like glimpses of a precious dream, and my sentiment for him was unlike the love and devotion I had for Leland. He was my savior, my mentor, and my guardian, and no matter what happened, I could always count on Leland to be there. In all the years I had been with him, he had never let me down once. He never would, either, and I was so sure of it that I would bet my own life against anyone who dared to challenge his intentions.

Leland and Switch were the last bit of family I possessed, and I vowed to protect their lives with my own, up until my very last breath. I wasn't going to let anyone harm them—not Stoney, not his cronies, not anybody. And although I had let down Harvey and Bill, I would not fail this time. I was coming for the vampires, and none were safe from my wrath.

****

It had been a cool, grey evening the night my parents were murdered. I remember it vividly, as if it had only happened yesterday. I could still hear the sound of my mother's screams—the violent sound of my father thrashing about on the kitchen floor. It was a memory I wished I could forget, yet, at the same time I was grateful for it. As harsh as the memories were, it forced me to remember the evil I was eradicating, and it motivated me to keep on fighting.

At seven years old, I was already a very independent girl, and some would say I had disciplinary issues. I was not good at following rules, and I took pride in free thinking, so when my mother called me inside for dinner one late September evening, I disobeyed. I refused to come inside until I was ready, despite my mother's loud protests.

My mother had been a sweet and graceful woman, with beautiful blue eyes and thick brown curls. Although I frequently challenged her authority, my mother was always patient with me and valued my spirited personality. No matter how angry she was, she never struck me. The memory of my mother's tender heart was what I cherished most of all, and out of both my parents, I had loved my mother most.

Unlike my mother, my father was a rather quiet and timid man. Although he cared for me, he wasn't much for showering me with attention. Throughout my young life, I had always wondered if

I had done something wrong to cause my father's indifference towards me. Unfortunately, his isolation was caused by his own sullied conscious due to his resentment of me, and there was nothing I could do or say to make him love me the way I needed to be. All I could do was survive off of whatever scarce affections he tossed my way.

I was born early in my parent's life, out of wedlock, and with my birth came responsibilities they were not yet ready for. Having a child prevented my father and mother from accomplishing all of the dreams and goals they had set for themselves, and though my mother forgot all about her childhood aspirations, my father had not. He resented me for stealing his youth, and he could not shake that bitterness no matter how hard he tried. In his last moments of life, however, he tried his best to make it up to me by giving up his blood in exchange for my safety. It was a sacrifice I would never forget.

I was playing on my swing set the night it happened. Wanting to swing higher, I kicked my legs, my head whirling as I swung and swung. My mother called to me, begging me to come in for dinner, but I ignored her and kept swinging. I could see her watching me from the kitchen window, a frown on her face when I continued to play.

My mother always gave me a trademark expression of disapproval when I disobeyed, and I loathed the look. It always made me feel so rotten. After some mental deliberation, I decided to head inside. The sky was growing rather dark anyway, and I did not like to be alone outside once night fell. I just wanted to swing a little bit higher before I succumbed to my mother's wishes and trudged inside.

I kicked and kicked my scrawny legs, and once I finally reached maximum height, that's when I heard it. The blood-curdling scream. It came from inside the house, and my entire body tensed up. My small hands gripped the rope of the swing tightly as my heartbeat raced from fear. The quiet that followed the scream was unbearable, and it made me antsy. The only sound to be heard was the creaky swing as it slowed down. When the swing finally slowed to a stop, my feet dragging against the dirt, I hopped off, but lingered by the play set, unsure if I should investigate the scream. Neither my mother nor father had come to get me.

My frightened inner voice told me to stay put, but it was my protective instinct that pushed me up the porch steps and into the hushed house. Once I crossed the threshold and entered the dining room, I called for my mother, and when I received no answer I began to shake. Without thinking, as many young children are incapable of doing once frightened, I rushed into the kitchen. I intended to find my mother cooking or cleaning, and waiting for me there with a smile. Unfortunately, what I found instead was a scene so horrifying it still gives me nightmares to this day.

There, lying in the middle of the kitchen floor was my mother. Her throat had been slashed open, and a thick pool of blood surrounded her frail body, staining the white and black checkered flooring. Although I was disgusted by the sight, it wasn't the blood that terrified me the most. It was my mother's eyes, once a vibrant blue, were now glazed over and empty as they stared up at the ceiling. The sight of her lying like that in the middle of the kitchen was too much for me to bear, and when I turned to flee the room, I bumped into a tall figure.

The man had long black hair that hung past his shoulders, and his skin was an eerie white color that reminded me of milk. He had a strong jaw and a sharp nose, and I noticed that his eyes were black and void of any emotion. He wore a long black leather jacket and pants, attire I was not used to seeing. He stared down at me, and as I held his gaze, I swore I could see my reflection in his cold eyes. Then, he smiled suddenly, and I stiffened at the sight of the bright red blotches that stained his lips and teeth.

"Hello, little girl," the stranger cooed. He reached out his hand to touch me, but I backed away, almost tripping over myself to avoid the unnaturally long stained fingernails. When I finally noticed how long and stained his nails actually were, it caused me to gasp and back away even further from him.

He continued to advance towards me, but I remained still, unsure of what to do next. I may have been a young child, but I wasn't dumb. This man was responsible for my mother's death—he was dangerous. Then, once he got too close, I finally did what I was trained to do with strangers. I screamed.

The man chuckled, but his black eyes narrowed at me. "I'll give you something to scream about, child," he told me, in a sinister voice.

His comment caused a chill to run down my spine, and I screamed louder, hoping a neighbor or passing pedestrian would eventually hear my screams and come to my rescue. However, I was not expecting my father to return home from work at that very moment, and when he rushed into the room with a wild look in his eyes, I breathed a sigh of relief. I knew my father would save me from the evil man.

Many emotions passed over my father's face in the few short moments after he walked into the kitchen. Confusion morphed into surprise, then grief, which finally shifted to anger. In the last seconds of his life he displayed a sign of bravery that I had never witnessed from him before. Without a word, he attacked the stranger in his kitchen, while shouting at me to run from the house. I obeyed and ran to the open archway of the kitchen, but paused to watch my father—my hero—struggle with the mysterious man in black.

The strange man didn't seem to be threatened by him. In fact, he was grinning, even after my father dealt a few successful punches to his jaw. He was unperturbed by the confrontation, and instead of focusing on the adult male attacking him, he placed his undivided attention on me. His cruel sneer mesmerized me, and I watched as two of his teeth suddenly elongated, becoming more profound than the others. I realized they were fangs, and the sight of them frightened me to the core. He was no normal man—he was a monster.

I watched him bite into my father's neck in horror, and it was then that I finally fled from the room, screaming as I went. I ran out through the sliding glass door and down the backyard, passing by my swing set. There was a small gate attached in the far left corner, and I hurried towards it. I hesitated only a moment. Tears stung my eyes as I fumbled with the metal latch, but I dared not to turn around for fear the creature was coming up on me.

Once I finally unlatched the gate, I scrambled into the neighbor's yard, rushing to the front of the house and then onto the sidewalk, searching for someone to help me. But by now it was late in the evening, and there was no one outside to hear my cries for help. I started sobbing once I came to the sad realization that I was on my own, but I kept running down the street, hoping to find some caring soul to take me in before the monster tracked me down.

As I crossed the dark and vacant street, a large blue van came speeding around the corner and screeched to a halt directly in front of me. Suddenly, a tall man with shoulder-length grey hair exited the vehicle and walked in my direction. I noticed then that he had some type of big weapon in his hand. The man insisted that I climb aboard his vehicle, and he told me that the thing following me was not human, and if I didn't come with him now, I would surely die.

Though I was hesitant to trust him, I knew that I couldn't remain outside with that creature hunting me down. Suddenly, the old man gasped, and my eyes grew wide with fear when I realized his gaze was fixed on something over my shoulder. I turned my head around, afraid of what I would find behind me, and I immediately wished that I hadn't looked. There, standing off in the distance, was the creature. He was smiling at me, with his head bent slightly forward; his brows narrowed in a menacing way. Just the sight of him caused me to burst into tears, and once unreserved fear took hold of me, I leapt at the man and buried my head into his arm.

I begged him to protect me from the creature, and explained to him what he had done to my parents, in-between my sobs. The man did not try to console me or ease my fears, but instead picked me up in his arms and ran back towards the van. He had me slide into the passenger's seat while he jumped into the driver's side and slammed the door shut. He turned the key in the ignition and I grabbed onto the armrests of my seat, squeezing them as I hard as I could.

The next few minutes passed by agonizingly slow. We drove off down the road, but the man followed us, eventually jumping on top of the van. He struck at the man driving, smashing his fist clean through the window. I watched the two men struggle with fear-stricken eyes from the safety of the passenger seat. I was unable to wrap my mind around the creature's amazing strength and invincibility. Even I knew that nothing should have the abilities that the strange man possessed.

Finally, the man driving the van slammed on the brakes, sending his assailant flying into the trunk of a tree. Before the creature in black could get his bearings, he reversed and drove off in the opposite direction, his foot now planted firmly on the gas pedal. I released a loud squeal of approval once the creature was nothing more than a speck in the passenger mirror. Now, finally relieved, I smiled at him, and he gave me one in return. It was as if both of us realized the same thing at the same time. We had gotten away safely.

Leland Olcoste was the man's name, and he explained the grave reality of the situation once we were finally safe. Paranormal beings, such as vampires and werewolves, existed and lived among humans. According to Leland, it was up to humans with certain abilities to rid the Earth of them, and although it was no easy task, he enjoyed protecting people like me in their desperate hours of need. He called himself a vampire hunter.

It was tough for me to process this frightening and life-changing information at first. I knew that the creature chasing us hadn't been human, but I would have never thought it was a vampire. Sure, I had heard of vampires and werewolves before, but I was told that they were make-believe. My parents had always assured me from a young age that monsters didn't exist. Now, suddenly, I was supposed to believe that everything they had told me about them was a lie?

After Leland explained his job as a vampire hunter, I tried to leave, but Leland assured me that I was safe with him. I wasn't frightened of him, but I was afraid that the monsters he hunted might come after him, and me. If I had had anyone to take care of me, I would have left right then. Sadly, I had no family to look after me. I was alone in the world, and that single thought made me burst into tears.

Once he learned that I had no living relatives, Leland promised to take care of me. I could tell that he was a slightly uncomfortable with the idea of me living with him, but he vowed to keep me safe from the vampires nonetheless.

The first few months weren't easy for me, and it was tough adjusting to my new life. When my parents' bodies were found, it was all over the news. Every night, I would watch the news reports, and my heart flared with anger the day the police declared that my parents had died of an animal attack. They said that the bites on their necks resembled that of a wolf's, and the case was closed shortly thereafter. Oh, but how wrong they'd been.

Although I was reported missing, Leland never came forward with information on my whereabouts. He said I had to leave my old life behind, especially since the vampire who had killed my parents may have been looking for me. Leland explained that vampires didn't like to lose their prey, and would always feel a need to track down the ones that got away from them. I would be safer if I started a new life with him.

Chelsea Lynn Charters

Leland was stricter than my parents had ever been, and I detested having to follow rules simply because I was a child. Despite my hatred for chores and lessons, my feelings towards Leland drastically changed over the years, and as my love for him grew, I realized I wanted nothing more in life than to be like him. He was strong, wise, patient, caring, and everything I hoped to be as an adult. I loved to watch him train in the gym; attacking the rubber vampire dummy like it had a death wish. It was because of his unparalleled skill with a stake that I knew I wanted to be a hunter too, and Leland couldn't have been more proud of my determination to fill his shoes.

As I grew, so did our family, and two boys Leland rescued from vampire attacks came into his care. Their cases, although two separate incidents, were both caused by vampires. Bill was the only child of a family in Philadelphia, and it was there that Leland had tracked a vicious vampire by the name of Savle. With the help of a fellow vampire hunter, Leland was able to slay the vampire and save Bill in the nick of time, but his parents hadn't been so lucky. Bill became an orphan that night, and Leland had no choice but to take him under his wing.

Harvey's circumstance was quite different. A teenage runaway, he was guilty of leading a troubled lifestyle and forced to make money a less honorable way in order to survive. Harvey accidentally came face to face with the undead during a drug deal that went south, but fortunately Leland had been patrolling that night. He vanquished the vampires and offered Harvey a chance at a better life, giving him the choice to stay with him and become part of the team, a part of a family. Although doubtful at first, Harvey eventually succumbed to Leland's persuasive argument and joined the group. We'd been a lethal trio ever since.

Because of Leland's good heart, all three of us were given a fresh start, and we became a part of something bigger than just a close-knit family. Teaching young children to slay vampires may have been unconventional, but it was Leland's guidance that kept us aware of the evil living within the shadows, and it was because of his skills as a hunter that we were still alive in the first place.

Bill, Harvey, and I protected people from vicious beings that only wanted to do wrong, and we were good at it. To us, slaying vampires had always been a sort of civic duty. We never saw it as a burden or a chore, and as we matured into adults, so did our skills. However, my abilities surpassed all. I was Leland's star pupil, reaching a potential not even the infamous hunter himself had expected. He trained me harder than the others, pushed me past my limits. I was strong because he wanted me to be.

To the vampire community, my teammates and I were a trio nobody wanted to mess with, and most of the time the undead were minding their own when my group came along and turned them into goo. We gave the vampires hell, especially Stoney's group, and it was only a matter of a time before our enemies decided to get even. Stoney was the vampire solely responsible for the deaths of my parents, and ever since the day I had learned his identity, I had made it my personal mission to have him die by my hand.

It was because of this vendetta that I was on the verge of losing everything near and dear to me. Just like before, Stoney had taken away the lives of more loved ones, but this time the responsibility rested on my shoulders alone. Stoney knew of my quest for vengeance and he used it against me, luring me into a vicious game where my friends paid the ultimate price. Even though the vampire sought to eliminate my comrades, killing me was not his intention.

No, I knew that Stoney had bigger plans for me, and unfortunately, he now had me right where he wanted me: in the palm of his cold dead hand.

Chapter Five

Since my bike had been stolen, I had to borrow one of the run-down extras we had locked up in the vault. I parked it on the street just outside of Casey's bar. It was nearly three a.m., but Casey's was still open. The bar remained in business until sunrise, due to it being located in the run-down parts of the Lower West Side of Chicago. Although known for its leniency towards the vampire community, there was a strict policy at Casey's that all patrons, whether dead or alive, had to follow: No conflicts were permitted inside the bar, and those who violated that policy were tossed out into the night, or in a vamp's case, staked in the back alley.

The bar was an exclusive establishment, and not many people were aware of its existence. Only those who were on the list made personally by the owner were granted entry. There were a few humans who, infatuated by the bloodsucking undead, found out about Casey's through unconventional methods, and they paid outrageous cover charges to get in. All of the non-vampire hunters were given a code to use to gain entry into the bar. Those who were found selling their code, they were eliminated. Everyone, vampires and humans alike, were required to keep Casey's a secret. It was beneficial to its success.

Among the hunters who enjoyed a night at Casey's, Leland was considered a regular there. I often asked him why he preferred to share drinks among the undead, and his response was always the same. He did it for the information. You could learn a lot from a vampire that couldn't hold his liquor, and though many vampires were turned off by the mere scent of alcohol, it only took a few drops of fresh blood mixed in with their booze to get them started. Leland had confessed of using the tactic often.

I walked up the concrete steps towards the bar, and the bouncer greeted me. He verified my name on the guest list before I was allowed to enter through the heavy, green double-doors. This was my second time visiting Casey's, and just like before, I had done so strictly on business. Unlike my father, I detested the idea of vampires and humans mingling together in a false state of harmony. It was unnatural, and in my opinion, a deadly combination that could only end in disaster. Harvey and Bill also shared my view on the matter, and so my team stayed away from the bar, interested in collecting information the old fashioned way: through sheer physical violence.

Upon entry, I was immediately put-off by the sight of how crowded it was. Human and vampire patrons were engaged in conversations with one another, and the sight of them enjoying themselves disgusted me to no end. Vampires were evil, plain and simple. They didn't deserve to be treated as equals to humans, and I couldn't understand why someone would pay to be around such monsters.

I passed by the first row of booths, and I watched a pretty woman lean her head on a vamp's shoulder as she toyed with the collar of his black polo. I wondered how the woman could be attracted to him. He was undead after all. The vampire grabbed the woman's breast suddenly and kissed the side of her face, keeping his eyes locked on her bare neck. As I observed the two share a kiss, I couldn't even fathom the idea of them sharing an intimate moment together that didn't end in the woman being torn to shreds and drained of all her blood.

As I made my way towards the counter, I side-stepped a drunk who was on the verge of falling out of his chair. He called out to me, hoping to gain my attention, but I kept on walking, ignoring him until he called me an obscene name. I froze in my tracks and twisted my head around to stare at the man. If he wanted my attention, he certainly had it now.

The drunk grinned at me and he hopped off of his bar stool. He hobbled in my direction, and I released a loud sigh as I stared at the man, my right eyebrow twitching from annoyance.

"Hey there," he said, still grinning. "What's a pretty thing like you doing in a bar like this?" The man burped suddenly, then leaned in to whisper, "There are vampires in here, you know."

My pissed off stare didn't falter as I replied, "Yes, I'm quite aware of that."

"Then why would you want to hang out in such a place? With a face like yours, I find it hard to believe you can't find company with somebody whose body temperature isn't below zero."

I rolled my eyes and turned away from him, eager to reach the bar and talk to Mike, the owner of Casey's. Mike was a middle-aged man, with blue eyes and a salt and pepper goatee. He was of Irish descent, like Leland, and they were close friends because of their shared heritage. I had known Mike since I was a young girl and he had helped me out of a few binds when I first started vampire hunting. Even though I preferred to stay away from his bar, I still considered him an ally.

Suddenly the drunk jumped in front of my path; a big toothy grin displayed on his face. "Hey, don't run away from me, honey! I'm just trying to talk with ya." He was holding a glass of whiskey in one hand, and with his free hand, he reached out and tried to grab my arm, but I moved out of his reach in time.

"Fuck off," I told him. "I don't have time for your bullshit, you miserable drunk!"

"Well!" the man remarked with a gasp. "That's a filthy mouth you've got there, baby. Somebody ought to teach you some manners."

My patience with the drunk had finally reached its limit, and I found myself biting down on my tongue to keep from spewing out a wide range of curse words. "I suggest you hop back on that barstool and get out of my way, before I break your nose."

He laughed at me and replied, "Ooh-wee! I like a girl with spirit."

"Get out of my face before I vomit," I told him with a sneer. "Your breath is making me sick."

I made another attempt to turn away from the stranger, but he this time he successfully grabbed hold of me. He wrapped a hand around my arm and forced me back towards him. I struggled with the drunk, and although I could have fought him off if I wanted to, I didn't want to cause a scene, as I was aware of Casey's number one rule. I was here on an important mission; I couldn't afford to be tossed out of the bar on account of one lousy drunk.

"Now, now, now," the man cooed, reaching out to touch my hair. "You and I are going to settle this dispute somewhere more private."

I laughed at his comment and said: "Keep dreaming. I'm not going anywhere with you."

"You're in no position to refuse me, little lady. Now, be a good girl and do as I say."

The drunk reached around to place his palm flat against my butt, and that's when I lost it. I could withstand dirty looks and catcalls—I could even tolerate derogatory insults, but when someone got physical and invaded my personal space, that's when absolute fury took over. With a smirk, I bawled my right hand into a fist. When I made the attempt to strike, however, Mike caught me by the hand.

I frowned up at him, disappointed that I hadn't succeeded in throwing a punch. "Mike, what the hell did you do that for?"

Mike shook his head as he released his hold on my hand. "You know the rules, Lina. I came over here to stop you before you did something regrettable." He paused to give me a smile before adding, "You know I don't enjoy tossing my friends out of my bar."

The drunk grinned and dropped his hold on me; his brown eyes twinkling with delight at my chastising. "Ha!" he yelled at me, pointing his index finger directly in front of my face. "See! Even this guy knows that a woman should stay in her place."

Mike turned to scowl at the man, his cheeks turning red. "Excuse me?"

The drunk patted Mike on the shoulder before replying, "I'm glad you came over here, buddy. I need to teach this bitch a lesson."

I frowned and crossed my arms. "Oh, I'm a bitch now?"

He laughed again. "Don't act surprised about it. All women are bitches." Then, the drunk turned to Mike and gave him a wide smile, "Aren't they? Good for nothing but a sweet fuck, am I right?"

Mike's face suddenly twisted into an expression I had never seen him make before, and I watched with wide eyes when he grabbed hold of the drunk by the collar of his shirt and growled, "You'll watch how you to talk to the lady, buddy, or I won't think twice about tossing you out of here."

"What's the big deal?" the man yelled back, now gaining everyone's undivided attention in the bar. I noticed that the mixed couple I had come across earlier had detangled themselves from each other and were now staring in our direction. All eyes were on us, and it made me feel a little uneasy.

"I own this establishment, and I don't appreciate trash like you coming in here and harassing my patrons."

The drunk looked me up and down with a confused expression before muttering, "What? You mean this stuffy bitch?"

"That's it," Mike said with a huff, now dragging the man towards the door of the bar by his neck. "Get the hell out of here— now, before I change my mind and let this bitch kick the shit out of you."

The drunk grumbled a few curse words as he stumbled towards the door, but he left without a fuss. I let out a loud sigh of relief, but I still possessed the itch to punch someone. As I shook my hands and balled them into fists a few times to release my pent up aggression, I glanced over at Mike and said, "You should have let me teach that a guy some manners."

Mike grinned, the anger melting off of his face. "I know."

"Who was he?" I asked Mike. I knew that only a few select people were granted access to his bar, so it surprised me that the drunk had been allowed to cross the threshold.

"He was a vampire hunter, one of the best. He's been retired for a few years now, and it looks like he's really let himself go."

"I'd say," I responded with a laugh. "The guy is mental."

"I'm already regretting letting him wander off into the night. Who knows who he'll harass next?"

"Oh well," I responded with the click of my tongue. "Not our problem now."

I plopped down onto an empty bar stool, steering clear of any patrons, either alive or dead, and waited patiently for Mike to walk behind the counter. Once he was standing directly across from me, he gestured to a bottle of vodka over his shoulder. I gave him a nod. After the night I had, I definitely needed a drink.

Mike went about pouring me a glass, returning with my fresh drink a minute later. I grinned at the sight of the maraschino cherry lying in the bottom of the clear glass; he had remembered.

"It's nice to see you again, Mike," I told him with a smile. "It's been a while."

Mike sat the drink down onto the counter, and pushed it towards my hand with care. He forced a smile, an odd expression of worry came over his face, and it roused my interest.

"Is something wrong?" I asked him, before taking a quick drink. "You're looking a little on-edge."

He shook his head and replied, "No, nothing's wrong. I'm just curious as to why you're here."

I had another drink, and this time I swallowed enough of it to burn my throat. I clicked my tongue against the roof of my mouth, waiting for the burning sensation to cease. After a sharp inhale, I said, "Why? You're not happy to see me?"

"I'm always happy to see you, Lina," Mike began. "But you and I both know you don't normally show up here unannounced." Then, after a swift survey of the patrons in his bar, he asked, "What happened?"

I also took a look around the packed establishment, searching for any familiar faces—particularly ones that belonged to Stoney's group—then leaned towards him. Even though I struggled to remain calm, once I noticed the concern on his face, my emotions broke free.

Before I fulfilled the urge to cry, I bit down on my tongue and glanced at my hands, which were now lying flat on top of the counter. I noticed that blood still stained the web of skin connecting my index and middle finger, and with a soft cry, I rubbed at the dried fluid.

Mike must have witnessed the anger and regret in my eyes, which was a dead giveaway that something terrible had occurred. Mike had known me all my life, and no matter the situation, I never let anyone see me cry. I had always been the toughest person in our group, but even the toughest people eventually cracked, and now something had finally caused me to fall apart.

With a heavy sigh, Mike placed his hand over mine and whispered, "Lina, whatever happened, you don't have to keep it to yourself. Just know that you can tell me, and I will try to help you the best way I can."

I rubbed at the corners of my eyes, disgusted by a lone tear that slid down my cheek. "You can't help me, Mike. Nobody can."

"Of course I can, but you have to tell me what's going on first."

I glanced back at him, my bottom lip trembling when the words started forming on the tip of my tongue. It broke my heart to tell him the truth, but if I wanted to find Leland, I knew that I had to tell Mike the whole story.

I eventually explained the entire dreadful situation—how my teammates had been killed due to my careless actions. Once I had finished spilling my guts, I couldn't help but to hang my head and await his harsh words of judgment. However, I was surprised when Mike never spoke one ill word against me.

Instead, he squeezed my hand and said, "I'm sorry for your loss. Harvey and Bill were good men, and they were always good friends of mine."

"That's it?"

"What do you mean?"

"You're not going to yell at me, or tell me how foolish and reckless I am?"

"Reckless—?"

"For getting my team killed!"

He paused a moment, his brown eyes looked me over. "It wasn't your fault, Lina."

I frowned up at him, confused. "Didn't you hear what I said, Mike? Harvey and Bill, my best friends—my family, are dead. I was in charge tonight—I gave the orders. It is most definitely my fault."

"No, it wasn't. Harvey and Bill knew what they signed up for. Their job has always been a dangerous one, and they've been putting their lives at risk since day one."

"Yeah, but—"

"They could have acted different too, and how do you know that Stoney didn't set you up?" Mike inquired with a curious frown. "You may have been in charge of your group, but if that tip turned out to be false, how would you have known you were heading into a trap? How would any of you have known what you were really getting into?"

I paused, scratching my head as I mulled over Mike's analysis. I wondered if he was right. Had the entire night been a set-up? If so, I couldn't believe that I had actually fallen for such a ruse. I thought I was smarter than that.

"Do you understand what I'm telling you?" Mike asked, after a quiet moment had passed.

"Yes, I understand what you're saying, but it simply can't be," I replied, still unsure if I should even consider the possibility. "I think I would have known if Stoney was pulling a fast one on me, Mike."

"Stoney's no fool, Lina," he told me with a sigh. "You've always had it out for him, and it was only a matter of time before he took advantage of your hatred. He's been around a lot longer than you."

I dragged a hand through my hair and then brought it down to my neck. My throat was burning, but this time it wasn't from the vodka. Anger and regret now replaced the grief I'd felt only moments before, and I cursed my foolish self. What if I'd actually allowed Stoney to succeed in duping me? If what Mike said was true, then it was most definitely my fault that my teammates were dead. All I had ever been able to see was red when it came to Stoney, and it was because of my nonstop search for vengeance that I'd played right into his hand.

My eyes welled up with tears again, and I whispered, "I'm sorry, Mike. I didn't come here to get all emotional on you."

"I know you didn't. You came here for my help, so let me help you."

With a thin smile, I rubbed at my wet eyes and tried my best to get a grip on my emotions. What was done was done—I couldn't bring my friends back from the dead, and my sorrow couldn't deter me from the task at hand. No matter how horrible I felt, I had to stop Stoney and his undead groupies from causing mass murder in the city. Unfortunately, the first step to stopping him was finding my father.

"Actually, I could use your help, Mike," I told him. "I'm looking for Leland. Have you seen him?"

Mike nodded. "Yes. He was here, but he left a few hours ago."

58

"Do you know where he was headed?"

"He mentioned checking out the old theater on 54th Street. Apparently, he was supposed to meet someone there tonight."

"Who?" My brows rose at the mention of the decaying movie theater. I wondered why Leland would be snooping around there, but I was even more curious about the mysterious person he was meeting. He had never mentioned it to me before, and it wasn't like him to leave me out of the loop. And normally, he would never go alone; it was rule number one.

Mike frowned and said, "I don't know who it was, but I remember Leland was pretty tense when I had asked him about it."

"Tense?"

"Yes. Actually, now that I think of it, he wasn't really acting like himself tonight, Lina."

"How do you mean?"

Mike glanced about the bar, before turning to face me again. "It was as if he was hiding something from me."

"Hiding what?"

"I have no idea, but when I questioned him about it, he took off."

I detected fear in Mike's tone, and it was obvious that he was worried about Leland. Alarms suddenly went off in my head at the possibility of Leland being in danger. Whoever was meeting him at the movie theater must've had a connection to Stoney, or knew of his plan for vampires to take over Chicago. He could be walking right into a trap, just as I had earlier. Divide and conquer— rule number two.

I reached for my drink and downed the remaining liquid, eager to resume the hunt for Leland. Once I thanked Mike for the free drink and the information, I hurried out of the bar and ran towards my parked motorcycle. I breathed a sigh of a relief that this one hadn't been stolen, and popped open the small compartment in the back. I quickly tugged on my black helmet and kicked the bike off of its stand, then sat down onto the leather seat. I turned the key in the ignition, and just as I was about to press my foot on the gas, I was pulled off of the bike and tossed onto the hard pavement.

I gasped from surprise, not expecting to be thrown off guard. It was then that I noticed the drunk who had been harassing me earlier was now towering over me, a half-filled bottle of Jack Daniels in his left hand, and a crowbar in the other. I glared up at him, annoyed that I still had to deal with him, and when I searched for the bouncer at the door, I noticed he was missing.

"Don't worry about your friend," the man said with a laugh. "I knocked him out with this," he told me, motioning towards the crowbar. "He won't be waking up anytime soon."

"Where is he?"

"I dragged him into that alley over there."

The man turned his head to glance at the small alleyway behind him, and although he was only distracted for a moment or so, it was all I needed to knock him to the ground. I kicked his shins, and when I rolled over and hoisted myself up, I used my other leg to sweep him, causing him to fall backward. Although I had had no choice in the matter, and was forced to subdue him, I grimaced at the loud sound his head made when it hit the pavement.

He may have assaulted me—more than once—but I had a strict policy against killing humans. In the event that it was truly necessary to take a human life, I would, but even then it always left a bad taste in my mouth. Killing vampires was easy—they had no pulse, no soul, therefore they weren't really alive. Humans, even the worst ones, had both, and I didn't agree with being in the position to take someone's life away.

I waited a cautious minute before I checked his vitals, and I was glad to find that the man was still alive. He was unconscious however, and upon realizing I couldn't just leave him lying in the gutter, I hoisted his body and dragged him towards the alley, where I spotted the bouncer leaning up against the side of a dumpster. I rushed over towards him, fearing the blood I saw dripping down his forehead.

The bouncer's name was David, and although he wasn't a friend of mine—I'd conversed with him only a handful of times, I prayed he was okay. He didn't deserve the blow to the head that the drunk had dealt him. I checked to see if he was still breathing, and he was. Once I had established that both men were all right, I hurried back towards my lopsided bike, and hopped back on it. If circumstances had been different, I would have sorted out the mess. But my father needed me, and I was running out of time.

On my way, I made a call to Mike, explaining the gruesome events that had occurred outside his establishment. He wasn't pleased that the drunk had returned to harass his bouncer and me, but I explained calmly that I had subdued him. I told him that both men were unconscious and that he should probably call an ambulance, just in case one of the men's conditions was worse than what I had assessed. Then I ended the call.

I prayed that I would reach Leland in time, and that he wasn't another one of Stoney's targets. I loved Bill and Harvey with all of my heart, and no one could ever replace them. However, I knew that if I lost Leland tonight, I wouldn't be able to handle it. I couldn't survive without him. He was my strength, and if he perished because of my vendetta against Stoney, I knew it would be the end of me.

Chapter Six

All was strangely quiet on 54th street, and the stillness only gave me cause for concern. The loud sound of my motorcycle seemed to shake the windows of the surrounding shops, and when I parked my bike outside the dark and empty theater, I noticed that all of the signs were displaying the word 'closed.' Even the windows of the twenty-four-hour tattoo shop were black. That business thrived during the early hours of the morning, when drunken customers came by for tattoos they would most likely end up regretting, and a chill shuddered through me. It was a bad omen.

Once I secured the bike, I ran up towards the entrance to the theater. The empty ticket booth was covered in cobwebs and dust. Various old newspapers were scattered around the floor, and the four entrance doors, which were usually barred shut with large pieces of wood and chains, were open. The building was falling apart, and it was far too dangerous for the public to inspect its interior, which is why it was supposed to be boarded up.

The movie theater was ancient, built in the 1920's, but it had been closed since the eighties, when a newer theater was built a few blocks away. Most people, especially the business owners on the same street, considered it an eyesore and wished for it to be bulldozed. Unfortunately, they'd never gotten their wish, and so the theater remained, collecting dust and continuing to decay as the years passed.

I glanced cautiously over my shoulder before proceeding inside; my right hand positioned near my holster, ready for anything or anyone who jumped out of the darkness.

Now paying close attention to the wreckage surrounding me, I stepped lightly around fallen columns and beams. I stepped on a large glass plane, which most likely belonged to a movie poster casing, and stiffened as the glass cracked and broke beneath my feet. The sound of it breaking apart echoed throughout the silent theater. Wondering if the sound had alerted anyone, I waited with my gun drawn. When no one appeared, I holstered my weapon and continued down the narrow entrance hall.

The main lobby was also empty, and there was no sign that anyone had been there recently. Heavy dust lined the floors and counter tops of the concession stand, and even the outdated machines were thickly covered. There were two sections of theaters, and as large as the place was, I was unsure of which side to investigate first. When I caught sight of light footprints heading towards the right wing, I hurried in its direction.

As I walked down the dark hall, trekking over discolored posters of actors and actresses that once used to be in the limelight, I glanced around the decaying building and imagined what the theater looked like in its prime. By the design of the solid ornate pillars and dark red velvet walls, I had no doubt that it had once been magnificent.

I traveled deeper inside the dark building; the footprints leading the way, and I relaxed a bit when I came across the separate theater boxes. I prayed that I would find Leland inside one of them. When I passed by the first two theater entrances, which were boarded up tightly, I noticed another fresh set of footprints. They seemed to appear out of thin air, which was rather odd, but I didn't let my suspicious nature ruin my optimism.

Which set of footprints belonged to Leland? Had he been here? Was he still in this theater somewhere? I needed those questions answered, and my heart rose with hope as I followed after both sets of footprints. They led me to the sixth theater in the wing, and before heading inside, I paused just outside the door and listened closely for any voices. When I heard none, I knew that two things could be reason for the silence. Either my father hadn't shown up yet, or Leland was either incapacitated, dead, or abducted. I tried to push those frightening thoughts out of my mind, but they still compelled me to rush inside the theater at full speed.

I vaulted down the hall, hurdling over heaps of trash, but when I finally reached the belly of the theater, my heart dropped from despair. The theater was empty; there was not a soul to be found. I searched the bottom rows of the empty theater warily, wondering just where he and the mysterious person could be. As I examined the grimy and dust-covered floor, I detected only one set of footprints. It was evident that someone had been inside the theater, but I didn't know who. Had my father been stood up? If so, where had the other person gone? Perhaps the meeting hadn't taken place after all, and he had returned to the base and was now waiting for me.

That scenario seemed plausible, however, I wanted to inspect the top of the theater before heading out. Once I had ascended the steps to investigate the remaining rows of seats, I overheard movement from below. I reached for my weapon as I twisted my body to face the direction of the sound; the barrel of my gun searched for a threat. It took my eyes a few moments to adjust to the darkness in the room before I noticed a figure standing at the foot of the stairs. I could only make out the person's outline in the dark, and I wondered if I had finally found Leland.

My hands wavered as I took a few slow steps down the stairs, but I kept my gun aimed directly at the dark figure. In the event they turned out to be a threat, I would be ready to neutralize them. My last steps were cautious as I neared the bottom of the staircase, and I watched the person reach into the back right pocket of their pants to remove a small item. I assumed the item they were holding was a weapon, so I moved to a crouched position, my finger hovering over the trigger.

"Drop the weapon," I commanded, my eyes squinting as I tried to make out my assailant's face. When the person made no effort to move, I shouted, "Drop it, or I will shoot."

He lifted his hands in front of him slowly, the item in his closed right fist. Then, with a swift flick of his thumb, a small flame appeared directly above his finger. "You can lower your gun now, hunter. It's just a lighter."

I scowled at the tone of the man's voice, and disappointment hit me hard when I realized I had not found Leland. Although the light illuminated the stranger's face, I was too far away to get a clear visual. "Yeah, that's not going to happen," I replied.

"Are you always this untrustworthy?" the stranger asked, after a quiet moment had passed.

"Yes."

"Why is that?"

I snorted at his question. "Why do you think? I'm a vampire hunter—trusting people is a privilege I'm not allowed to possess."

"Not everyone you meet is a threat to you."

"Are you telling me that you're not a threat?"

"That's right. I'm not."

"Oh really? And how do I know you don't have a weapon hidden somewhere on you?"

He sighed with exasperation at my inquiry. "Because I didn't come here for that."

I laughed and said, "So, you didn't follow me into an abandoned movie theater in the middle of the night to kill me?"

"No, I have no intention of harming you, Lina Holiday—and I wasn't following you." I tightened my hold on my gun, ignoring the sweat that was beginning to trickle down my back.

"Then what are you doing here exactly, and how do you know my name?" When he didn't answer my question right away, I said, "Listen, I've already fallen for one vampire's ruse today and I won't make that mistake again."

I watched the stranger move away from the stairwell and walk towards the front of the torn movie screen. He leaned up against it then, and I noticed that he was still holding the lighter in his right hand. "Sorry to disappoint you, but I'm not a vampire. I know how much you hunters get off on slaying vamps, but you can keep your stake sheathed. It won't be necessary."

"Who are you?" I asked, as I descended the stairs, making sure my eyes never left his dark outline. "If you're not a vampire, and you're not a threat to me, then show me your face."

"Why does my appearance matter?"

"I want to see who, but more importantly what, I'm dealing with."

The man took a deep breath and said, "I don't think that's such a good idea."

"What's the matter? Are you completely fuck-ugly or something?" I asked him curiously. "Listen, if that's the case, I deal with vampires on a daily basis—and not the rare, gorgeous ones either. There's nothing more hideous to me than a vampire, so you don't have to be shy with me."

"It's not that," he retorted. "I'm not deformed or mutated. I would just prefer to keep my identity concealed, for personal reasons."

"Which are?"

"My safety for one."

"Okay, well, you have two options. Either you tell me who you are right now, or I decide that you're my enemy and put a bullet in your brain."

"Those are my only options?" He sounded amused, and that aggravated me.

"If you're not honest with me, I'll assume you have something to hide. We'll be right back where we started, which is me not trusting you."

"Fine," he replied after a moment, his tone bitter. "If it will put your mind at ease. But first, I want your word that you will remain calm."

"We'll see. It depends on how ugly you turn out to be."

The man's voice hardened as he said, "Your word, hunter."

"Jesus," I mumbled, rolling my eyes at his request. "Okay, sure. I promise I'll be calm."

He seemed hesitant at first, but the stranger eventually removed the hood from his head, letting it fall against his back. He brought his hand below his chin, and the tiny flame from the lighter lit up his handsome, yet rugged face. I realized the man was a complete stranger—no one I had ever come across before, and although he was human and seemed normal enough, his bright amber eyes were a dead giveaway of the monster he truly was.

Since I was quite knowledgeable on the subject of the paranormal, I knew that the person standing before me was definitely not a vampire. In fact, he was something much worse. The man I was currently having a conversation with in the abandoned theater was a werewolf.

"Holy shit," I muttered, my hands gripping my gun even more tightly now. "You're a werewolf?"

In my long span of hunting vampires, I had never come across a werewolf before. Leland himself had confessed to having hunted only one, and he had explained that it had been a terrifying and unorthodox encounter. He had wished to never face one again. Hunting werewolves required instinct and bravery—which couldn't be taught.

Whenever our group got wind of a werewolf tramping around in Chicago, we stayed out of it. Werewolf hunting was quite dangerous, and although I was aware that many hunters had perished in the pursuit of werewolves, I had always wanted to track one down at least once in my lifetime. My father, as careful as he was, never allowed me to, no matter how many times I voiced my interest to him about werewolf hunting.

As I stared at the beast in the dark theater, my pulse raced with excitement and another emotion—one I wasn't used to feeling. It was fear. I wondered if I possessed the ability to subdue the creature. In the event a fight took place between us, I wasn't convinced that I could make it out of the skirmish as the victor. As skilled as I thought I was, I wasn't naïve. Facing off with a werewolf wasn't as simple as taking on a few vampires. I was aware that a full-fledged werewolf could tear me to shreds in a matter of seconds, and torn flesh was not a look I was willing to try.

"You promised to be calm," he said.

I swallowed hard and shrugged my shoulders. It was then that I realized my gun was trembling in my sweaty palms. "Who's not calm? I'm very calm—as calm as a person could be in this type of situation."

"I can smell your fear," he replied with a chuckle. "It's not something you can hide."

"I'm glad that I amuse you," I said dryly.

"Please, Lina," he began. "There's no need to fear me—"

"No need to fear you?" I interrupted with a laugh. "Are you completely insane? There's plenty of reasons why I should fear you! Let's begin with the fact that you transform into a man-eating wolf when the moon is full!"

With a low growl, the man glanced down at his feet and mumbled: "I knew revealing my nature would only make things more difficult."

I frowned, curious as to why he seemed so upset. "Well, can you blame me?" I asked him, after a moment of awkward silence passed between us. "It's not every day a person comes across a bona fide werewolf."

"I understand … but as I said before, you have nothing to fear from me."

"Yes, well, I'm sorry, but I don't believe you. And if you think I'm just going to stand around here and wait for you to—"

It was at that moment that I realized the wolf had called me by my name—for the second time. I watched him closely then, wondering how he knew who I was. With my gun still aimed at him, my eyes narrowed as I asked, "How do you know who I am?"

"I came here to meet Leland," he said suddenly, catching me off guard. His amber eyes glowed from satisfaction once he realized he had captured my undivided attention. "And I know all of the hunters who operate in Chicago."

I glared at him. "You were the person who was supposed to be meeting him here?" I muttered the words in disbelief. Leland had arranged a secret engagement with a werewolf. I couldn't believe it. That was something I was sure he'd never done before.

"We arranged a meeting for tonight, and I must say I was quite surprised to find you in his place."

"Why? What business do you have with Leland?"

"My name is Gabriel. I'm the son of Brulin, pack leader of the clan Arcane. I contacted your father a few weeks ago, when I got wind of some very interesting information regarding a certain vampire's plan of rebellion. Leland wants to stop it from taking place, and my clan feels the same. We formed a truce, and are now working together to prevent the vampires from destroying our city."

"You know about Stoney's plans to take over Chicago?" I asked with raised brows. Although I didn't doubt he was the person Leland was supposed to meet with, I was still unsure if I should trust him. "How could you possibly? I thought werewolves and vampires were mortal enemies? There's no way they would share that kind of information with you."

He nodded. "That's very true, but there are some impartial vampires who can be trusted to obtain valuable information, and in exchange we offer them a substantial payment of what they desire most."

I could tell by the grave expression on his face that he was telling the truth, and I lowered my gun. "You mean blood," I muttered, disgusted by the thought.

"Yes."

"So, you pay these vampires with blood, and in exchange they relay information from vampire overlords like Stoney?"

He nodded. "Yes."

"Werewolf blood?"

"That's correct."

"How do you know they aren't giving you false info?"

"They wouldn't dare. Also, our arrangement is too good for them to turn their back on. A vast supply of fresh werewolf blood is hard to come by easily nowadays, especially since the increase in hunters these past few years."

"You never know," I began with a huff. "I've met quite a few shifty vamps in my day. Trusting those blood suckers is not a wise idea."

"I know this is hard for you to understand, given your history with vampires, but you have to believe me, Lina," he told me with a sharp inhale. "The information I possess is not false."

I studied his grim face for a considerable moment, and the idea that I should trust a werewolf seemed comical, if not absolutely ridiculous. However, I was aware of the fact that if Leland trusted him, I had to as well.

"Okay. So, let's say I believe you. What is this supposed information then?"

"I intended to deliver this information to Leland personally, but if the old man trusts you enough to take his place, then I suppose I can convey it to you."

"Wait a second. Leland didn't order me to meet you tonight. I came here looking for him."

Gabriel stared back at me dumbfounded. "I don't understand?"

"I thought you knew where he was!"

He shook his head, looking confused. "No. When I saw you, I figured he had sent you in his place."

"Shit!" I muttered. "This cannot be happening!"

If Leland hadn't shown up at the theater, then where could he be? And what about the footprints I had followed here? Had my father made it inside the theater at all, and if he did, where was he? Had someone gotten to him? More importantly, was he still alive? So many unanswered questions were swimming around inside my head, and the idea that my father was in mortal danger pushed me over the edge.

I pulled out my phone and tried calling him again. Earlier, when I had called, it rang a few times before reaching voicemail. This time, I kept getting a busy signal. It was not a good sign. I looked to Gabriel and said, "He hasn't been answering his phone all night."

Harvey and Bill were dead, and I had no idea where Leland was. I had gone through too much in such a short span of time, and even though I had tried my best to not fall prey to my emotions, I was not able to control them now. Tears sprang at my eyes, and I brought my hands up to my face to hide my grief from the werewolf. Before I realized it had even happened, all of the strength in my legs gave away and my knees buckled from under me.

Expecting my body to collide with the grimy floor of the theater, I was surprised when a pair of strong hands caught me just in time. Gabriel held me against his chest, and I could hear his heartbeat as his amber eyes stared down into mine. I felt breathless as I stared up into his unusual eyes, mesmerized by the odd flecks of gold. They seemed to glow in the absolute darkness, and although the flame from the lighter had long been extinguished, I was somehow able to make out every line and curve of Gabriel's strong features.

I had never been this close to a paranormal being without the intent to kill it, and when a strange feeling of warmth began to spread inside my stomach, I figured his closeness was making me sick. If the sensation was caused by anything else, I was too ashamed to admit it. I was already disgusted by showing weakness in front of the wolf, admitting I was attracted to him would have caused me to question my own sanity.

"Let go of me," I said abruptly, tearing my gaze away from his face as I tried to wriggle out of his grasp.

"As you wish."

Gabriel did as I commanded. He rose to a stand and lifted me onto my feet, but when he withdrew his arms from around my body, his eyes never left my face. I chose to disregard the werewolf's unyielding scrutiny and moved away from him, smoothing down my hair as I ignored the heavy beating of my heart. I was confused over my mixed emotions for the wolf, and I wanted nothing more than to flee the dark theater and continue in my search for Leland. However, I still needed the information Gabriel possessed, but the idea of spending another minute alone with him caused my skin to grow hot.

Realizing I had no choice, I took a deep breath to steady my nerves before glancing over my shoulder at him. "I need to know what you were going to tell my father about Stoney, and then I'll be on my way."

He nodded. After replacing his hood over his head, Gabriel replied, "Of course. It's not much, but it's imperative that you and your team know as much as possible." He cleared his throat before continuing. "Stoney and his pack of vamps have already begun to increase their numbers, siring just about anyone they can get their hands on. Although these vampires are newborns, they are still dangerous to humans in their desire to feed. Even more so since they have almost no control over their blood lust yet."

"I've noticed there have been quite a few young vampires tramping around town lately," I admitted.

"That's because Stoney plans to turn half of Chicago into vampires."

My eyes grew wide at Gabriel's admission. "What?"

"It's true. Siring half of Chicago is Stoney's first step. Once he's completely expunged the city of its inhabitants, he'll move on to the next city, and then the next. Soon, half of our beloved country will be overpopulated with vampires."

"That's complete insanity!" I exclaimed.

Gabriel nodded in agreement. "Yes it is, which is why Stoney needs to be stopped."

"Wait a second," I mumbled, a sudden thought occurring to me. "You just mentioned that he plans to sire half of Chicago."

"That's what I said."

"Okay, so what happens to the other half?"

"They, along with all of the werewolf clans in the city, will become his slaves. We will have the unlucky fate of becoming their donors." Gabriel stiffened before saying, "Those who don't comply or try to escape, will be killed."

"Donors?" I said the word with a frown, knowing its true meaning. "You mean blood donors."

He nodded. "Yes. We will be bred for our blood alone."

I winced. The idea of the human race being farmed like animals was simply too much for me to fathom. "That is disgusting."

"We have to stop him, Lina, before he and his pack sire any more vampires for their cause. As their numbers rise, our chance of success decreases considerably."

"This cannot be happening," I moaned, rubbing at my temples. "No wonder he planned to get rid of me, Harvey, and Bill. He doesn't want anyone to interfere with his scheme."

"What do you mean he planned to get rid of you?" Gabriel inquired. "Has something happened?"

I froze, now cursing my big mouth. I was unsure if I should inform Gabriel of the deaths of my teammates, but I ultimately realized that if we were to work together, it would only benefit him if he knew everything that had transpired earlier. I decided to inform him of the night's events, explaining how Bill and Harvey had perished at the hands of Stoney's lackeys. Gabriel listened intently, but as soon as I told him of the notebook I found on Leland's desk, he became angry.

"I never told your father about Stoney's scheme to take over Chicago!" He shouted, his bright eyes sparking with rage. "How did he find out about that?"

"What?" I remarked in surprise, taken aback by the wolf's fury. "What do you mean? You just said you contacted him a few weeks ago!"

"That's right! I did reach out to him, but I never mentioned what Stoney's specific plans were. I wasn't even aware of them until a few days ago!"

"But—"

Before I realized what was happening, Gabriel grabbed me by the throat and slammed my body against the wall. He raised me up by my neck and bore his fangs, and his eyes turned wild as he snarled, "What sort of game are you playing here, hunter? Are you setting me up?"

I fought to speak, but his grip around my throat was much too tight. All I was able to express was a soft gasp, and my eyes grew wide with fear. I reached up to beat at his arms, but it made no difference. The wolf was lost in his anger, and the idea that he was being deceived was driving him deeper into a heated frenzy. I continued to pound my fists against his arms, but I was no match against the werewolf's strength.

He squeezed my neck tighter, his body now pressing up against mine while he growled. His sharp teeth snapped at my face, and I was deathly aware of the terror I faced if Gabriel transformed into his true form. His conscience would be lost, and I would be doomed to suffer the werewolf's extreme fury.

With pleading eyes, I struggled to beg Gabriel to stop, but all I was able to mumble was the word please. It must have been my weak voice and the fear conveyed on my face that snapped Gabriel out of his rage. His heated stare vanished within a matter of seconds, and he seemed appalled by the damage he had just inflicted on me.

Gabriel released me and I slid down against the wall, falling onto my knees as I gasped for air. I rubbed at my neck and my eyes teared in pain. I avoided looking at him, but I could feel his unwavering stare. Although he seemed calm, I was afraid that if I met his eyes, his beastly aggression would be triggered again.

"I …" Gabriel began, clearing his throat. I watched from the corner of my eye as he rubbed at his face, which was now damp and flushed with shame. "Lina, I'm so sorry. I lost control …" His voice fell and he looked away, trying to hide his embarrassment. "I don't know why I lost myself like that."

"I do," I whispered, fighting back tears. It was difficult for me to even speak.

"I apologize—"

"It doesn't matter!" I interrupted him, my voice hoarse. "Nothing matters to me right now except finding my father. I don't care about you, or your apologies—hell, I don't even care about Stoney's plan for absolute world domination. All I care about is finding Leland and saving him from whatever trouble he's gotten into."

I paused to catch my breath before saying, "I can't lose anyone else … I just can't."

"I'm sorry about your father," he said, after a moment. "I'm sure he's fine. There's no lingering scent of blood here—no sign of a struggle. In fact, I can't trace his smell at all, which is a good sign."

I rose to my feet then, shaking my head as I went. "There were footprints leading to this exact theater. I know they were his."

"They could have been anybody's, Lina. It doesn't mean—"

"You and I both know he's not fine, especially if the vampires got to him!" I stated. "He could be their prisoner—or worse. He could be lying in a ditch somewhere with his throat slashed, and maybe I could have prevented it from happening, if I hadn't been wasting my time by being assaulted by a werewolf!"

He frowned at my remark and replied, "You can't be certain Stoney has him."

"Maybe not, but I know Stoney. He's coming after me— he's made that very clear."

"How?"

"He's been hunting me ever since I was a child. The night my parents died—when Leland saved my life, he warned me that Stoney would never stop until he found me again. He was right."

"I'm sorry … I didn't know that Stoney murdered your parents."

I nodded. "He plans to hurt the ones I love, in the hope it makes me weak." I laughed suddenly, when I realized that the vampire had already accomplished his goal. "And you know what? It's working."

"You can't give up, Lina. You can't let him win," Gabriel said. "It may sound cliché, but you just need to have a little faith."

"Faith," I remarked with a weak smile. "Right. Because faith will bring my friends back to life, and faith will stop the creatures of the night from destroying the world." As I stared at Gabriel, at one of the monsters I had vowed to protect the innocent citizens of my city from, I felt my blood boil. "There is no room for faith in my line of work."

"I know all seems lost, but you're not alone," he said, taking a sudden step towards me. "I apologize again for losing my temper, but no matter what has transpired between us here tonight, you can count on me and my clan to help you."

I moved towards the open hallway and spat, "I don't need your help, Gabriel, nor do I want it."

He growled and hurried after me. "Don't be naive! This is not a task you can handle on your own!"

"Maybe you're right," I said, pausing by the divider of the wall. "But I would rather perish than accept help from someone just as evil as my enemy."

"You're making a grave mistake, Lina."

"Maybe so," I replied, unperturbed. "But at least I won't constantly be wondering what the outcome will be after you lose your cool again."

"I'm not your enemy. Why can't you see that?"

Gabriel reached out to grab hold of my arm, but I evaded his hand, jumping backwards towards the exit. I faced him with a true expression of hatred, hoping it would send him a message. If he tried to touch me again, it would only provoke me to retaliate.

"Whether you like it or not, hunter, you're going to need my clan to help you stop this vampire rebellion. If you choose not to accept our help, I can't be sure that you will make it out of this battle alive."

"Well, I guess that's just a chance I'm going to have to take."

"Don't turn away from me, Lina!" Gabriel begged. "Please! I don't want to see you or your father suffer at the hands of those bloodsuckers."

"Why do you care, Gabriel?" I asked him after a moment. "Why would you, or your pack, care about us, when our sole mission is to exterminate you?"

"Because, whether you believe it or not, Lina, I feel that we can help each other. I'm willing to risk my clan, my life—everything, to aid you and Leland." He paused to clear his throat. "If I'm willing to trust you, why can't you see past my form and trust me?"

"Because no matter what you say, you're a werewolf, Gabriel, and I've dealt with enough supernaturals to know that I should never trust one."

I trekked out of the theater without another glance in his direction. I was eager to return to the vault, on the off chance that

Leland was waiting for me there. I knew it was childish to hold onto the hope that he was all right, but it was all I had left to keep me going. Until I knew for certain that Stoney had gotten to him, I would continue to believe he was alive and well, and that he would help me put an end to the threat that was plaguing us.

****

Once I retreated back onto the cold and darkened city street, I began to doubt my choice in turning my back on Gabriel and the Arcane clan. Without their help, I was unsure how I could defeat the vampires on my own. I had no team—no one to guide me for the time being. I was on my own now, but I chose to ignore Gabriel's forewarning that my stubbornness would only get me killed.

Today, it had cost me two friends—I was determined to not let it claim anymore.

Chapter Seven

It was morning, nearly an hour or so before the sun would rise over Chicago, so I wasn't worried about running into any of my undead assailants. Vampires rarely strayed far from their underground hideaways and murky covens at such a dangerous hour.

When I finally returned to the street that led to the rundown warehouses of Chicago, where the vault was located, I thought I was home free, but as I pulled up, I noticed that at the end of the lane, a tall figure was standing in the middle of the road.

I came to a squealing stop, shifting the bike sideways. I kept the motor running with one foot planted on the road while I watched the figure walk towards me. As he got closer I finally got a good look at his ashen face, realizing he looked vaguely familiar. Then it dawned on me; he was one of Stoney's vamps.

Without a moment to waste, I reached for my gun. As I attempted to remove it from the holster, the vampire lunged at me, shoving me off of the motorcycle and onto the cracked pavement. We rolled around on the ground, and I struggled to keep him from gaining the upper hand. When the vampire noticed that my neck was bruised, he went for my throat, cruelly wrapping one hand around my still tender flesh.

I hollered in pain, the skin feeling as if it was on fire. I watched with wide eyes when he began to lower his mouth down towards my shoulder, his fangs unsheathed. Before he was able to take a bite, I reached for one of the stakes on the inside of my jacket, and once I tugged one free, I shoved it clean through his arm. He howled, his red eyes growing dark with fury, but he released my neck and backed off, without fear.

Finally able to grab hold of my gun, I aimed it directly at the vampire's heart, keeping my hand steady as I clicked-off the safety. The vampire yanked the stake out of his arm and looked to the gun in my hand, then back at me, his lips curling upwards into a smile. He laughed, seemingly amused, and flashed his fangs at me.

"What's so funny?" I asked him with a scowl.

He pointed at my gun and replied, "You think that puny weapon is going to subdue me, hunter?"

"No," I admitted. "But the tiny silver bullet inside the chamber will. Once it hits your cold, un-beating heart, you'll blow up like a firecracker on the fourth of July." I told him with a grin, and the arrogant expression on the vamp's face disappeared.

"It doesn't matter!" he growled. "Go ahead and kill me. There are hundreds of vampires in this city, and you can't take us all on at once!"

"Who's says I'm going to kill you all on my own? Surely you're aware of the other hunters in the city, and my teammates. I won't be the only one hunting down the rest of Stoney's disgusting band of bloodsuckers."

"Teammates?" the vampire remarked with a smirk. "You mean that cowardly doctor and the old man?"

My eyebrows twitched at the mention of Leland and Switch. "What did you do to them?"

"Let's just say they won't be much help to you now, hunter."

"You son of a bitch!" I screamed, my temper now fully out of my control. Before I even realized it had happened, I was on top of the vamp, digging my nails into his eye sockets. The vampire hissed and swiped at me, scratching the bottom of my jaw. I vaulted to my feet before he could cut me again, kicking my silver-tipped boot into his side. I kept him pinned to the ground underneath my other foot by pressing it deep into his ribcage.

"Where are they?" I asked him, striking the vampire with my foot again. "What have you done with them?"

He growled, his red eyes now glaring up at me. "Maybe if you hadn't been conversing with that mutt Gabriel, you could have saved them!"

My blood boiled at the vampire's admission. "You were watching me with Gabriel?"

The vampire smiled and said, "We're always watching you, Lina Holiday."

Panic coursed through my veins when I realized I'd been followed the entire night. With a cry, I pressed the silver toe of my boot against his bare skin, and I watched as his ashen skin began turning a charcoal grey. The vampire writhed beneath my foot, howling with pain. "You tell me where they are!" I screamed.

"Stoney has them!" the vampire finally admitted.

"You're lying. There's no way any of you could have gotten passed the UV lights! You and your undead friends would have fried."

"Am I lying? Or are you just blind to the truth?"

"And what truth is that?"

"That you were outsmarted."

I stiffened at the vampire's remark. "Outsmarted?"

"That's right," the vampire sneered. "You fell right into Stoney's trap, hunter."

"Oh, really?" I remarked with a smirk. "Because I'm still standing."

"Not for long," the vampire replied with a grin.

Irritated by his amused expression, I delivered a cruel kick to his head. "Tell me how you got into the base!"

The vampire sneered and snapped his fangs at me. "We have our ways."

"Tell me!" I commanded, hastily kicking him again.

The sneer on his face quickly morphed into a look of sheer amusement. "You can keep torturing me all you like, but knowing how we beat you won't change the fact that you failed. And now you have no one left. Tell me, who will protect you when Stoney comes for your head? The wolves? Can you really trust them to spare your life?"

"Shut up!" I warned.

"Face it. You're alone now, and there's not a soul on this earth that will weep for you when you die."

"I said shut up!" I screamed, aiming the gun at his crown. I fired once, the bullet blasting through the side of his head. I had missed on purpose, and the silver pieces that exploded inside the vampire's head caused him to screech and squirm beneath my boot. There was a now giant hole where his hair and skull once were, and I had to fight back a gag when I realized I could see his brains beginning to leak out.

"You fucking bitch!" he screamed, his fangs glaring at me as he fought to get back on his feet.

"Lie still," I commanded, aiming the gun at his head again. "Or I'll shoot another bullet into that thick skull of yours."

"Just kill me!" he told me. "I'm not afraid of death. It's why Stoney chose me to deliver his message!"

"And what message is that? To tell me that my entire team has been massacred at his command?"

He sneered before replying, "They're not all dead, unfortunately. Stoney has them locked up on our island."

My pulse raced at the news. "Which ones?"

"Why does it matter?"

I pressed the barrel deeper into his temple. "Tell me!"

"Stoney wants you to come for them. If you don't, they will all be slaughtered."

"And where am I supposed to go?"

"There's a small harbor on the edge of town. He'll be waiting for you there at midnight tomorrow with a boat to take you to our coven." The vampire eye's flashed with mischief as he added, "And he wants you to come alone."

"Of course he does."

"If you want to save your friends, you'd better be there."

"Why didn't he just deliver his message himself?" I asked him with raised brows. "Is he that much of a coward that he refuses to face me on his own?"

The vampire snarled. "He has more important issues to deal with than you, hunter!"

I clicked my tongue against the roof of my mouth before saying, "He is a coward. If he wasn't, he wouldn't be playing these childish games! He would have faced me a long time ago."

"Do you honestly think you're the only vampire hunter in this city with a vendetta against him? What makes yours more important than any of the others?"

I dropped down on one knee and pressed the barrel of the gun even deeper into the vamp's temple. "Stoney murdered my parents in front of me when I was just a little girl, and he's been hunting me ever since. He tore away the only family I had, and because I was a child, I was helpless to stop him. But I'm not helpless anymore. He's going to pay for what he's done, and I'll be damned if I let him take another person away from me again!"

The vamp's face twisted into an expression of pure amusement. "Are you still going on about your parents?" he chuckled, his mouth wide and gleaming. "They've been dead for years. Deal with it."

I pulled the gun away from his head and with a sharp exhale, pressed it against his chest. The vampire's eyes went wide with fear, but before he could get a word in, I fired, this time shooting him straight through the heart. He was able to release a violent howl before he erupted into a bloody mess. His blood sprayed up onto my face, and I used the crook of my right arm to wipe it off before rising.

"Deal with that," I muttered, to the red gooey pile beneath my boots, and shoved the gun back into its holster.

I glanced over at the building where the vault was located, wondering if I should expect more vampires waiting for me within the shadows. I doubted it, but I honestly didn't know what to expect. Stoney might have been coercing me into another trap. It wasn't like him to send one vampire, even if it was just to deliver a message. And why did he want me to come to his coven? What sort of sick game was he playing now?

****

I jumped back on my bike and sped towards the factory, where I parked just outside the main door. Remaining vigilant, I maneuvered with ease through the fallen beams inside the building, leaping over piles of stone and debris with haste. I didn't even mind when my pant leg got snagged on a metal rod and tore a large hole in the fabric. My only concern was getting back to the vault, and assessing the damage the vampires had done to my home.

Once I reached the vault door, I detected no undead in my midst, but when I walked within the perimeter of the UV lights, I came to a standstill. I gazed up at the dark lamps above my head, and I was stunned when I remained clouded in darkness. The lights weren't turning on. Fear ran up the back of my neck when I realized that the vampire had been telling the truth.

I waited in the dark, expecting to be attacked from behind. To my surprise, nothing came at me. When I realized I was in the clear, I hurried towards the vault door, but when I attempted to place my palm against the scanner, I noticed fresh blood stained the metal panel. My hand froze in mid-air, and my pulse began to race as my mind concocted the worst possible scenarios. The vampires had my friends in their custody, so I wondered whose blood was smeared across the scanner.

After realizing I had no choice but to come in contact with the blood, I ignored the sick feeling in the pit of my stomach. I placed my hand against the cool metal, trying my best not to assume that the blood belonged to Switch or Leland. Once the scanner recognized my fingerprints, the door slid open, and I ran across the threshold. Although I was doing my best to remain calm, I was afraid of what awaited me inside.

As I wiped my now bloodstained hand against the front of my pants, I prayed that I would not find bodies within the hushed vault. If I did, it would mean I was responsible for two more deaths, and the thought was too much for me to bear. I searched the front entrance first, finding broken furniture and weaponry scattered all along the floor. It looked like there had been a struggle. Thankfully, Switch and the civilian were nowhere to be found among the wreckage.

My throat burned with anger once I realized Stoney had taken both of them hostage, and I couldn't help but imagine that he was most likely torturing them. It was my fault that they had been kidnapped. I shoved a bookcase in a fit of rage, knocking it over onto its side.

"God damn it!" I screamed, kicking at the fallen bookcase. I fought against sudden tears that threatened to spill, trying to remain strong, but the thought that I was the only person left caused me to fall to my knees in despair. "This can't be happening!" I cried out, my head bowed as I sat crouched on the ground. "Switch," I whispered his name in grief. "I'm so sorry."

I rocked myself back and forth, allowing myself a moment of frustration. No one was around to see me cry, and so I let out all my emotions at once. As fresh tears flowed down my cheeks, I cried out in agony. For the first time, in a long time, I felt utterly helpless and alone. I wasn't sure how I was going to stop Stoney without my teammates, and I was afraid that he had won.

The sound of metal hitting the ground echoed in the empty vault. The noise startled me, and I jumped to my feet. I paused, waiting, but all was quiet afterward. With a deep breath, I reached for a discarded silver stake that was lying on the ground a few feet away from me and crept forward in the direction of the clatter. It had come from the infirmary, and I expected to find a vamp rummaging through the room, possibly stealing blood. However, once I made it to the doorway, I dropped my stake in surprise.

There, lying askew on a stretcher, was Harvey. His eyes were closed and he appeared unconscious. There was an ice pack resting atop his head, and I noticed there were various bruises and scratches on his face. The black clothes he wore were tattered and torn, and his left pant leg was drenched in blood. I noticed that his entire body was soaking wet and he was dripping water onto the floor, creating a small puddle underneath the stretcher.

Seeing Harvey again was quite a shock, and for a split second I wondered if it was just my imagination. However, when he coughed and his eyelids fluttered open, I knew it was no dream. I approached him then, whispering expressions of gratitude to the higher powers for sparing my friend's life. I was curious to know how he had trekked back to the vault in his condition, without being jumped by any of Stoney's goons, but I ultimately realized it didn't matter. All that mattered was that he had made it out of the sewers alive.

The sound of my footsteps startled Harvey, and he stiffened, his eyes darting to the open doorway. His expression eased when he realized it was I standing before him, and a smile eventually formed on his face.

"Lina … thank God it's you. I thought it was one of those fucking vamps coming back to finish me off."

I walked over towards him and sat down carefully on the edge of the stretcher. "Nope, it's just me. It looks like they ransacked the place though, and Switch and the civilian are gone. Stoney has them captive. I think Leland is with them too."

"I know," Harvey sighed. "No one was here when I returned. I assumed the vampires had gotten to them too."

"So, it was your blood on the scanner then."

"Yeah." He nodded, grimacing.

"Are you okay?" I asked him, my voice breaking, as I looked him over.

Harvey appeared touched by my concern. He nodded and said, "Yeah. I'm more exhausted than anything else. I've got a killer headache and a small gash on my left calf, but it's not too bad."

I checked his wound, surprised to find that it wasn't too deep. I wasn't the greatest healer, but I could stitch it up myself. Other than the bruises and the few small cuts on his face, Harvey seemed to be okay. I was shocked, given the fact that he had gone up against Scarlett. I wondered if she had fled the battle, or if he had finished her off.

As I looked him over, the painful truth of the situation hit me hard. I hung my head suddenly and confessed, "I'm so sorry, Harvey."

"For what?"

"Everything. It's my fault that Bill is dead, and that Switch was taken. If I hadn't run off looking for Leland, I would have been here when the vampires attacked. I could have protected them … but instead, I let Switch and that poor woman both down."

Harvey lifted hand to place it on top of mine. He took a deep breath before saying, "You can't blame yourself, Lina. The vampires would have waited to attack regardless of when or why you left the vault. It seems as if this was their plan all along."

"What do you mean?"

"Haven't you figured it out yet? This entire night was one big set-up. The tip that Stoney was hiding out in that building downtown was just the beginning of this little ruse. We took our cues from the enemy. We played right into their hands."

"How do you know this, Johnson?"

He frowned at my question and replied, "I don't know for sure, but look at everything that has happened tonight. It's pretty obvious that the vampires wanted to separate you from everyone, starting with me and Bill. It was their intention to pick us off one by one—it wasn't a coincidence, and if Leland is also missing, my guess is that they got to him first. Stoney knew you'd go into the building if you thought he was inside it."

I nodded, knowing full well that Harvey was right. "There's just one thing I don't understand about Stoney's plan."

"Which is?"

"If this was Stoney's plan to get back at me, why would he want to take you guys out beforehand if I'm the one he's after?"

Harvey scowled at my response. "Jesus, Lina. Try to put aside your ego for a minute.."

"You know what I mean, Harvey," I responded with a huff. "The vampires have a vendetta against me—especially Stoney. I've eliminated at least one hundred of those bloodsuckers single-handedly, not to mention I've faced countless vamps that claimed were hired to kill me. They want me dead."

"You're absolutely right. The vampires do have a vendetta against you, but what better way to torture you than to kill off your entire entourage before coming for your head?" Harvey coughed suddenly and rubbed at his throat. After clearing the phlegm from his pipes, he said, "It makes sense doesn't it?"

I said nothing, but I knew he was right. Mike had even come to the same conclusion at the bar. My stomach churned with disgust at my naivety. I fell for Stoney's trap–there was no doubt about that now. What Harvey proposed was right; Stoney was never in that building to begin with. He had sent me there only to separate me from my team. "He thinks he's won," I mumbled. "He really thinks it's over."

"It isn't over," Harvey replied. "Stoney thought I would go down without a fight, but he was wrong. I completely annihilated his red-headed playmate."

"Did you?" I asked him, unconvinced that he had defeated Scarlett on his own.

Harvey grinned, coughing once more. "Well, you know … I may have screamed and hollered like a little girl when she slashed up my leg and bit me, but I got the job done nonetheless."

"Scarlett's dead?"

He nodded. "Stuck a stake straight through that bitch's cold heart."

I chuckled at his response, relieved that Scarlett was dead. That was one less vampire crony to deal with. Sadly, I knew that Stoney would not take the news of his beloved's death well.

I leaned my head onto Harvey's shoulder, careful as to not disturb his wounds. "Stoney's going to be pissed when he finds out."

"Good," he replied.

I gazed up at Harvey's face then, my eyes tracing over his boyish features. Harvey was my age, but he looked five years younger. I always gave him shit about his looks, but there was something new and strangely mature about him in this moment. I wasn't sure if it was because he had taken care of Scarlett on his own, but whatever it was, I found myself oddly attracted to him because of it.

Harvey must've realized I was staring at him, because he peered down at me suddenly, and our eyes instantly locked. I stared up into his brown eyes, noticing for the first time that there were tiny flakes of amber within them. I was taken aback by this, and by the sudden warming sensation in the pit of my stomach.

"I'm glad you made it back, Johnson," I told him after a quiet moment passed between us. "I was having a hard time imagining my life without you."

"You were?" Harvey replied sheepishly. I noticed his cheek had flushed at my admission.

"Of course. How could I possibly live in a world without Harvey Johnson or Bill Sects? You guys are the two most important men in my life—besides Leland of course." I reached down to squeeze his hand before saying, "We may be a team, but we're also a family."

He smiled at me, but I detected some disappointment behind it. "Yeah, that's true. We are a family."

I felt myself choking up, and I suddenly buried my head against his neck, hoping to hide my tears from him. He tensed up at the action, and I figured I had caught him off guard. I fought back my tears, but when my breathing turned ragged, I realized I was powerless to stop them from falling.

"You and I are the only ones left," I whispered, my face still hidden from his sight. "We have to save them, Harvey, no matter what."

Harvey reached down to lift my chin, and when he realized I was crying, an expression of genuine shock passed over his face.

"Lina? Are you okay?" Harvey looked terrified to see me in such a state. In all the years we hunted vampires together, he had never seen me cry—I had made sure of it.

"I failed everyone, Harvey," I told him in-between sobs. "Even if this whole thing was a trap, I should have known better—I should have thought it all through before rushing into that building and putting everyone at risk. Now Bill is dead, and Switch and Leland are hostages." I wiped at my eyes, disgusted by my overwhelming emotions. "I put my family in danger, all because of my stupid feud with Stoney."

"Shush," he told me, as he smoothed down the back of my hair. "It's not your fault, so stop blaming yourself. Like I said before, it was out of your control."

"But if I had just listened to you on that rooftop, Harvey, none of this would have happened. If I had just followed protocol—"

Harvey shook his head and replied, "It would have happened sooner or later. Stoney is aware of your unbridled hatred for him, and he would have used it to his advantage. He wants you to suffer, and he would not have stopped until you lost everything and everyone."

"That's exactly what Mike said."

"It's true, Lina."

"I want Stoney dead," I murmured. "I want to ram my fist clean through his chest and rip out his lungs with my bare hands."

"Lina, you and I both know that won't kill him," Harvey told me with a knowing smile. "Play around with his guts all you want, but that monster needs to be staked, shot with a silver bullet, or decapitated, maybe all three for good measure."

I frowned up at him, but then I began to laugh. I smiled when Harvey wrapped his arms around my shoulders and squeezed. "Simply staking him will do, but maybe I'll just torture him for a little while before that happens."

"Ha. Fat chance," he responded. "If you cornered Stoney, and you had the advantage, you would kill him without a moment's hesitation."

"You're right. You know me so well, Johnson."

"Well, that's what happens when you spend as much time with a person as I have with you. I know what you're thinking before you even think it, Holiday."

I grinned up at him suddenly and whispered, "I'm so glad you're alive, Harvey."

"You've already said that," he replied, holding my stare.

"I know ... but I mean it."

We stared into each other's eyes for a moment or two, until I broke eye contact. I cleared my throat and glanced down at my hands resting in my lap, trying my hardest to avoid Harvey's intense stare. I was frightened of the way he was looking at me, and I thought back to the moment on the radio, when he had tried so desperately to confess something to me. Although I was curious, I knew now wasn't the time to bring up the subject.

"What do you think Stoney will do when he finds out that he didn't get rid of you as planned, Harvey?" I asked him suddenly, hoping to keep the conversation on more important matters.

Harvey frowned at my question. "I'm not sure. I hadn't thought of that."

"Well, I guess I need to figure out what his next move is."

"Yeah."

"I'll tell you one thing though, you are going to lie here and rest. I don't want you overexerting yourself, Johnson."

He frowned at me and shook his head. "Lina ..."

"I mean it, Johnson. No one else is going to die on my watch."

He laughed and nodded, knowing full well there was no point in arguing with me, but I had a feeling that there was no place in the world he would rather be than by my side. He had always had my back no matter what. I promised to protect him and he would do his best to do the same for me, even in his current injured state. That was one thing I loved about him.

"Whatever you say, boss."

I managed a smile, but my thoughts turned dark as I recalled my parent's horrific deaths. Watching them die had scarred me for life, provoking me to despise all vampires that roamed the earth. Stoney was, and forever would be, an evil creature, and it was my job to rid the world of him–especially now. In the beginning, it had always been about exacting revenge for the death of my parents, but the rules of the game had changed.

Now, killing Stoney was about absolute justice. He may have had the upper hand, but I vowed to finish the job. No matter what. He had Leland and Switch in his clutches now, and I had to do everything in my power to rescue them.

"I can't lose Leland, Harvey," I whispered, choking up again. "I just can't."

Harvey carefully wrapped his arm my shoulder and squeezed it tight. "I've never seen you like this before, Lina. You're kind of freaking me out."

I laughed at his remark. "I know everyone thinks I'm this ruthless, vampire slaying bitch, but deep down, I have my share of weaknesses too."

Harvey raised his brows at my admission. "You have weaknesses?"

I pushed his arm gently. "Yes. You guys are my weakness. My love for my team—my family. I'm nothing without you."

"Lina, come on. That's not true."

"It really is," I confessed. "I know I didn't always give you and Bill the praise you deserved, and I'll admit that at times I was hard on you two, but I owe my life to you guys. You've always had my back—you were always there for me."

"You don't have to thank us. It's an honor to fight alongside you."

I gave him a weak smile, but whispered. "The sad thing is that Stoney figured out my one true weakness. It's just like you said earlier. What better way to get to me than to kill you all off? Which is why I know that if I fail and Leland dies, I will die along with him."

Harvey wrapped his other arm around me and pulled me into a warm bear hug in an effort to comfort me. "Don't say that," he replied softly. "We'll save them, I promise."

I gazed up at him then, giving him a serious look. "How can you be sure?"

"Because, it's like you said: you're a ruthless, vampire slaying bitch. Stoney doesn't stand a chance against you."

I laughed at his statement. "I'm glad I have you on my side, Harvey."

He didn't respond. Instead, he rubbed my shoulders gently. His soft touch sent a chill down my back. "I believe in you, Lina," he whispered. "I always have."

Then, to my surprise, he bent down to kiss my forehead. The action was out of character for Harvey—for us, and I found myself gazing up at him in bewilderment. Before I could even question the action, he bent down to kiss my lips. My eyebrows rose the moment his lips touched mine, and they remained there for a moment or so before he pulled back to stare into my eyes.

I don't know what came over me, but I leaned in and kissed him back. Maybe I was just living in the moment, with the grim thought in the back of my head that Harvey and I weren't coming out of our meeting with Stoney alive. Or, maybe I was finally giving in to feelings I had for Harvey that I'd kept bottled up for years. Either way, all I knew was that at this moment in time, I wanted to lose myself. I wanted the memory of the night to fade away, even if it was only for a couple of hours.

My display of affection caused Harvey's thin lips to curve upwards in a grin. He gently wrapped his hands in my hair and kissed me deeper, causing my eyes to slip shut, and all of my worries about Leland and Stoney to wither from my mind.

Still, I wanted to lose myself even more. I kept my mouth against his as I began to unbuckle his pants, but he dropped his hands down to grab mine, sliding his fingers between mine and locking our hands together. I was confused as to why he had stopped from going any further, and so I promptly questioned him.

"What's the matter?"

Harvey was out of breath and his cheeks were flushed, and he was looking at me in a way that he never had before. My stomach fluttered from his intense stare, and when he asked me if I was confident that I wanted to make love, I silenced him with another kiss.

"I don't want to talk anymore," I told him, in between heated kisses. "I don't want to think, or care, or feel! I just want to exist, here in this moment with you."

"Lina …"

"I want to feel something other than pain, Harvey, even if it's just for a little while. Please."

He nodded, and thankfully didn't say another word on the matter. Once he let go of my hands, I tugged off his pants, and then lifted my arms, allowing him to remove my shirt. We took off the remainder of our clothes and then laid back down onto the stretcher, our bare bodies pressing together tightly as we held each other close.

Time seemed to stand still as we gave ourselves over to one another, and Harvey was as gentle and considerate throughout as I expected he would be. In that scared hour that we shared, we were no longer vampire hunters. We weren't mourning the loss of our friend, or fearing for the lives of the rest of our comrades. Harvey and I were simply man and woman, and during that brief time, Lina Holiday, the bad-ass vampire slayer, ceased to exist.

Chapter Eight

After our brief and intimate reunion, I fell asleep bare naked on the stretcher next to Harvey. I had taken up most of the space on the small rigid bed, but he didn't seem to mind. He made space for me, encircling his arms around my waist before we both succumbed to sleep.

It was nearly mid-day by the time e we woke up, and I rushed to get prepared for the meeting with Stoney. After what had happened between us, I could barely look at Harvey, but I felt his eyes on me as I dressed. Last night had been a mistake, I was sure of it, and I hoped that he wasn't expecting anything more than friendship from me. However, I wasn't about to have that conversation with him now. We had more important things to be worried about.

To my relief, Harvey didn't bring up what transpired last night, but he did try to talk me out of the meeting with Stoney. He confessed that he was afraid I wasn't emotionally prepared for a showdown with him. After my breakdown Harvey must have figured I was in a fragile state of mind. I was, but I couldn't let that stop me.

Before leaving, I tended to the gash on Harvey's leg, stitching it up nicely. I also cleaned the cuts on his face and hands. Although he appeared to be fine to fight, I couldn't ignore the nagging fear in the back of my mind. I had just gotten him back. Did I really want to chance losing him again? I knew I couldn't go through that pain again, and I pondered the idea of meeting Stoney without him.

When I confessed my fears to Harvey, he strongly disagreed with my plan to leave him behind. I told him it was in his best interest if he remained in the vault and rested, but he wasn't having it. He pleaded with me for nearly an hour until I finally gave in to his pestering.. I was fully aware of the warning that I was to go alone, but I figured it'd be a wise idea to bring along as backup.

As soon as night fell, we collected our things and made for the harbor. I knew I had to be there at twelve and not a second after, or there would be hell to pay. Stoney had a violent temper, and I was sure he would make an example of me if I showed up late. I decided not to give him the satisfaction, and so we had left the vault with time to spare.

Harvey and I pulled up to the entrance of the harbor and parked the SUV by the front gate, then exited the vehicle. We stayed alert, and on the lookout for any undead. I may have appeared calm, with steady hands and a straight face, but my heart was on the verge of popping out of my chest. I couldn't trust Stoney, and that there was a good chance that my team was dead. If that was the case, it would only put me right where he wanted me: defenseless and isolated. Harvey, even in his current state, would hold his own in battle, but I was still going to worry about his safety.

I kept my senses alert as we walked down the shaky, wooden dock, and Harvey and I headed towards the end of the row of boats. I kept my right hand dangling near my holstered gun as I surveyed my surroundings. We were unsure which boat was Stoney's, but I was positive that we were at the right place. The harbor was small, restricted, and empty—the perfect place for a vampire to dock his boat. It was an ideal spot for an ambush, but all was quiet.

"Where are they?" I whispered to Harvey. "I figured this meeting with Stoney was most definitely a trap, but there aren't any vampires skulking about. You would think they would show their ugly faces by now!"

"Yeah," he murmured in agreement, his forehead beginning to perspire. "I knew from the moment you told me about this meeting that he was setting us up. Again." Harvey sighed and shook his head. "I don't know why we're here ..."

"Because, he has Leland and Switch. I need to know that they are all right." We just have to be on guard until we find the right boat."

Harvey rolled his eyes. "Lina, please. You and I both know we aren't making it to that boat in one piece."

"Harvey, don't start ..."

"No, there's no smoothing this over," he said with a harsh whisper. "I'm not a child—you don't have to coddle me."

I frowned and glanced over at the stubborn expression conveyed on his face. "I'm not coddling you, Johnson. I'm ... just trying to remain positive."

"Positive?" Harvey muttered the word with a forced smile. "We're going to die out here, Lina." His face took on a blank expression as we carried on down the wooden path. Then, he glanced over at me and asked, "Are we ever going to talk about what happened last night?"

"Harvey, not now."

"Why not? I think now is as good a time as any, since we're moments away from death!"

"Harvey, keep your voice down!" I scolded, my own voice hoarse.

"Sorry," he responded, his brown eyes darkening at my chastising. "But I think I have a right to know."

I ignored his question and kept advancing down the dock, trying to keep my mind focused on the task at hand. I should have trusted my instincts earlier and left Johnson behind. We were about to face off with Stoney—now was not the time to be having a lover's quarrel.

"You're ignoring me now? That's just great."

I had finally reached my breaking point. I spun around to face him and said, "Harvey, I can't do this with you right now. I know you want to get closure on what happened last night, but you're just going to have to wait. We have more important things to be worrying about, like where our friends are being held captive and if they're even alive."

He uttered a forced sigh, but eventually nodded in agreement. "Okay, okay. You're right. I'll let it go."

"Thank you," I responded, relieved.

"I'm sorry, Lina. I guess I don't know where my head's at."

"Don't fall apart on me," I begged. "I need you. I can't do this on my own!"

He coughed and rubbed at his forehead, wiping the sweat away with the back of his hand. "You know I've always got your back." He paused a moment before saying, "I just don't want to die."

I nodded. Hoping to comfort him, I reached out and squeezed his hand. "I know. I don't either, but we're not going to die. I promise I won't let anything happen to you."

"That's not a promise you can keep, but I appreciate the offer nonetheless."

****

As soon as the last boat on the dock came into view, I drew a deep breath, and my pulse raced from anticipation. It was an average looking boat, medium-sized with a cabin and a deck large enough to fit at least ten people. However, there was something sinister about it. I noticed there was mild corrosion on the hull, and when I stole a closer glance, I thought I saw blood splatters on the railing. Once I concluded there was no one aboard, I tossed my hands in exasperation.

"What the hell is going on?" I muttered, growing angry. "Where is Stoney?"

"I don't know. Maybe he's messing with us?"

"Does he expect us to sail the boat ourselves?"

"Don't be ridiculous," a mysterious voice said. Harvey and I were both taken aback when Stoney emerged from the cabin of the boat. He looked just as frightening as usual; his long, black hair fell in waves over his broad shoulders, and his eerily stark white skin was blinding. Stoney's gaunt face curved into a sneer as he stared down at me from the deck of the boat; his large, black eyes baring down on me. A chill shivered down my spine when he continued to stare at me.

"Stoney." My voice was ice-cold. I glared up at him from the dock. Due to habit; I dropped my right hand quickly, leaving it dangling near my holstered gun. It had been quite a while, but I was finally face to face with the monster who had killed my parents. The rage I had been harboring for the vampire all my life was burning through, and the ability to restrain myself from shooting him was proving to be more difficult than I thought.

"Hello, beautiful," he said, with a wide, toothy grin. I wanted nothing more than to smack the satisfied look right off his face.

He leapt off of the boat with ease and landed directly in front of me. We stood only a few feet apart now, his lifeless eyes ogling me while I continued to stare daggers at him. I hoped to appear unaffected by his nearness, but I had a feeling the vampire could see right through the smokescreen.

He flashed his fangs at me. "Did you miss me?"

My response was a swift punch to his face, but instead of scolding me, Stoney simply laughed. Once he no longer found my brash action amusing, he grabbed me by my neck and hoisted me high into the air. I struggled to breathe, and I pawed at my throat when Stoney began to crush it.

"How many times do I have to showcase my strength to you, Lina?" he asked me with a disappointed scowl. "You never learn, do you, girl?"

"Drop her, Stoney!" Harvey shouted, now gaining the vampire's attention. "Or I'll shoot."

Stoney glanced in his direction and dropped me back onto my feet. I rubbed at my sore neck, cursing all paranormal creatures and their sick fascination with squeezing the air out of my lungs. Once I had gained my bearings, I glanced over at Harvey, noticing that he was now aiming his pistol at Stoney. Fearing for his safety, I shouted at him to drop his weapon. He refused, but was now inching away from the vampire. Unfortunately, the Stone was relentless.

"You were told to come alone, Lina," Stoney remarked with a sigh. "So much for following my orders."

"Do you think Lina would be dumb enough to come face you on her own?" Harvey asked him with a smirk. "Screw you and your orders, Stoney!"

"Ah, Harvey Johnson, the heroic hunter who's always so eager to jump in and save the fair maiden from the evil vampires." Stoney chuckled and shook his dark locks, sneering. "I see you've barely survived the encounter with my fledglings. It's such a shame to see you all battered up."

"Yeah, well, you should see the other guys."

"Unfortunately, they were just fodder." Stoney glanced back at me before saying, "I always leave the best for last."

"Oh, really?" Harvey murmured, looking surprised. "Was Scarlett just another insignificant vamp to you too, Stoney?" When Stoney didn't respond, Harvey added, "Well, I guess you won't miss her then."

The vampire's gaze hardened, and he twisted his head back around to face him. Stoney charged Harvey without a moment's hesitation, knocking the gun out of his hand and shoving him down onto his back. He stood poised over him, his fangs unsheathed once more.

"You dare belittle Scarlett in front of me?" Stoney roared, his pale, bony hands shaking with anger. "I should rip out that tongue of yours, hunter, and shove it down your throat!"

"Stoney!" I shouted, trying to gain his attention. I approached him with haste to say, "Your quarrel is with me! Harvey has nothing to do with this."

"It appears that now he does," Stoney retorted, and gripped Harvey by the collar of his shirt. He bent down towards his neck, his mouth ajar, showing off his sharp, elongated teeth. He made the attempt to bite him, but my plea gave him pause.

"Please don't harm him! I'm begging you."

"Oh, you're begging me now?" he asked, amused by my outburst. "Get on your knees then. Do it properly."

I froze, unsure if he was serious or not. "What?"

"You heard me. Get down on your knees and beg me to spare this detestable man's life." Before he gave me a chance to respond, Stoney dragged one of his long, black fingernails over Harvey's cheek, and with the swift flick of his hand, a fresh cut started leaking blood. The vampire brought his finger to his mouth, sucking the blood from his fingertip slowly. "Or, perhaps you would prefer to watch me drain the blood from him slowly and painfully?"

"Okay, fine." I dropped to my knees and lowered my head until my forehead touched the wooden dock. "I'll do anything you want, Stoney. Just don't hurt him."

"Look at me, Lina," Stoney commanded, and I did as he wished. His black eyes flashed with amusement at my hunched over form. "You'll do anything I want?" he asked curiously.

I nodded. "Yes. I swear it."

"Excellent. I'm glad you see it my way." He released his hold on Harvey's collar, but not before he said, "You're a lucky man. The only reason you're still alive is because Lina wishes it."

Harvey mouthed me a thank-you once the vampire had backed off.

As I rose to my feet, Stoney came towards me, and I immediately stiffened. I dropped my hands down at my sides, and my right fingertips grazed the cool metal of my gun. I wanted to be sure I could defend myself if the vampire made a move to attack. But, instead of striking me, he maneuvered around my defensive stance and climbed back aboard the boat without as much as a second look in my direction.

Once he was back onboard, Stoney reached his arm over the side and offered his hand to me. "Come with me now," he said, and his smug grin resurfaced. "We have much to discuss."

"Do we?" I replied with a frown. "I believe the only thing we have to discuss with each other, Stoney, is where my friends are."

"You already know where they are, Lina. They're back at my coven, safe and sound, and if you come aboard this boat, I will tell you how you can reclaim them."

"Don't do it, Lina!" Harvey yelled, now rising to his feet. "Please! You don't have to sacrifice yourself like this!"

I looked to Harvey and contemplated refusing Stoney's offer. Sadly, after a few moments of mental deliberation, I came to realize that I was not in the position to. If I did not heed the vampire's commands, he would certainly force me onto his boat regardless, and Leland, Harvey, and Switch would be killed as punishment. Bill was dead because of me, and I did not want the rest of them to suffer the same fate.

Staring at Harvey with sorrow-filled eyes, I watched as fear flashed across his face. He knew what I was about to say before I even said it. "I don't think I can refuse his offer, Harvey."

Harvey hurried towards me then. "If you board that boat, you will be in his complete control, Lina! Don't you understand? It's what he's wanted all along!"

"What about Leland?" I asked him with a frown. "I can't just turn my back on him. This may be the only chance I have to save him, and Switch."

"We can find another way!"

Stoney growled at Harvey, his face twisted with fury from the hunter's outburst. "I believe I was talking to Ms. Holiday, and besides, there is no other way to save your merry band of vampire killers. You can come willingly, or against your will, it matters not to me. Either way, neither of you are leaving this dock unless you're on my boat, and just so we're clear, rejecting my offer will leave your friends to the horrid fate of becoming my dinner. The choice is respectfully yours, Lina."

The frown on my face remained as I studied the vampire's cold expression. Once I had carefully considered his ultimatum, I asked, "How can I trust that you won't kill us once we get to wherever the hell it is we're going?"

"You know that you can't ... but then again, you don't really have a choice, now do you?"

"What if we just kill you now?" Harvey asked him with a grunt.

Stoney laughed at the question and said, "I'd love to see you try." He then turned to face me and said, "Don't get any ideas. I've left orders, and in the event I don't return, they are to slaughter your precious family."

I flinched at his admission. "Bastard."

"I keep all my loose ends tied, Lina. You should know that by now." Holding out his hand to me once more, he whispered, "This is the only way you can save them, Lina, so don't be foolish. I know you don't want your team to perish, so be a good girl and take my hand now."

I sighed and glanced back at Harvey, who was undoubtedly more anxious than I was. However, as wary of Stoney as I was, I knew that the vampire had the upper hand. He had my family, and in order to save them I had to do whatever he requested. If I refused him, he had made it clear that he would not hesitate in killing them all. I was right where he wanted me, and there was nothing I could do about it.

"All right," I whispered after a moment. I eyed the vampire's outstretched hand with apprehension, but I eventually placed my hand in his, allowing his bony fingers to curl over mine. I jolted from his icy grip before declaring, "I'll go with you."

"Lina, no!" Harvey screeched. "It's suicide!"

As soon as Harvey made the attempt to pull me away from Stoney, a pair of vampires emerged from the shadows. They grabbed both of his arms, holding him at bay. As he struggled against their firm grasp, one of the vampires broke off a piece of the wooden railing and bashed him over the head. The harsh blow was enough to knock Harvey unconscious. I gasped when I watched his body go limp.

"Harvey!" I tried to pull my hand out of Stoney's grasp, but it was too late. He yanked me up onto the boat, and was holding me up against his body as I fought to get free.

"Let me go!" I hollered, watching with tear-filled eyes as the two vampires lifted Harvey high into the air. They hoisted his body over the edge of the boat's railing, and proceeded to drop him onto the deck. "Be careful with him!" I shouted at the vamps, still struggling to fend off my own vampire assailant.

"Hush now," Stoney commanded as he smoothed down the back of my hair. "Your little boy toy is fine."

"If you hurt him, Stoney—" I began, my tone stricken with fear.

"You'll what?" the vampire remarked with a laugh.

Stoney motioned for his vampire goons to approach us, and as they came forward, he said, "Take her weapons."

I glared at him, but remained still as the two vampires frisked me. They removed the gun from my holster, the sliver stakes from my vest, and even the small knife I kept hidden in my boot. Once they had collected all of my weapons, Stoney ordered them to remove Harvey's as well.

"Where are you taking us?" I asked, as the two goons walked away.

"You know the answer to that question, Lina."

"No, not really."

Stoney ceased stroking my hair to grab a hold of my chin, forcing me to face him. His dark eyes were aglow with triumph as he whispered: "I'm taking you to a place where you will never see the light of day again."

Then, suddenly, he dropped his hold on me and moved over towards the steering wheel. Stoney turned the key in the ignition and placed his hands on the wheel, routing the boat away from the dock. I crawled across the slippery deck of the boat to get to Harvey. Once I reached him I wrapped my arms around his unconscious form and held him tight against me.

It was then that I noticed Stoney's vampire cohorts now towered over us, and I glanced up at them, their lust-filled eyes causing me to worry. They were only fledglings—weak vampires who were at the bottom of the supernatural totem pole, but to fend off two of them on my own without any weapons would still be difficult.

"You smell delicious, hunter," the vamp on my right said. He had a thin blonde mustache, and he rubbed his fingers over it slowly as he said, "I'm starving. I haven't dined in hours."

The other one laughed, his dark gaze heavy as well. "You know what, Gavin? I just realized something."

"What's that?"

"I've never tasted the blood of a hunter before."

"Oh, you've got to try it. It's the most delicious blood of all." Gavin paused, pondering his statement. "Well, second to the blood of a newborn, of course." He licked his lips next and whispered, "Don't worry, hunter. This won't hurt—much."

I glanced over at Stoney, who still had his back turned towards them, wondering if he was honestly going to stand by and allow the vamps to feed freely. When I realized he didn't seem to be interested in the impending doom I now faced, I decided I had to deal with the unruly vamps on my own before I became their entree.

My arms still embracing Harvey, I stayed on defense, and as soon as the first vampire made his move, I would be ready for him. My plan was to swipe at his eyes, with the intent of gouging them out of his head.

However, neither were given the chance to put a hand on me. Before the vampires could even take another step in my direction, Stoney rushed them, baring his fangs as he shouted, "You will not touch her!"

The vampires cowered before their master, but they snarled as they gazed back and forth between Stoney and I, confusion etched on their ugly faces.

One of his goons frowned and said, "We weren't going to kill her, Stoney. I swear! All we wanted was a taste!"

Stoney's violent expression turned blasé as he stared at the vampire. "You just wanted a taste, eh?" He chuckled at his request, his black waves bouncing freely in the wind. It was at this moment that I realized that our boat was now sailing without a captain, which did nothing to soothe my already frazzled nerves.

"That's all you wanted?" Stoney asked him, still laughing.

The vampire nodded and laughed along with his master, seemingly relieved. Then, without warning, Stoney picked him up and lifted his body directly over his head. In a matter of seconds, he broke the vampire's spine and tossed him overboard into the black water. I was shocked by the action, and watched as the vampire sank below the water's surface.

Gavin stared up at Stoney with wide eyes, cowering in fear when he approached. The vampire dropped down onto all fours and pleaded with his master for forgiveness. Stoney chuckled at Gavin's cowardice, but his amused expression wore away in a matter of seconds.

"Lina is mine," he informed him with a snarl. "Do you understand? No one is to put a hand on her, but me. No vampire is to taste her, but me. If I catch you even looking at her the wrong way, I will rip your head off and throw you over the side of this boat! Is that clear?"

Gavin nodded, still crouched down at Stoney's feet. "Yes, master. I promise no harm will come of her."

"Good. Now get out of my sight."

Gavin trudged over towards the doorway to the cabin, but he paused and glanced back at Stoney, as if waiting for him to change his mind. Stoney said nothing, only waved him off. With a disappointed look, Gavin finally disappeared inside.

Once he had left the deck, Stoney looked to me, his left eyebrow raised. "Happy?" he asked after a quiet moment had passed.

I frowned, confused by his meaning. "What?"

"I could have sensed your fear and desperation from a mile away, hunter," the vampire responded with a huff. "You're losing your touch."

I said nothing, only glared at him, my grip on Harvey tightening. I glanced off in the distance, watching as the shore grew farther and farther away. Stoney was taking us to some unknown coven, and I considered the possibility that it might be on an island in the middle of nowhere. Although I wasn't aware of any islands near Chicago, I knew there were some farther up the lake, near Michigan, but I didn't figure that was where his base was located. He could be found in Chicago frequently, and I doubted he would travel that far. No, Stoney's coven was somewhere in the city— where exactly, I wasn't sure.

"We're getting close!" Stoney said loud and dramatically, and spun the wheel to the left.

I surveyed my surroundings, confused. "Close to what?" I asked him with a loud snort. "There's nothing but miles and miles of water."

"Yes."

"Yes?"

He was on me in a flash, tearing me away from Harvey, who still lay unconscious on the deck of the boat. My eyes grew wide with fright as I stared at the monster who had his hands around my throat once more; genuine confusion etched on my face. Stoney's grip was rough as he forced me onto my feet, simply to slam me against the wall of the nearby cabin wall. I gasped and pawed at his right hand, but his hold on me was so tight I could scarcely breathe. I was no match for his strength.

"Why are you doing this?" I managed to wheeze. "You promised you wouldn't kill me!"

"I'm not killing you, my dear," he retorted. "I simply can't have you remembering the route to my coven. Suppose you managed to escape—although highly unlikely, it could happen, and we wouldn't want you running off for help, now would we?"

"But—" I hollered in pain when he used his free hand to press his nails deep into my shoulder, cutting through the tender flesh.

"Does that hurt, Ms. Holiday?" He asked with a perverse grin.

"Fuck you!"

"Now, I believe it's time to say goodnight."

After blowing a kiss, he lifted me away from the cabin, only to slam my body against it once more. This time, the back of my head hit the metal wall just right. The last thing I recalled seeing was the disturbing toothy smile displayed on his wicked face, before blackness claimed me.

Chapter Nine

"Wakey, wakey!" a blaring voice hollered, bringing me back to harsh reality.

My eyes fluttered open; the back of my head throbbing as I came to. Once my sensations were fully roused, I examined my surroundings in a daze. Cold grey walls enclosed the space: I was sealed inside a dark room. There was a metal door parallel to where I lay, but there were no windows, and a lone light bulb flickered above my head, providing a miniscule amount of light. The room was dark and forbidding, and its coldness chilled me to the core.

It took me about a minute or so before I even realized I was lying on an uncomfortable metal bed with a mattress that could've been only five inches thick; my ankles and wrists were bound to the legs by leather straps. I pulled my arms downward, hoping my wrists would slide free, but the straps around them were too tight and the leather cruelly bit into my skin. My pulse raced with fear at the idea of being unable to defend myself in a coven full of vampires, and I anxiously tried to yank my legs out of their binds, but it was no use. I cried out in exasperation; my forehead beginning to perspire.

"Poor girl," the same voice whispered. "So young and beautiful, but so foolish too."

"What's going on here?" I asked, trying once again to tug my wrists free. I could not recall how I came to be in the room, and the last thing I remembered before blacking out was drifting out to sea, with Stoney's hand encircled around my throat.

"Oh, I wouldn't try to struggle too much. You don't want to wear yourself out before the master comes to see you."

"Huh?" I searched for the source of the voice, but I found no one in the room. It was only when I lifted my head backward that I noticed a figure positioned directly behind the bed. I gasped, startled by the dark figure, and watched with wide eyes when it maneuvered around the side of the bed to come before me.

It was an old woman, shrouded in a shabby navy dress. Her grey hair was pulled into a tight bun, and her face was weathered and pale. She was holding an object in her gloved hands, and when I stole a closer look at it, I noticed it was a white handkerchief spotted with blood.

"So beautiful …" the woman said again, and this time she reached out her hand to touch my face. I withdrew from the woman, worried. She scowled at me and grumbled something under her breath.

"Such beauty wasted!" she exclaimed, suddenly. Her tone had turned vicious, and I winced.

"I'm sorry?"

"You should be sorry, whore!"

I stared up at the woman, taken aback by her rudeness. "Whore? Why would you call me that?"

The old woman sneered and replied, "Because that's what you are! Tramping around in the middle of the night. You lack morals! You are impure!"

I was certainly confused by the woman's crude accusations, wondering how she had the right to judge me when I had never even met her before. "Ma'am, I don't understand—"

"Of course you don't!" she shouted, her cloudy eyes narrowing in anger. "You, with your beauty and your perfect health! You have the world in your hands, but you waste it hunting vampires!"

I remained silent as I watched the woman withdraw from the side of the bed. She began to pace near the door, waving her hands in the air, her eyes wild and fervent. While the woman was preoccupied, ranting and raving, I leaned my head to the right and tried to lift my mouth towards the strap around my hand. I hoped I could tug it loose with my teeth. Unfortunately, the old woman realized what I was doing and rushed at me before I could make any progress, snapping her decaying teeth in disapproval.

"Don't do that!" She screeched.

"Okay!" I responded hastily, swallowing the lump of fear that formed in the back of my throat.

"The master said he would make me like him—he said he would make me feel strong again! But has he? No! He's too busy chasing you all over Chicago!" the woman snarled, jealousy conveyed on her weathered face. "What about me? What about what I want?"

When I did not answer her, the woman pounded her fist on the metal post of the bed. Then, with a sudden harsh cry, she bent her face down towards mine. Our noses were only inches apart now. "What about what I want?" she repeated, her voice barely above the sound of a whisper.

"I'm sorry," I replied slowly. I was growing increasingly uncomfortable by the woman's nearness.

"You're sorry?" the old woman cried, a smile creeping onto her face. "Apologies won't make me young again, missy! Nothing will stop the cancer from spreading but immortality!"

The old woman grew silent as she hovered over me, her hands quivering as they clutched the blood-stained handkerchief. Then, with a far off look in her eye, the woman suddenly dropped the handkerchief from her hand to reveal a glimmering pair of metal scissors. They had been shrouded all along, and the sight of them in the hands of a deranged lunatic only caused my anxiety to worsen.

I wasted no time. I leaned my head over again to the right, this time my teeth successfully gripping the strap around my wrist. After a few harsh tugs, I was able to lift the strap out of the teeth of the buckle, until finally, the strap was loose enough for my right hand to slide free. I quickly reached over towards the other strap and unlatched my left hand, but when I went for my bound feet, the woman slammed the scissors down onto the mattress, into the empty space between my legs.

"I said not to do that!" she hollered, her wrinkled lips forming a deep scowl. Then, her angered expression melted away as she stared at the scissors in her hand. A look of absolute understanding came over her, and she murmured, "Perhaps if I kill you, master will save me. If he has no more distractions, he can focus on what's really important …"

"No," I explained, hoping to reason with her. "You don't want to kill me—"

"Don't tell me what I want!" she screamed, her brows raised high. "You must die, because if you're alive, you have all of his attention … and I refuse to suffer any more!"

Without another word on the matter, she swiped the scissors at me. She didn't lie about her weakness and her thrust was slow. I dodged the attack, and grabbed at the old woman's wrist before she could stab me. We struggled with each other, both of my hands now wrapped around hers, preventing the sharp blades from reaching my flesh. I was positioned wrong, unable to move my legs but I was still stronger and younger, and once her vivacity began to give, I ripped the scissors from her hands and stabbed her in the neck.

I watched the woman stumble backwards in shock, her back colliding with the wall behind her as she felt around for the handle of the scissors. Before I could command her to stop, the old woman yanked them out of her neck, revealing the fatal wound I had inflicted on her. Blood streamed smoothly from the open wound, the ripped flesh bubbling with blood. It poured down the front of her dress and down her arm to puddle on the floor.

The woman tried to put pressure on the wound, but it was no use. She was dead in a matter of seconds. She slid down the wall, leaving a trail of her blood as she went. I grimaced at the sight: her eyes wide in horror, her feet slick with her blood. I turned away and began to work on freeing my legs. As I unlatched the straps around my feet, I blamed Stoney for the woman's insanity.

Once I was free from my binds, I hurried towards the only door in the room. I tried the handle, and was surprised when I found it was unlocked. Stoney misjudged me. Instead of rushing out at full speed, I waited patiently, listening for any sounds outside of the door. When I heard none, I proceeded to escape, but not before grabbing the bloody scissors off the ground.

I opened the door and peered out of the cracked doorway, praying there were no vampire assailants waiting for me. Once I realized that the coast was clear, I left the room, tip-toeing down the dark hall. I kept my grip on the scissors tight, knowing it was the only weapon I had on me. If I came across a hostile vampire, the scissors would be somewhat useful.

As I continued down the narrow hallway, I wondered where Harvey had ended up, and it was then that I noticed the hall was lined with doors. Was Harvey hidden within one of these rooms? I tried to open a few of the doors, but they were all locked, which seemed unusual. If all of these doors were secure, why was mine left open? Surely Stoney would keep a lock on my door above all others, wouldn't he? Unless the old woman had crept inside my room without him knowing and left it open.

Before I even realized it, I came to the end of the hall, and face to face with another door. To my surprise, this one was not secure. I opened the door to reveal a large storage room, where large metal crates stood stacked upon each other, at least five high into the air. I entered the room prepared, with the expectation that someone was inside, but it was empty.

I suddenly realized how chilly it was inside the storage room, and I found it very odd. As I wandered about, I felt as if I was walking through a freezer at a grocery store. I rubbed my hands together furiously in effort to warm them. "Why the hell is it so cold in here?" I whispered as I crept deeper into the storage room.

As I looked about the room, I briefly wondered what was inside the crates, but I decided that I didn't want to know. All of a sudden, a high-pitch alarm sounded above my head, and I covered my ears. I glanced at the rafters above, a large beacon was going off, its red light spinning. I glared at it as I hurried towards the opposite end of the room. Another door appeared around a stack of crates but as I reached for it, it began to swing open. Before the person on the other side of the door caught sight of me, I ran back in the direction I came from. But that door was also in the process of being opened. I was trapped.

"Shit!" I muttered under my breath.

Without an escape route, I crept around the boxes, holding my breath as I struggled to slide in between them. Then, as soon as it had come, the alarm ceased flashing its lights, and the room went silent. However, my celebration was put on hold when I overheard footsteps echoing inside the room.

I brought a hand against my mouth, hoping to mask the sound of my breathing, but I knew it was no use. Vampires would be able to detect any human within a fifty-foot radius. I knew then that I had no choice. The best chance I had at avoiding a run in with the person wandering around the storage room, was to climb into one of the crates and hope that whatever was inside would overpower my scent. They looked to be at least 7 feet tall and 7 feet wide—large enough to hide me.

I didn't have much time until my hiding spot was found, and so I slid out from between the crates, breathing a sigh of relief when I recognized the sound of the footsteps were coming from the other end of the room. I climbed one stack of crates that were positioned on the far wall, hidden behind a mountain of others. Sadly, it was padlocked.

Staying low and out of sight, I began searching the remaining crates, hoping to find one that was open. I had begun to give up all hope, until my eyes fell upon a metal crate a few feet away with its side panel slightly ajar. I hoped I was small enough to fit through the crack. It was a long shot, but I prayed the metal panels would be thick enough to mask my smell.

I scaled back down the stack of crates, keeping my eyes and ears peeled for the unknown person who was walking around the room. I was surprised that they hadn't come across me yet, but I was thankful for their negligence.

Once I made it over towards the broken crate, I sized up the opening, and after finding I could fit through the gap, I sucked in my small gut and squeezed inside. It was oddly cold within the crate, and as I backed away from the crack of light and into the shadows, I wrapped my arms around my body for warmth, trying my best not to shiver. I made no attempt to examine the crate's contents when I overheard the footsteps drawing nearer.

The footsteps grew louder until they stopped right outside the crate. I took a few careful steps backward, hoping the outline of my body was still concealed by the darkness inside the crate. However, once I did, I felt my back press up against something large and stiff. I froze, my eyes growing wide with fear, and I reached my hand back to feel along the object. It took only a moment or so until I recognized what, or who, I was feeling up.

Against my better judgment, I turned my head to examine the person I had my hands on. When I realized it was the frozen corpse of a dead woman, I bit my bottom lip to keep from crying out in surprise. The woman was completely nude, and her body was a deep blue color and covered in a thin ice coating. Wanting to put distance between the corpses, I stumbled backwards, and I cringed when my back hit the empty panel of the crate. I kept still, hoping whoever was on the outside hadn't overheard the sound of the dull collision, but unfortunately I had no such luck.

The metal panel of the crate was torn off in an instant, revealing a very pissed-off looking Stoney. Before I had a chance to defend myself, he grabbed my arm and yanked me out of the freezing crate. I glanced back at the interior of the same crate I'd been standing in only moments ago, and I shuddered with disgust when I realized it was filled with frozen corpses.

"Lina, Lina, Lina," he greeted me with a sneer. "Where do you think you're going?"

"Nowhere now, obviously."

But then I remembered I still had the pair of scissors I lifted off of the old woman. I made a quick move to stab him, but the he only laughed as he caught me just before I could pierce the skin above his heart. He grabbed the scissors from me and tossed them over his shoulder carelessly. They made a soft clank when they hit the ground.

"Damn," I muttered.

"I see you've made quite a mess already, hunter," he told me. "Killing a defenseless old woman? Shame on you."

"She wasn't defenseless! She tried to kill me!"

"Well, it seems like she failed."

I glared up at him. "What do you want with me, Stoney?"

His black eyes sparkled at my question. "What do you mean?"

"Why did you bring me here? What are you planning to do to me and my family?"

With the click of his tongue, he replied, "All in good time, my dear. All in good time."

Before I could demand answers from him, he reached into his pockets to remove a long piece of twine. He forced my hands behind my back and tied them together in a fierce knot. I knew it would not be loose enough for me to wiggle out of.

"Really?" I asked him, with raised brows.

"There's nothing wrong with taking extra precautions, especially where you're concerned."

Stoney wrapped his arm around my waist and led me out of the stacks of crates, towards the door I had come in through. As we walked down another empty hall, I noticed the doors lined along the walls again.

"What's inside these rooms?" I asked. "More prisoners? More frozen corpses?"

"Perhaps."

I rolled my eyes at his remark. "Perhaps is not an acceptable answer, Stoney."

"It will have to do for now."

"Is Harvey in ones of these rooms, Stoney?"

His grip on my arm tightened, as he said, "Worried about the young man, are you?"

"Of course I am. He's my partner."

Stoney laughed at my reply and said, "He's more than just your partner, isn't he, Lina?"

I stiffened at his remark. "I don't know what you mean."

"Of course you do," he cooed. "I sensed something between you two at the harbor. A kind of closeness that I never detected before."

"You're imagining things."

Stoney's gripped my arm even harder now, causing me to wince. "Don't lie to me, Lina! You let that weak, insignificant man touch you. Didn't you?"

"That's none of your business!" My face heated at his accusation, and I wondered how he knew. I sure as hell hadn't told him, but I had the sudden thought that maybe Harvey had. My stomach churned and I grew pale at the thought.

We abruptly stopped walking; Stoney twisting me around and pushing me up against the wall. He brought his hands down my back before grabbing hold of my hips. "It would be wise to not lie to my face, Lina Holiday. I can make your life a living hell."

I glared back at him; his threat not scaring me in the least. "You already have."

He reached out to touch my cheek, sweeping his cold fingertips over my skin. I grimaced at his touch, but I was not able to turn away as his other hand kept me in place, facing him. "Such

118

fire, such spirit. For a human, you're quite extraordinary. I've always admired you."

"I can't say the same about you."

Stoney sneered down at me, not looking very pleased. "You're mine now, Lina, It's time you come to terms with it. You belong to me."

As Stoney's bony hands moved to caress my back, I came to the sad realization that what he said was true. I was his prisoner, in his coven, and the chances of escaping with my life were near nonexistent. It was after I had this epiphany that I wished I still had the scissors. A swift cut to the throat is all it would take, and I would finally be free from the monster who had haunted me since childhood.

Burning in Hell for all eternity was a far better fate than having to spend another day with my sadistic, blood-sucking captor.

Chapter Ten

Stoney's grip on my arm was brutal as he led me down the dusty and dismal halls of the warehouse. He kept his pace brisk as he dragged me along the empty corridors, never once stopping to let me catch a glimpse of anyone or anything. I remained quiet through every twist and turn, trying to keep a look out for Leland, Harvey, or for anything peculiar. As if being in an abandoned warehouse with a cult of vampires wasn't odd enough, I couldn't shake the feeling that something unusual was about to go down. I was suspicious of Stoney already, but now that he'd stripped me of my weapons and separated me from Harvey, I wondered just what he had planned for me. He could have killed me by now, but he hadn't, and I wanted to know why.

Finally, after ten minutes of wandering inside the old building, Stoney stopped outside of a black metal door. He reached for the rusty handle and pulled the door open, revealing a large, open room with nothing but a single metal chair sitting in the middle of it. There were no windows, just four solid grey walls and a cracked cement floor.

I lifted my brows in curiosity, surprised that this is where we ended up. I barely had any time to take in my surroundings before Stoney shoved me into the room, propelling me towards the chair. As I stumbled through the threshold, I missed the chair and fell to the floor, knocked off guard by his strength. After rising up onto my knees, I heard Stoney laugh as I struggled to stand. My hands still tied behind my back, I winced as my left shoulder throbbed from the impact when I'd hit the ground. With a sharp inhale I finally rose to my feet.

Stoney gave me no time to recover. He strolled in my direction and took hold of my arm once again. The vampire forced my body against his, and when I looked away, his free hand tugged on my chin and yanked my face back to his own. His black eyes glistened with lust as he stared at my bare neck, and he licked his lips.

I squirmed in his hold and said, "Don't even think about it."

Growling with eagerness, Stoney couldn't control himself any longer, and he bent down toward my neck to lick at my skin. He appeared intoxicated by me, and he leaned his ear towards my chest, as if he was trying to listen to the beating of my heart. He continued to caress me with his tongue as he did this, now reaching for the zipper on my leather jacket.

Before I could protest, he made the attempt to yank it off of my body, but he noticed that my hands were still bound together. Instead, he slid the jacket off of my shoulders, his grip growing tighter at the sight of my flesh. The vampire's tongue was rough on my skin and it got to the point where his fervent licking began to hurt.

I trembled from disgust as he continued to suck on my neck, the skin now sore, and I knew it was only a matter of seconds before he unsheathed his fangs. As he continued to slobber all over me, I found that I couldn't move; it was as if I was frozen to the spot. My eyes grew wide with fright when I felt him nip at my skin. Unable to push the vampire off, I wondered if I was doomed to be fed on. However, it was when he ran his hands over my breasts that I finally found the strength to react.

I ducked down to thrust my bruised shoulder into his gut, and I jumped backwards when he howled in anger from my defiant action. Stoney glared at me, his eyes had become a black void, just like a shark's when it feeds. His expression turned vicious, and I stared back at the monster in front of me, wiggling my hands against my restrictive bonds. I struggled with rope while I continued to inch away from him.

121

"Keep away from me!" I cried out. He did not heed my command, and I cursed my bound hands as he came towards me. I looked around the room for something to defend myself with, but I found nothing, and I sadly realized I was running out of options.

Stoney kept advancing until he was on me again, pinning me up against the wall with one hand. Once again, I couldn't move as I stared into his lifeless eyes. The vampire smiled with mischief as his hands roamed my body again, and when he squeezed my breasts, I squirmed from the pain.

"What's wrong, Lina? Harvey was good enough for you to fuck, but I'm not?"

"You bastard! Take your hands off of me!" I groaned, writhing from his touch.

He continued to smile as he let his hands slide lower until they were near the tops of my thighs. "I could take you right now, Lina." Stoney said, his voice smooth, and he gripped my hips. His dark eyes transformed into a bright red, and the intensity of them worried me. I tried my hardest to break free of his hold, but the vampire was just too strong.

Upon licking my cheek, Stoney said, "I want to hear you beg, Lina. Beg me to stop!"

"You make me sick!" I spat, squeezing my hands into fists as I felt him rub up against my crotch. I squeezed my eyes shut and ordered him to stop. "Let go of me, Stoney. Now!"

To my surprise, Stoney did as I commanded and backed away, an odd expression now displayed on his face. "You're right. I don't want you that way," he told me after a moment. Stoney frowned when he noticed my relief. "Don't act so thrilled, Lina. I will have you, eventually, and when that time comes, nothing will be able to stop me."

I glared at him and replied, "Don't be so sure, Stoney. I may be tied up and unable to defend myself right now, but I will get my hands out of this knot, and when I do you're one fucked vampire."

Stoney grinned and shook his head. "You're wrong, Lina. I think your days of hunting vampires are over."

I didn't respond. Stoney took hold of my arm and proceeded to drag my body over towards the metal chair. The vampire sat me down and I watched as he removed a long rope from his back pocket.

"You've got to be kidding me," I mumbled, frowning when he began to wrap the rope around my body. When he was finished, he tied it to the bonds on my hands. "Well, that seems like overkill to me," I smirked. "Are you really that afraid of me, Stoney?"

"I can't have you getting loose," Stoney explained, tugging on the ropes and making sure they were tight and secure. "I wouldn't want to get sidetracked by searching for you again. That would deter my plans."

"Stoney, no matter how hard you try and contain me, it isn't going to work! Mark my words, I'm going to find a way to get free."

"No, you're not," he replied with an amused expression. He patted my shoulder and after turning his back on me, he moved towards the door. However, instead of leaving, he paused and brought his hand to his chin, in sudden thought.

"Okay, Stoney …" I began, trying to get comfortable against the metal chair. "I agreed to play by your rules. I'm tied up to a fucking chair now, so it's time you let me see Leland."

Stoney twisted his head to glance at me. He frowned and replied, "The old man? You may see him later."

"We made an agreement—"

"Not now, Lina," he replied with a huff, waving his hand at me. "I'm thinking." He began to pace, back and forth, which vexed me to the point of screaming.

"I'm not going to play these games with you anymore, Stoney! Where is Leland? Furthermore, where is Switch and Harvey? I want to see them—all of them, right now!"

"You'll see your pathetic little family soon enough. Remember, patience is a virtue," he grumbled, still pacing. He completely disregarded my presence as he continued to pace and pace, until he came to a sudden halt, a realization seemingly befalling him. With a wide and toothy grin, the vampire said, "I'll be back later to check on you. Sit tight."

Furious that he was leaving without giving me the information I needed, I shouted, "Where are they, Stoney! You tell me where they are, or I'll⌐⌐—" My voice broke just as Stoney's face brushed up against mine. I narrowed my eyes at him, detesting his nearness.

"Or you'll what, huh?" He barred his fangs, sending a slight chill down my back. "You'll kill me? Was that what you were going to say?"

"Put those away," I replied, my tone hardening.

Stoney growled, taking my chin in his hand and forcing me to stare into his cold, hollow eyes. "You think you're so tough, Lina, but you're no match for me. Beneath that hardened exterior lies nothing but veins and blood."

Without warning, he pulled my face towards him and slowly licked up the side of my face. I gasped from disgust and pulled away, wishing my hands were free to wipe his saliva off of my face. I glared at him and spat, "If you're trying to scare me, it's not working, so why don't you just back the fuck off!"

Stoney chuckled, his deep voice echoing in the small room. "Such absolute resistance to my charms. You're the strongest human I've ever met."

"It's easy to resist you, Stoney. You're repulsive."

His hand shot out to slap my cheek, and he grinned at the pain that flashed across my face. "It's unwise to offend me, Lina. I just might forget how important you are." Stoney licked his lips and reached out to touch my neck. "I might do something rash."

My face twitched with hatred when he began to caress my neck again. "Tell me what you want from me, Stoney!" I screamed suddenly. "I'm sick and tired of playing your twisted games."

Stoney withdrew his hand and replied, "Don't worry, Lina. You'll find out soon enough." He blew me kiss and headed over towards the door. Before exiting, he turned back around to face me and said, "Until next time, my love."

Once Stoney had left the room, I heard a scuffle outside the door. My ears perked up at the sound of an argument, but I couldn't understand what they were saying. Then, the lights were turned off, and I was forced to sit in complete darkness. I tilted my head back and closed my eyes, trying to calm my nerves. I had to find some way to free my hands from their binds, but I was at a loss for ideas. Dismayed, I recalled that the vampires on the boat had taken all of my weapons, even the small pocketknife I kept hidden in my left boot. My face crumpled up at the thought of the impending doom I now faced.

I was at their mercy.

****

As I sat there, in the damp, dusky room, I envisioned Leland in the same condition, or possibly worse off. I grimaced at the thought of him bound and gagged, undoubtedly awaiting a horrid fate. He didn't deserve this—none of my teammates did. I had gotten them into this mess. If I had only listened to my team's objections on that rooftop, none of this would have happened. My heart sank to my stomach and I screamed out into the darkness, hoping the action would help ease my frustrations. It didn't.

"Damn him!" I screamed, recalling Stoney's arrogant sneer when I'd first arrived. I growled as I cursed him, wishing I could destroy his ugly, immortal face.

The door to the chamber opened, startling me, and a sliver of light shone into the room. Within seconds, a body was thrown into the sliver, but when I tried to get a closer look at whoever it was, the door was slammed shut, once again shrouding me in darkness.

I wrinkled my brows in thought, wondering who the fallen person could be. Fear gripped my throat as I thought of Harvey, lying only a few feet away, seemingly unconscious. Peering over at the black lump lying in the middle of the room, I called out, "Hello? Who's there?" When I didn't receive an answer, I spoke again. "Harvey? Is that you?"

The person didn't respond and they were not moving, causing me to assume the worst. I frowned, determined to learn their identity. Deciding to take action, I once again struggled to get free. Twisting my hands against the rope, I winced in pain as the skin on my wrist began to wear down. Frowning, I let my hands fall back as I studied the large lump on the floor.

I tried hopping forward on the chair, but it barely moved at all. It was made of metal, and I knew I wouldn't be able to break it on my own. With a groan, I stopped all effort to try and get closer towards the person lying on the floor.

The person was still unmoving, and now, growing frustrated, I shouted, "Hey! Wake up!" I shook the metal chair, trying to make as much noise as possible. "I need some help over here!" I sighed when they continued to lie still, and a sick feeling settled in the pit of my stomach. The person before me was dead.

I prayed then, begging whatever higher power was listening, to keep Leland and Harvey and the others safe until I could get to them. "I'm coming for you guys, I promise."

I wasn't sure how long I sat alone in the quiet room before sleep took hold of me, but when I finally drifted off, I thought I heard Leland calling my name.

Chapter Eleven

"Rise and shine!" Stoney hollered, startling me from my slumber.

He was crouched down near my chair, studying me as I came to. His dark eyes traced over my face, and I realized he was leaning in towards me, as if to give me a kiss. When I realized what he was doing, I gasped and jerked my head away from his. Stoney chuckled at my reaction and straightened up.

I was surprised to find him next to me, in a metal chair identical to my own, and I wondered how long he had been sitting there, watching me. I shuddered to imagine what he had done while I slept.

"What do you want?" I inquired, my voice sounding groggy. I was rather annoyed that I awoke to the sight of his hideous face..

"I want *you*, Lina. Surely you know that?" Stoney grinned, tucking a strand of his long black hair behind his left ear. "Why won't you just succumb to me? It would make things so much easier."

"For you maybe."

Stoney sighed then and shook his head. "Why must you be so difficult? Can't you see that I can give you everything you desire?"

"What I desire, is seeing my family."

He waved at my request and replied, "In due time."

"Stoney, I want to see Leland! I need to know that he's okay."

"You should have thought about that before you tried to escape."

"You're right, I'm sorry." I motioned my head in the direction of my bound arms and added, "I won't be going anywhere now, so you don't have to worry about me escaping again."

He flashed me a grin and muttered, "I'm well aware of that."

"So then let me see Leland!"

"Stop your pestering!" He yelled, now glowering down at me. "Can't you see I am trying to have a serious conversation with you?"

I ignored his outburst and simply stared at the floor, but this upset him even more. "Look at me when I'm talking to you!" he growled, and grabbed ahold of my shoulders roughly. Stoney stood before me now, waiting to hear a response to his demand.

My face conveyed no emotion as I continued to stare blankly at the grey stone flooring beneath my feet. Once a few minutes of silence passed, Stoney snapped. He picked up his chair and tossed it across the room, grinning at the loud clatter it made when it hit the ground. He went to strike me, but he balled his hands into fists and turned away, not allowing himself to act on his rage.

I was, on the other hand, yearning for Stoney to make a rash move. I planned to somehow push him over the edge, so that we would be forced to fight one on one. It was my best shot at getting out of the binds. As I thought of how to handle him, I suddenly realized that the person from the night before was still lying on the floor in the same spot. There was light in the room now, on account of Stoney leaving the door to the cell open, and I examined -the body, noticing it appeared to be a man. He was lying on his stomach, and I couldn't see his face, but he had dark brown hair. My stomach dropped when I recalled that Harvey was a brunette. I glanced over at Stoney next, and I was disturbed by the satisfied smile on his face.

My voice shook as I asked him, "Who is that, Stoney?"

Stoney chuckled, waving his hand rudely at the question. "He's dead, Lina. Just forget about him."

Fidgeting in my seat, I bit my lip as I continued to stare at the body. "Please tell me." The concern in my voice did not appeal to Stoney, and he simply shook his head.

"I can't do that, Lina. It'll spoil the fun."

The horrid thought that the dead body lying in the middle of the room could belong to Harvey caused me such anxiety that I could bear the suspense no longer. "God damn you, Stoney! I need to know!"

"Are you afraid it's your lover?"

"Show me who that is right now, you son of a bitch!"

"All right, fine! You want to see his face, Lina? Is that what you want?"

He strode towards the body and picked the corpse up with one hand. In a flash, the vampire was beside me again, holding up the man's face for my viewing pleasure. My eyes grew wide from horror as I stared at the dead man's gruesome appearance. I turned away, catching my breath as I tried to forget the horrible image.

"What's wrong, Lina?" Stoney inquired with a snort. He stared into the deep hole in the man's neck, not the least bit affected by the shocking wound. Most of the man's neck had been ripped off, and his head was being held up only by his spine. Stoney's hand trembled when he realized there was still a drop of blood lingering on the man's cheek. I watched as lust took over the vampire and he licked the corpse's cold face.

"Delicious," he said.

The corner of my mouth twitched at the sight of the vampire's tongue scraping the dead man's cheek. "Why did you kill him in such a grotesque way?" I asked.

"No reason, really. He was just in the wrong place at the wrong time, and my crew was starving."

"Did you put him here just to taunt me?"

Stoney grinned sheepishly. "Something like that."

"You're despicable."

"Am I?" Stoney asked. He carelessly dropped the body to the floor before saying, "You should just be grateful that it isn't Leland or your pitiful sidekicks lying dead at your feet."

"Oh, I should be grateful?" I remarked with a frown. "For what? Locking me up in a dark room as a prisoner, without any contact with my family? Tell me, Stoney, why are you such a heartless bastard?"

"Would you prefer me any other way?"

"Yes, actually. I would prefer it if you were dead."

His eyes flashed with anger at my remark. "Sorry to disappoint you, but I have no intention of dying, Ms. Holiday."

I faced Stoney, now locking my eyes with his. "I'm going to kill you. I swear I will."

"With your hands tied behind your back?" he said with a sneer. "That would be a difficult feat to accomplish, even for you."

I ignored his mockery, and my tone remained stern as I said, "I don't know how or when, but I refuse to die until I've taken you out. I will not let you win!"

"So tough, so serious..." The vampire took a sudden step backwards and said, "I wonder how Harvey Johnson is holding up. Is he acting as brave as you are, or is he crumbling under the pressure?"

"Johnson's no lightweight," I responded with a snort. "He won't break, no matter what you do to him."

Stoney shrugged and replied, "I don't know about that, Lina. He's not as strong as you are." Now walking a circle around my chair Stoney stopped behind me to place his hands on my shoulders again. He lowered his lips just above my ear to whisper, "Persuading Harvey will be too easy."

"You're in denial, Stoney. He'll never join you!"

"Oh, I'm sure I can strike up a deal with him."

"A deal? Harvey wouldn't make a deal with the devil, let alone you!"

Chuckling, Stoney gripped my shoulders and added, "Don't you realize I have what the man wants? The only thing he cares about?" Stoney's voice faded when my shoulders tensed up.

"What are you talking about?" I inquired, my face growing hot at his suggestion.

"You know that he would do just about anything to save you, Lina," Stoney whispered into my hair. "After all, you're Mr. Johnson's weakness."

I stiffened at the vampire's remark, finding myself growing short of breath. I imagined Harvey being tortured somewhere in this warehouse, wondering if I was safe or not. Although I would never admit it, I knew Stoney was right. Harvey would do just about anything to protect me, even give himself over to the vampire overlord. The mere thought caused my eyes to well with tears.

"You're wrong," I managed to say, after I got a hold of my emotions. "Harvey is a lot stronger than you think."

Pursing his lips at me, he replied, "Like I said before, I know how he feels about you."

"It's not like that! Harvey and I, we're not–."

"You mean to tell me that you're not lovers?" Stoney interrupted.

I glowered at the vampire, but I said nothing. I knew lying to him was futile. Somehow, Stoney had figured out about me and Harvey. I was confused as to how he knew, but more so as to why he seemed to care so much.

"Your silence says it all."

"I don't have to explain myself to you, Stoney!" I shot back. "My personal life is none of your fucking business."

He struck me across the face; the surprise blow was strong enough to cause my vision to go blurry for a minute or so. I grimaced when Stoney lifted his hand again, but with a grunt, he dropped his hand back down at his side.

"To think that someone as remarkable as you chose to lay with that vile human is just disappointing."

"Go to hell!"

"Watch that foul mouth of yours. I wouldn't want to bruise up your pretty little face."

I glared at him and spat, "Your threats don't scare me."

He struck me again in the same spot, but this time considerably harder, and I cried out from the pain. I held back the tears that formed in my eyes as the left side of my face throbbed profusely.

"Damn you."

Stoney sighed and crossed his arms, watching me with a disapproving look on his face. "You're bringing this misery upon yourself. Do you want me to keep hurting you? Is that what you want?"

"I don't care what you do to me, Stoney," I confessed, refusing to let him get to me.

His brows rose at my response. "Is that so? Well, perhaps you might care about what I plan to do with Mr. Johnson."

His statement sent chills down my back. "What do you mean?"

"I have no use for him in his current state, surely you know that, Lina. However, I have toyed with idea of making him an ally."

I shook my head and clenched my fists, already wise to what Stoney planned to do. "Don't even think about turning him, Stoney!" I warned, struggling against the ropes; my rage boiling over. "If you turn him into a blood-sucking monster, I'll—"

"You'll kill me?" he interrupted with a harsh laugh. "I believe you've already made that threat at least a dozen times already. But who's counting?" Taking a step closer, Stoney added, "You're in no position to do anything, Lina. Face it, I have defeated you."

I stared back at him, fury etched in my eyes. "You haven't won yet."

Stoney laughed at my confidence and wandered off behind the chair. He paused at my back and circled his hands around my neck, squeezing gently. "I could kill you right now. It would only take a moment."

"Then do it!" I shouted angrily. "Why are you keeping me alive?"

"I still have hope you'll come around," he told me, his fingers now caressing my skin.

My pulse throbbed as his fingertips grazed my veins, and I began to struggle when his hold grew firmer. He moved back around me, now kneeling directly in front of my chair. His black eyes bore into mine, and I couldn't look away as his tough grip prevented me from turning my head. As I stared into his dark, soulless eyes, I felt myself growing weak. I tried to close my eyes but Stoney commanded me to open them, and I found myself unable to disobey.

"I want you, Lina," he whispered, dropping his hold on my neck to touch my face tenderly. The vampire brought his face close to mine, and his sharp nose poked the left side of my face as he inhaled my scent. "It's obvious that I want to make you mine. Why else would I have brought you here? You're a smart woman—you must have figured that out by now."

"Yes … but why? Why me?" I managed to ask him, feeling breathless just from attempting to speak. "I loathe you."

I was slipping farther and farther away, and when the thought of him touching me didn't cause my stomach to churn with nausea anymore, I came to the sad realization that I was succumbing to his charms. This wasn't the first time I had fell under a vampire's spell, but this was the first time I hadn't been able to snap out of the trance as soon as I went under.

My eyes rolled into the back of my head when he dropped his hands to my chest, where he caressed the skin just above my breasts. I was growing more intoxicated with his nearness with every second that passed, and I feared how willing I would be if he kept me under for much longer.

"I've been obsessed with you since that day in the kitchen, Lina—since the day I let you escape me."

"I was just a child," I whispered.

"You were the first human who had ever eluded me, besides Leland of course. At first, the thought of you safe in the arms of a vampire hunter drove me insane. There were many times I tried to track the old man down, to finish the job, but he was good at staying hidden. After a while, I came to the conclusion that you were meant to live, and that you were meant to be with me."

"That's crazy," I mumbled.

"Is it? Or do you feel a connection to me too?"

I was at a loss for words. His question disturbed me, and I refused to even entertain the idea. When I tried shaking my head, in effort to deny his claim, he reached up and kept my head in place. Stoney's expression turned serious as his black eyes looked over my face. "Such pretty green eyes," he whispered. He then lifted his right index finger to trace down my nose, and along my lips. "You're so beautiful, Lina...so full of passion...How could I resist you?"

I tried to respond, but I was so far gone now that I was unable to speak. The vampire seemed proud of his ability to break me, and without a word, he dropped his head down to taste my skin. I shuddered when he nipped at my neck, and I felt his tongue trace my veins, underneath my chin, and then finally, he made it to my lips. Now staring at me, Stoney made a move to kiss me, and being in the position I was in, I was unable to deter his advances. His lips were cold at first, but I felt them grow hotter each time his lips grazed mine.

Still under his spell, I did not fight him off. Instead, I was receptive to the vampire's kisses, and when his tongue entered my mouth, I groaned from eagerness and my entire body tingled with pleasure. I strangely found myself wanting more..

I was startled by my actions, but I wasn't able to control myself. My mind was foggy and all I could think about was Stoney and my desire for him. It frightened the sensible part of me that still lingered, but Stoney was in control of me now. So long as he had me under his trance, I was putty in his hands.

Then, Harvey's face popped into my mind, and it seemed as if Stoney's spell waned. My eyes still closed, a sweet feeling of déjà vu swept over me, and I began to experience all of the feelings and emotions I had felt the night Harvey and I made love for a second time.

"Harvey," I whispered his name, and Stoney broke away. He studied me for a moment or two, and then sighed and glanced off, and I felt the haze in my head starting to clear.

"I thought it would be so easy to have you, Lina ..." he said after a quiet moment. "But it seems as if your love for Mr. Johnson is strong enough to block my method of *persuasion*."

"I will take what I want from you eventually, mark my words, but I'm afraid that it's not going to be very enjoyable for you."

Finally back in charge of my own body, I gagged and pulled back from him, disgusted from what had just transpired between us. I spit onto the floor, and then used my tongue to scrape at the insides of my mouth. I was shaking with rage and fear, having a hard time coming to grips with the fact that I had actually been turned on by the vampire.

"You seem upset, Lina," Stoney said, still watching me.

I glared at him. "Don't ever do that again."

"Why not? You seemed to enjoy it."

"It wasn't real, Stoney."

"Alas, you're right," he responded, his candor startling me. "I yearn for you, but I won't be satisfied until you give yourself up to me willingly."

"That's never going to happen," I replied with a snort.

"You say that now, Lina, but I can be persuasive."

I rolled my eyes at his denial. "Stoney, even if you blackmail me into it, it still won't be real. No matter what you do, I will never be yours."

He growled at my defiance, and it was obvious that I had pushed him too far. "Damn you! I have gone above and beyond for you, Lina. I gave into your demands and kept you and your precious family safe, yet you still reject me!"

"Are you expecting a thank you?" I asked with a laugh.

"I expect you to get used to the fact that I am in command here. This is my coven and you will heed my demands, not escape your confines the first chance you get! You being here is turning out to be more of a liability than I thought."

"What? You thought breaking me was going to be easy, Stoney? How could you possibly think that when you know how much I hate you?"

"I have done so much for you, but no more. I can't let you jeopardize everything that we have built!"

"We?" I breathed, curious as to who he was referring to.

Stoney backed off and retreated to the door, and my suspicions grew. What did he have to hide? He remained quiet as he reached for the handle of the door, on the verge of fleeing, but I wouldn't let him get out of answering my questions so easily.

"Where are you going, Stoney?" I called out to him.

He froze at the door, his hand in mid-air. "You should be thrilled that I'm leaving you alone."

"Why are you avoiding my question?"

"Which question was that?" Stoney replied coyly, finally turning around to face me again.

Narrowing my eyes at him, I said, "You know damn well what question. Who else is helping you do this, Stoney?"

"My affiliates are none of your concern, Lina. However, I'm sure you'll learn their identities soon enough."

Stoney frowned as he gazed at me from across the room. "I feel sorry for you. You poor, poor woman. You have no idea that your world is about to topple." Then, his frown lifted into a grin and he added, "But, your downfall is inevitable of course ... and when you're at your weakest, that's when you will become mine. Make no mistake about that."

With a boorish wave of his hand, he made the attempt to exit the room, but he stopped just before the door and turned back around to glance at the dead man lying near my feet. He reached down to grab one of the arms, then proceeded to drag the corpse towards the exit.

As he reached for the handle of the door with his free hand, I began hollering at him to tell me where he was keeping Leland. Stoney slammed the door shut behind him, leaving all of my questions unanswered. When I heard the cruel click of the lock, I cursed him for once again leaving me in solitude.

Chapter Twelve

Stoney returned later that evening, much to my unpleasant surprise. I wasn't expecting to see him back so soon after his last visit, and especially not with a tray of food in his hands. I wondered what game he was playing at when he brought the tray before me, and the delicious aroma floated up my nostrils, teasing me. I hadn't eaten in what seemed like eternity, and I winced when my stomach growled loudly.

"You brought food?" I asked him, my curiosity getting the best of me. He crouched down before me and then rested the metal tray carefully on the tops of my thighs. "Why?"

Now that the meal was in clear view, I couldn't divert my eyes. I stared at a thick piece of steak, and two large sides of mashed potatoes and broccoli sitting on the plate. When my eyes fell on the large glass of water, I could suddenly feel how dry my mouth actually was. Even though I tried my best to appear unaffected by the sight of the food and drink, I sadly realized that my hunger most undoubtedly showed.

"I can't let my guest of honor go hungry, now can I?" he remarked, with a grin.

"You poisoned it, didn't you?" I asked him as I stared long and hard at the tantalizing food. "It's the only logical explanation."

"Why on earth would I do that, Lina? You're far too precious to me alive."

Stoney walked to the back of my chair and proceeded to loosen the binds on my hands and legs. Once the ropes had been removed, I breathed a quiet sigh of relief and rotated my arms, enjoying the ability to move them around once more. Although I

138

was starving and dying of thirst, I refused to make a move for the food or the water. Instead, I crossed my arms and looked off, not allowing myself to even glance at the meal sitting in my lap.

Stoney moved back around to stand before me, and I realized he was watching me with a stern expression. "You need to eat," he told me.

"I'm fine."

"Nonsense."

"I said, I'm fine," I replied.

"Do you honestly believe I'll think less of you if you slake your hunger?" he asked incredulously. "You've already lasted two days without eating. There's no need for you to go another day without food and water, so don't allow your pride to influence you."

"Perhaps I'm just tougher than you think."

"Right."

He then moved towards the door of the cell, catching me off guard.

"You're going to leave me alone in here with my hands untied?" I asked, surprised by the change in his behavior. "What if I manage to get loose inside this warehouse?"

He smirked at my suggestion and replied, "I'm not too worried about that happening anymore." Stoney reached out to pat the metal door and added, "This door now has three padlocks on the outside, all of which possess different keys." The vampire's smile widened as he said, "There's no way you're getting out of this room, Ms. Holiday."

Infuriated by the news, I glared at him, and the vampire blew me a smug kiss before he walked out the door. Once I determined enough time had passed, and that Stoney wouldn't be making a return, I made a move for the food. There were no utensils left for me on the tray of course, as Stoney must've anticipated I would use them as weapons, and so I was forced to eat with my bare hands like a barbarian.

The steak was tender and juicy, cooked medium with a pink center, and the broccoli and potatoes were drenched in a savory garlic and butter sauce. I then grabbed the cup of water and drank slowly, savoring the cool, refreshing taste. As I feasted on the meal, I wondered who had cooked the food. Vampires didn't possess a palette for mortal cuisine, and I was sure that whoever had prepared the meal had to have been human. I figured my meal had to be take-out from a nearby restaurant, as I doubted the vampires had a human cook held hostage in the coven.

Once I licked my plate clean, I stood, stretching out each leg as I did. I now had the chance to explore the dark cement cell, but as I looked about, I came to the depressing conclusion that there was nothing for me to examine but empty grey walls. As I felt along the cold walls, I could barely see in front of me, the lone light bulb nearly extinguished.

A few minutes of searching my cell for an escape turned into a half-hour, and as I continued to pace, I found there was nothing left for me to do. Although I had tried opening the door— more than once, I moved towards it, sighing as my fingertips grazed over cool metal. There was no way I was breaking through.

I didn't want to admit it, but I realized I was stuck. There was nowhere for me to go—there was nothing I could do to get free, and my heart sank with despair at the thought of never escaping the dark and depressing prison.

I finally gave up pacing and sat back down in the metal chair, leaning my head back to stare up at the light bulb above my head. It was then that I noticed it was flickering, just as the bulb in the room with the insane old woman had. My mind began to wander then, and my thoughts turned to Leland, Switch, and Harvey. My heart told me they were still alive, which brought me some joy. Stoney would not kill them, as he was holding their safety over my head, but I was worried about their accommodations. Were they all together, or were they locked in separate cells like I was?

As I fell deeper into my thoughts about their whereabouts, the door to my cell flew open and three vampires came rushing inside the room. Before I could get my bearings, all three grabbed at me, yanking me out of the chair and onto my feet. I opened my mouth to protest, but they shoved me out of the door and down the hall before I even had a chance to object. Two of the vampires kept their hands on my shoulders, while the third walked directly behind us, and when I tried to struggle out of their tight grip, the vampires countered with violence. They dug their nails deep into my flesh, until I finally stopped struggling.

It only took a few minutes before my undead entourage and I came across another door, but this one was red with a large black X spray painted unevenly across the middle. Before I had a chance to study the door further, it was opened from the inside to reveal Stoney standing in the open doorway. He was dressed in a long black satin robe, and he was holding a wine glass in his right hand. It was full to the brim with blood, and drops of it were sliding down the sides of the glass slowly and then falling to the ground below. His long black waves tumbled down across his pale chest, and when he swept them back with his free hand, I noticed a jagged scar near his heart.

"Bring her over to the bed," he instructed his goons, while looking me square in the eyes. The vampires did as they were told, towing me in the direction of the king-sized bed. They pinned me down on my back with my hands at my sides. My body was seized with fear when the vampires began to strip me down to my underwear, leaving me nearly naked on top of Stoney's plush sheets. Stoney commanded them to leave, and they fled the room moments later, leaving us alone together.. Stoney approached the bed next, and I felt bile rise in my throat when I noticed the lust in his dark eyes.

"What the hell is this?" I asked him, holding up my hands when he attempted to join me on the bed. "I thought you said you weren't going to force yourself on me!"

"I changed my mind," he said, his voice heavy and licentious. "You know I'm not a patient man."

"You're not a man at all," I shot back.

He grinned then, displaying two sharp fangs. "You're absolutely right. I'm not. Which makes this all the more interesting."

I was confused by his meaning. "What do you mean?"

"Have you ever had a vampire inside you before, Lina?"

His question took me aback and I glared up at him, absolutely disgusted. I could feel my face heating up as I snapped, "Never."

Stoney grinned, amused by my reaction. "Of course you haven't. Well, it's a very wild and sensual experience, far more exciting than sex with a human man." When he noticed how tense I had become, he added, "Don't worry. I won't hurt you too badly, and I promise you will enjoy it."

I began to shake, the idea of sharing another intimate moment with him almost caused me to scream. "You can't do this!" I shouted. "You tried to force yourself on me once, and you know how that turned out."

"It wasn't so bad."

"It was vile!"

"Was it?" he replied with a whisper, now joining me on his bed. He crawled over my body slowly, his long hair hanging down and tickling my bare skin. "Or do you want me just as much as I want you?"

I stiffened when he flashed me a smile. "I want you dead, Stoney! That's all I've ever wanted where you're concerned."

I tried to get up, but he pushed me back down onto the bed, his black nails digging into my shoulders cruelly. "Where do you think you're going?"

I searched his cold eyes, praying that he would see I was terrified of what was about to happen. Surely my displeasure would dissuade him from forcing himself on me.

"Please, Stoney," I begged. I could feel the tears collecting in my eyes as I lay weak underneath my vampire imprisoner. "Let me go."

"I can't," he responded, and reached out to touch my hair. He fisted his hand in my hair, and yanked hard, directing my head towards him.

"Why?" I whispered, my breath catching in my throat from fear when he dipped down to taste my lips. I had to fight the urge to vomit.

When he finally pulled away, I said, "Don't you know that I despise you? If I had the chance, I would not hesitate in driving a stake right through your heart."

Stoney chuckled at my admission. "Well, you seemed to be quite enthralled with me the other night."

"Only because you had me under a trance. I eventually snapped out of it!"

"I think it runs deeper than that."

"What the hell are you talking about?"

"You possess a secret desire for the paranormal, don't you, Lina?"

I found his remark absurd and I could not contain my amusement. "You're joking, right?"

"Ever since you were a little girl, you were made aware of vampires. You were taught to hunt and slay them because they were evil, but you can't deny the fact that you've always been fascinated by them. Their power and invincibility excites you."

"That is ridiculous."

"You're afraid of this dangerous attraction, because vampires cost you your parents. Not to mention how disturbed Leland and the others would be if they found out about your sick infatuation with the paranormal."

"This is absolutely ridiculous!"

Stoney ignored my heated response and continued to dig the knife deeper. "You've always kept your association with vampires strictly professional, in the sense that they were always your enemy, but you can't deny that a longing for the paranormal exists within you."

As Stoney's words sank in, I immediately thought of Gabriel and our close encounter in the movie theater. I recalled the sight of his bright amber eyes and the feeling of his hot breath on my neck when he held me close, and a chill ran down my back. Unshakeable warmth began to spread from chest all the way down to my toes as I thought of the burly werewolf, and I was dumbfounded as to why.

"Well, Lina?" Stoney inquired. He observed my quiet disposition closely. "Am I right?"

I opened my mouth to discredit Stoney's claim, but when I was on the verge of telling him off, I suddenly found that I could not utter a single word. Gabriel's handsome face popped into my mind again, and my cheeks grew hot. I stared up at Stoney then, a bewildered expression now on my face.

When Stoney realized he had been right all along, his lips furled upward into a smile. "I knew it," he breathed. "You can't hide your true feelings from me, Lina."

"No, it's not what you think," I managed to interject, after managing to get a grip on my emotions.

"Oh, I think it is," he murmured, still smiling. Then, Stoney bent down toward my ear to whisper, "You want me."

This time, I couldn't hold back my gag. "Are you insane? You cost me my parents! You and you alone! The only thing I'll ever feel for you is nausea!"

"Hear my voice, Lina." He whispered into my ear again, his tone silky smooth, "Stop trying to fight it."

"Stop it!" I shouted, finally having heard enough. "I won't fall for it this time!"

I tried inching away from him on the bed, but his bony hands were still wrapped in my hair. He gave the strands a sharp tug, and I was forced closer towards him again. We sat only a few inches apart now, and as I stared into Stoney's black eyes, I felt my strength fading away.

"Not again," I muttered, forcing my eyes to close as I struggled against the vampire. "Please, not again!"

Stoney commanded me to open them, and I was unable to resist. My eyelids flew open in an instant, and I was trapped by the fierceness of his gaze. His eyes were zoned in on mine, and it was as if everything around us faded into darkness. All I could see now were his big, soulless eyes boring down on me. They caused me to forget my unbridled hatred for him and our tragic past. This hypnotized trance I now found myself in was unbreakable, and so long as I stared into Stoney's eyes, I knew I would be lost.

"That's a good girl," he murmured. "Keep your eyes on mine."

I was under his spell now, and I was powerless to stop him as he laid me down onto my back gently, smoothing my hair away from my neck. His gaze lingered on my bare throat for a moment, but he then fixed his attention on my body. There was intensity in his eyes that overwhelmed me, and for a split second I thought he was going to take me right then and there. Instead, he grabbed my hand and placed it against his chest, directly over his heart. I found myself touching his scar, the one I had noticed upon entering his bedroom.

"Do you know how I got my name, Lina?" he asked me, his face now serious and forlorn. "I was turned in the beginning of the fifteenth century, but even before I became a vampire, I was a known ruthless killer. I plundered towns and murdered innocents, and it wasn't long until the people of the towns dubbed me as the man with a heart of stone. Soon after, the nickname Stoney began to catch on, and so it stuck with me. My true name, is Julian, but no one has called me that in a very long time."

I stared up at the vampire, surprised and confused as to why he was sharing such personal information with me. This was a side of Stoney I had never seen before, and I came to the conclusion that

145

I preferred his ruthless, blood-sucking side, rather than this emotional persona.

"I've been a vampire for more than 600 years and my heart hasn't pumped blood in centuries." His grip on my hand tightened as he whispered, "However, that doesn't mean I still don't possess a heart, or the ability to feel.

"In all my life, I have never met a woman like you before, Lina. You have such strength – such fire; it is hard even for a cruel man like me to resist your charms." He brought my hand before his lips to leave a trail of kisses. "I need a woman like you by my side. A true partner."

Although I was now spellbound, lost in the vampire's trance, there was still a sliver left that was untouched by his magic, and that tiny bit of consciousness worried over what he planned to do. If Stoney finally fulfilled his desires, I would never be able to live with myself knowing that my parents' murderer had tainted my virtue. As I continued to lay next to him, he began to caress my skin, and the idea that I would be unable to defend myself from his advances again triggered a lone tear to escape from my right eye. He made a move to kiss me, and when he noticed the tear sliding down my face, his behavior turned violent.

"Even now, as I pour my heart out to you, you still won't give yourself to me?" he shouted, crouched over my torso. "Do you realize how much I've jeopardized by bringing you here? By keeping you and your insignificant family alive?"

Still under his spell and unable to speak, I remained motionless, my eyes clouded with tears as I gazed up at Stoney's enraged expression.

"I did it all for you!" He stood from the bed then, his hands clenched into tight fists. Outraged by my refusal, he grabbed an antique brass lamp off of a table near the bed and threw it at the wall. I watched it take a huge chunk out of the cement wall. With wide eyes, I watched him as he shoved over one of his bookcases; I was frightened by his brash behavior. If Stoney decided to take his rage out on me in the state I was in, I would not be able to defend myself at all.

"I don't know why I even bother!" he hissed.

Stoney's power over me began to wear away when he began pacing at the foot of the bed, and I was once again able to move. I regained feeling in my toes at first, until finally, my entire body was free of his spell. I sat up straight on the mattress, observing the vampire nervously as he continued to pace back and forth. He was behaving like a jilted lover, and it chilled me to the bone. Stoney was frightening enough when I faced him one on one in a skirmish, but when he behaved this way, I didn't know what to expect him to do next.

"I should just kill you and your entire family—just be done with it all!" Stoney said with a fierce growl. He stopped pacing to stand motionless at the side of the bed, his dark eyes appearing even darker than usual. "Is that what you want? For your beloved family to suffer at my hands?"

"No," I pleaded with him. "Please, just leave them out of this."

"Fine," he said. "I won't hurt them, but in exchange for their lives, you're going to give me what I want!"

"I'm your prisoner, Stoney! What else could you possibly want from me?"

"You. To be mine."

"What?" I asked incredulously.

"It's like I said before, I want you to pledge your loyalty to me! I need you to promise to spend all eternity by my side."

I gasped at the vampire's declaration. I was shocked by his request, to say the least. "Spend an eternity with you? You're insane if you think I could ever agree to that, Stoney."

He inched closer to me, dipping his head down to whisper in my ear, "What if I offer your family's freedom in exchange?"

My eyes grew wide at his offer. "Are you serious?"

He nodded. "I will grant them their freedom, Lina, if you promise to stay with me."

I wanted to say yes—I wanted to be able to set my family free, but I knew that I couldn't agree to such a request, no matter how enticing his offer had been. I had to find another way to save them.

"How could I ever agree to such a thing? To commit myself to someone with a heart as black as their soul?" I paused then, a sudden thought occurring to me. "Oh, that's right. You don't even possess a soul."

He glared at me. "You refuse to surrender to me because I'm a vampire?"

"I will never willing give myself over to you, Stoney, because you are evil. You murdered my parents, and now you've taken away the only family I've ever known. No matter what you promise, or how many threats you make, I will never feel anything but hatred for you." My tone hardened as I said, "You might as well kill me now, because you're never going to get what you want from me."

A flash of anger crossed the vampire's pale face, but the look faded as quickly as it had come. He became cool, composed, when he finally said, "Perhaps if I take away your shiny mortality you will finally begin to understand."

"My mortality—?"

His words took a few moments to sink in, as my mind was still jumbled over his plea for devotion. However, when he yanked me on to my feet and pulled me into an embrace, I noticed his eyes were glued to my bare neck and I finally understood what he planned to do to me.

"No!" I screamed, writhing in his arms. "I won't let you do this!"

I tried to pry his hands off but it was no use. Stoney was far too strong, and his determination to sire me was stronger. Before I could beg him to reconsider, he bit into my neck. His fangs pierced my flesh smoothly, and I was surprised to find that the bite had been rather gentle. Stoney groaned once the blood hit his lips, and I shuddered when he began to consume my life force.

I could scarcely breathe as Stoney drank. It was as if I was hypnotized again, and as much as I tried to fight it, I could not ignore the warm sensations that flowed through my entire body. I felt as if a thousand hands were caressing me, rubbing all of my pleasure points—even some I didn't know I had. When he began to drink faster, I grew lightheaded and felt my legs give away. Stoney caught me just before I collapsed, and he cradled my body in his arms as he fed.

Time seemed to come to a standstill, and I sighed, my eyes rolling back into my head from pleasure. I felt as if all of my limbs had been removed, and all that remained of my body was my head and torso. The loss of sensation terrified me, yet I also felt peaceful. There was no pain, no anguish—I was simply lost in the warm embrace of ecstasy, and it was something I had never had the joy of experiencing before.

But, the pleasure couldn't last forever. Stoney stopped drinking just before he consumed the final drop and pulled his head back into view. I noticed a thin line of blood was trickling down his chin, and as I stared up at his ashen face, my breathing turned shallow. My heartbeat was almost nonexistent now, and it took a few moments before the pain hit me. When I finally understood the gravity of what was happening, I managed a smile, finding it oddly amusing that I was now at death's door.

"I'm dying," I murmured. "You killed me."

"Don't worry, my love," he said, touching my face. "You will be reborn."

I closed my eyes then, his remark causing me to cringe. "Please, Stoney, just let me die."

"I'm sorry, but I can't lose you, Lina—not now. I know you don't see immortality as anything but a curse, but eventually you will be grateful for this gift."

Stoney wasted no time. He bit into his wrist, slicing his veins with his fangs. His blood spilled from the open wound, and it splashed onto my face, my lips and jaw now coated in his thick blood. I tried to turn my head away to avoid it, but the action required too much strength. I kept my lips sealed as a last resort, but the liquid managed to seep through, and once the odd, metallic taste filled my mouth, I had no choice but to swallow.

Once I had swallowed the vampire's blood, I gasped for breath and felt a sharp ache in my chest. The sensation was dull at first, but it grew more intense, until suddenly, it felt as if someone had shoved a knife straight through my heart. The pain was so severe, I screamed and jolted upright, clutching my chest as I continued to howl in agony.

My face contorted from the pain and I hoped massaging the area would soothe the horrible agony I was enduring, but unfortunately nothing worked in subduing my suffering. As I remained cradled in Stoney's arms, I felt myself fading, until finally, I could take the pain no longer and I started to slip away.

As I allowed darkness to take me, I heard Stoney whisper, "You will live, Lina. You will live forever."

Chapter Thirteen

I woke with a scream. My eyes snapped open, and I sat upright, shoving off the plush sheets tucked around my torso. I realized I was still in Stoney's bedroom, but he was nowhere to be found. As I came to, I struggled to remember what had caused me to black out. Unfortunately, I couldn't recall what had happened after I was brought into his bedroom. All I was able to remember was his hypnotic eyes, and then everything went black. It was as if my memory had been completely erased.

I slid off the bed, finding that I felt strangely weak as I struggled to stay upright, but the sensation soon passed. I realized I was still undressed, and I began hunting around for my clothes. As I searched the floor of the bedroom, it suddenly dawned on me that my sight had changed drastically. My surroundings were much clearer than before—brighter even, and I noticed everything. Every crack in the floor, and every speck of dust on the furniture popped out at me. It was as if my eyes were on steroids.

Staring down at my hands, I examined them and realized they were shaking, most likely from fear. When I noticed that they too appeared more vibrant and detailed than ever before, I stumbled backward, smacking the back of my head against Stoney's wardrobe. My instincts commanded me to rub the back of my skull, but I was surprised to find that it didn't ache from the collision. I was beyond confused, but when I overheard the loud sound of footsteps drawing near, I realized I didn't have time to worry about my heightened sight. If I wanted to escape before Stoney returned, I had to act fast.

I reached for my clothes on the floor and began to dress. I tugged on my leather pants, blouse, and jacket, and as soon as I slipped on my black boots, I hurried towards the bedroom door. I was eager to resume the search for my family and when I reached my hand out to grab the handle, something stopped me from opening the door. There was a strong sensation of unease pressing on my mind, and as I stared at the panel of the door, I felt as if I was able to see through it. Somehow, I detected Stoney standing out in the hall, and I gasped and backed away, my confusion shifting into fear.

The door to the room opened, and Stoney sauntered inside. I wish I could say that I had been startled, but I wasn't, and by the amused expression on his face, I had a feeling that he knew I had been aware of his presence all along.

He greeted me with a grin. "Good evening, Lina."

I ignored his greeting, shaking my head as I continued to back away from him. I was feeling weak in the knees, and I tried to regain my bearings as I leaned up against his wardrobe. I refused to comprehend what was happening to me. I could see things a normal human being couldn't, but I didn't want to believe the worst. I couldn't bring myself to face the truth—not yet.

Eager to prove that I could, in fact, feel pain, I searched the room for something to injure myself with. I felt very foolish as I hunted for a blunt object, but I knew I had to put my sensory system to the test. Stoney watched me scurry around the room with raised eyebrows, but I turned my back on him and tried my best to ignore his presence.

"What are you doing, Lina?"

"Looking for something big and heavy."

"There's no need for you to beat yourself up." He knew what I planned on doing; I didn't even have to say a word. "You won't be able to feel anything," Stoney said, and a knowing smile appeared on his face.

"I'm not listening to you," I retorted. "You did this! You charmed me somehow to make me like this."

"Like what?" he probed, his dark eyes glowing with mischief.

I ignored his question and kept searching. When my eyes fell upon a bronze candlestick sitting on an end table next to the oversized bookcase in the bedroom, I hurried towards it. Once the candlestick was in my hand, I raised it and thumped my free arm with the candlestick, not too hard, but hard enough to cause injury. I waited for the pain to shoot through my arm, but unfortunately, the pain never came.

I waited a few minutes more, my hands shaking. I had lost the ability to feel. The candlestick fell from my hands to the floor with a thud, and the loud sound of it hitting the floor pierced my ears. When I stared down at my arm, I was shocked to see that no welt or bruise had formed there either, and the ivory tone of my skin had transformed into a fair porcelain color.

"I told you the attempt was futile."

My head shot up at the sound of his voice, and I sent the vampire a menacing glare. "What did you do to me?"

"What do you think?"

"What did you do?" I hollered again, now enraged, and once the idea to kill him filled my mind, it consumed me. I leapt at him, my hands outstretched with my nails pointed for his throat. After colliding into him, I swung at his face, but he was anticipating the action and snatched my arm before I could get my hands on him. He twisted my hand and yanked my arm behind my back cruelly.

"You need to calm down now, Lina," he explained, jerking my arm tighter. "Fighting with me isn't going to change your fate."

Now in the fierce grip of my enemy, I broke down, my voice breaking as I started to sob. "Why did you do this to me ..." I drew in a deep breath before whispering: "I'm a monster now!"

"I gave you a second chance—a better one. You should thank me for changing you."

"I never asked for this!" I shot back.

Stoney let go of my hand then, but instead of allowing me to gain my bearings, he lifted his foot and kicked me down to the floor. I collapsed onto my knees, now hiding my head in the palm of my hands. Still sobbing, I could feel nothing but anguish, and it caused me to cry even harder. Stoney sighed, as if fed up by my show of emotions, and knelt down beside me. He leaned his head over my shoulder, his lips pressed against my ear.

"You will stop crying now," he commanded. "It's unbecoming."

"I don't want this, Stoney," I replied, in between sobs. "I can't live this way!"

"Too bad," he said, and rose to his feet. "The only means of escaping this fate is if you kill yourself. However, I don't believe you're that foolish."

I wiped at my tear-stained cheeks and whispered, "How do you know?"

"Because if you do insult me by disposing of this gift, I will have no choice but to make your family suffer for the rest of their miserable lives. They will be my personal blood reserve, and believe me when I say that I'm not usually such a tender feeder."

I turned my head to glare at him, fully aware that he was telling the truth. If he didn't have complete control over me before, he did now. "I fucking hate you."

"You'll get over it."

There was a sharp knock at the door, and Stoney glanced over at it in surprise. He went to his bedroom door and opened it, revealing a tall, slender vampire standing in the open doorway. The vampire had an odd, elongated face, with shoulder length brown curls and bright grey eyes. He said nothing once he entered the room, but he looked to Stoney and nodded.

"Ah, Drake. Right on time." Stoney approached me once more. "Come now, my love," he said, lifting me to my feet. "We can't spend the entire day moping around."

He proceeded to drag me towards the door, and although I fought him at first, I eventually gave in, knowing he wouldn't stop until I did what he willed.

"Where are we going?"

"There's something we must do."

"Where?" I asked him again, this time more forcefully.

He smiled at me, his hands reaching out to cup my face. "You're going to finally get what you've been yearning for, my dear. You and I are going to pay a visit to your lovely little family."

Chapter Fourteen

Upon leaving Stoney's bedroom, I was escorted down the halls of the warehouse once again, with Stoney leading while the other vampire, Drake, prevented me from losing stride. I paid close attention as we trekked through the modern-day labyrinth, hoping the memory of where I was headed would be useful in the future.

The three of us wandered the halls for close to ten minutes, until we finally came upon an enormous-sized packing room. The room was filled with large machines and conveyor belts, which all led to a giant roll-up door. There were tons of boxes stacked up along the walls, and a large empty cement platform centered in the middle of the room. I wondered what it was used for.

Towards the back of the room, up the steep cement steps and hidden away in the corner, sat a large metal cage. Inside that same cage was my family. Harvey, Switch, and even the young woman I had rescued, were all sitting on the floor, leaning up against the bars. However, it was when I caught sight of my father that I could contain my excitement no longer. He was standing at the door to the cage, and I couldn't help but smile, overjoyed to see him alive and well.

"Thank God," I murmured. "They're still alive."

"See," Stoney whispered, tracing a lone black fingernail down my cheek. "I told you I would hold up my end of the bargain."

I shrugged him off and bounded up the stairs, eager to finally reunite with my family. Once I reached the cage, they all hurried towards me, save for the young woman. She was staring off, and seemed unaware of my presence. There was an expression of unwavering sorrow etched on her face, and I couldn't help but feel sorry for her. She was suffering because of me, and there was nothing I could do to help her. The poor woman had lost her son and her freedom to vampires, all in one night.

Harvey and Switch greeted me with smiles, but Leland's greeting was the warmest of all. He reached his hands out to me through the bars, trying to grasp my hands. I reached my hands out, but when I attempted to touch him, I faltered, knowing that my hands would be ice-cold. Leland would know what had transpired, and I didn't want this reunion to be any more depressing than it already was. I lowered my head, trying to hide my face with my hair with the hope that he wouldn't be able to notice the change in my appearance.

"Leland," I smiled, and grabbed the part of his arm that was sleeved. "I'm so glad to see you're okay."

"Has he hurt you, Lina?" Leland asked, giving me a quick once-over.

I shook my head. I had to lie, even though it pained me to do so. "No, I'm fine."

"Lina—"

"I promise," I replied, squeezing his arms tightly.

Leland leaned closer towards me to whisper, "You have to get out of here. I know you came here wanting to protect me and the rest of the team, but you need to forget about us. Save yourself."

My smile faltered, and I glanced back at Stoney, who was watching me from a distance. His goon, Drake, was standing protectively at his side. When I turned back to face him, I cursed the tears in my eyes as I said, "I can't."

"What do you mean?" he inquired. "Of course you can!"

I bit my lip, hating the fact that I had to lie to him once again. "I promised Stoney I would do as he says, so long as he keeps you four alive. We made a deal."

"Lina, you cannot negotiate with him!" he told me, his tone harsh. "He's a vampire! The first chance he has, he will betray you! Have I taught you nothing all these years?"

"I know, but I had no choice. He would have killed you all."

"That doesn't matter now," he replied. "You need to run! Do you hear me? I won't stand to see you suffer on my account!"

Harvey nodded in agreement and stepped forward, wrapping his hands around the bars. "Listen to him, Lina. It's too late for us."

"I can't just leave you all here."

Harvey forced a smile and whispered, "I care about your safety much more than my own."

"Harvey—"

"He's right, Lina," Leland agreed. "I can't stand to see you suffer the same fate as us, or your parents. You need to escape while you still have a chance!"

"Your both wrong. I don't have any chance at getting out of here now."

Harvey and Leland seemed confused by my response, but before they had the chance to question me further, Stoney appeared at my side, flashing his fangs at the men in the cage.

"Good evening. I see you're all doing well." Leland and Harvey glared at the vampire from behind their bars. I watched as Leland reached for his neck. He seemed eager to pull out the gold cross that he always wore to keep the vampires at bay, but he found the necklace missing.

Stoney chuckled and replied, "I'm sorry but that was taken from you a while ago, old man."

"What do you want with Lina?" Leland asked him. "Why are you holding our lives over her head?"

"Because ... I need her."

"For what?" Harvey remarked with a scowl.

Stoney appeared thoughtful for a moment, but that look morphed into an arrogant sneer. "Wouldn't you like to know?"

"Stoney, let her go!" Harvey shouted back.

"Ah, still pining after the beloved Lina, aren't you, Mr. Johnson?" He laughed at him. He placed his arms on my shoulders, leaned towards the cage and whispered, "I have a secret to tell you: you're not the only one who's had her."

Harvey slammed his hands against the bars. "You son of a bitch!"

"Harvey, don't listen to him!" I said, trying to squirm out of the vampire's hold.

Stoney laughed at Harvey's outburst, then took hold of my arm and began to steer me in the direction of the staircase. "It's time to go."

"What?" I whirled around to face him, panic rising in my voice as I said, "But we only just got here!"

"Sorry, pet. There's something I need to show you."

I glanced back at Leland and forced a smile. For days I had been searching for him, and during those seventy-plus hours I had imagined the worst. However, Leland was fine. He was alive, along with Harvey and Switch. They were all that mattered—I valued their lives more than my own freedom.

With a heavy sigh, I dropped my hand from his and said, "This isn't goodbye. I will see you again."

Leland held my gaze, and he disregarded Stoney's heavy stare as he said, "Lina, please remember what I said. You must take care of yourself."

I nodded, if only just to indulge him. "I will—I promise."

Before I could finish saying goodbye, Stoney turned around and led me back down the cement steps. I glanced over my shoulder at the cage while I descended, and my stomach twitched with guilt when I noticed that my father had tears in his eyes. Switch and Harvey seemed just as upset, and it saddened me to see them all in so much pain. As I grew farther and farther away from them, I wondered if I was even doing them a favor by keeping them alive as Stoney's prisoners.

I glanced at my captor then, feeling disgusted when I noticed how pleased he seemed with himself, and just the sight of him overjoyed caused me to rethink my situation and our so-called agreement. As Stoney continued to tow me down the stairs, he was oblivious to the fury that had begun to rise within me. I knew at that moment, that I had to stop feeling sorry for myself. He had what he wanted—he had taken my humanity. It was high time I received something valuable in exchange.

Once we neared the bottom of the steps, I yanked my arm out of his grasp. The vampire was shocked by my action, and he came to a stop, now standing on the platform. I stood on the second to last step, and I refused to budge when he beckoned me to follow him. By the fierce expression on my face, I had a feeling that he knew I meant business.

"All right, Lina," he said finally. "What's troubling you now?"

"I want you to let my family go."

Stoney raised his thick black brows, amused by my request. "Excuse me?"

"You heard me."

"You had the opportunity to gain their freedom, but you threw my generosity back in my face. Now, I'm afraid, the offer no longer stands."

"Damn you!" The stern expression on my face held as I said, "You have what you want now, Stoney! I'm a vampire for Christ's sake. There's nothing I can do about it now."

"You're right, there's not."

"So there's no reason for you to keep my family hostage. I'll do as you say—I promise I'll be yours … just please let them go free."

"Why on earth would I do something as foolish as releasing vampire hunters who happen to want me dead? Not to mention their freedom would impede on my plans. They would only get in my way."

"You don't need them, Stoney!" I countered. "And I know for a fact that they don't know where this coven is. They won't be a threat to you if they can't find you!"

It appeared as if he was considering the idea. "Why should I let them go now?"

"Because if you don't, the first chance I get, I will end this terrible curse."

"I'll stop you if you try."

I nodded. "You probably will, but let's face it, Stoney. You're a busy vampire—you can't always be with me every second of the day."

"You don't have the courage to end your own life. Besides, I already told you what would happen to your precious little family if you did."

"I don't care," I stated. "A life lived as your captive is a death sentence. Sooner or later, you will renege on our deal. This is the only chance I have at securing their freedom."

Stoney's lips curved upwards into a smile as he said, "The lengths you will go to protect these humans is very admirable, Lina?"

"I'll do whatever it takes to save them."

I paused a moment, choking up at the memory of listening to Bill's horrible suffering over my radio as Stoney's undead goons tore him to shreds. Although there had been a trap set for them from the start, I still blamed myself for his death, and I would never come to peace with it.

"I already lost one member of my team to you. I won't allow you to doom the rest."

"I respect your commitment to your family, Lina, but—"

"You will let them go," I interrupted. "Or this pleasant arrangement between us ends right here, right now, on these steps."

He sighed in response, obviously annoyed by my demand, and glanced over his shoulder at Drake, who was observing our conversation with raised brows. I figured Stoney didn't want to look weak in front of his subordinates, but he didn't have a choice. He either gave in to my demands or he would lose me. If I really was as important to him as he said, he would do what I asked.

"Well, Stoney? What's it going to be?"

"All right, my love," he remarked, tossing up his hands as if in defeat. "Have it your way."

"You'll let them go?" I inquired, a sense of relief washing over me.

"Yes, I'll let them go," he sighed. "Now, shall we carry on?"

"I need your word."

The vampire paused for a moment, but eventually agreed. "You have it."

"Thank you."

I glanced over my shoulder and up the steps behind me. Leland and the others were too far away to have been able to overhear our conversation, but I was excited nonetheless that they were being set free. It was the least I could do for them. As I celebrated the fact that my family's nightmare was coming to an end, I sadly realized mine was just beginning.

"Shall we carry on?" Stoney asked, now holding out his hand once again. "As I mentioned earlier, there's something important I must show you."

I took his hand without a fuss, and we continued down the remainder of the steps in the direction of the platform, where Drake was waiting patiently. Once he joined us, we left the packing room, and Stoney locked the door behind him with a brass key he kept hidden in his pocket. He refused to tell me where we were headed, and I had a feeling that whatever he had planned for me was not in my best interest.

Chapter Fifteen

We wound up at the storage room, the same one I had come across during my brief escape in the warehouse. The vampires ushered me inside the room, and I caught sight of three naked bodies clumped together on the floor. I gasped at the unpleasant scene, assuming that all three were either dead or unconscious, but as I drew closer, I could sense a heartbeat. It was coming from the man, who was situated between the bodies of two naked women. I noticed that both of the women's throats had been slashed open and their flesh was ashen and pale. They, unfortunately, had been dead long before I had arrived.

The man stirred suddenly, and Drake was upon him in a matter of seconds, dragging him away from the corpses of the women. His eyes fluttered open, and when he caught sight of the vampire towing him, he began to scream. He tried to yank his hand out of Drake's, but his hold was far too strong.

Stoney grinned and clapped his hands together when the naked man was presented before him. I watched all of this unfold with dreary eyes, wondering why I had been brought here. I was uncomfortable with the way the man looked at me, fear etched on his face upon realizing that I was a vampire too. It was the first time a human had ever truly feared me, and I found that I did not favor the idea of being seen as a monster.

"What is going on here?" I whispered, turning my head away to hide from the man's fear-stricken gaze.

Stoney smiled at my inquiry. "What do you think?"

Before I could respond to his question, Stoney approached the man. He knelt down to his level, and placed his palm flat on his

163

forehead before gazing into his eyes. The man hollered and squirmed from Stoney's touch, but as he looked back into the black eyes of his captor, he fell into a trance. After only a brief moment of gazing into the vampire's eyes, he became unconscious.

Stoney turned to me and beckoned me to come forth, but I remained glued to the spot, unsure as to what he wanted. He sighed and looked to Drake, who then shoved me towards his master. Stoney grabbed my arm and yanked me down onto my knees beside him. I was now only mere inches away from the body of the man, and I could feel the heat radiating off of his skin. I could also smell the blood pumping from his heart and through his veins, and the aroma caused my eyes to roll back in my head. I was surprised to find that I was tempted by this man.

A sharp cramp roused in my stomach, and I gasped at its ferocity. I massaged the area, wondering what had caused the pain. Stoney was watching me now, and he seemed rather interested in my current state. Another stab of pain jolted my stomach, and I groaned, gritting my teeth as I fought to ignore it.

"You feel it don't you?" Stoney whispered. "The thirst."

My eyes were heavy as the pain dissolved, and a thick sensation now blossomed in the pit of my stomach. The feeling was similar to that of hunger, but I found it was far more acute. It was more of a deep desire for sustenance than a need to feed, and my mouth began to salivate with each beat of his pulse.

"It won't be long now, before the thirst takes control of you. You're a newborn—you won't be able to resist."

"I … won't," I managed to say, my body beginning to shake as I crouched over the man. "I won't drink blood."

Stoney laughed at my unwavering defiance and shook his dark locks. He placed a hand on my backside to say, "Lina, my sweet, don't you understand? You've lost. You're one of us now. There's no need for you to keep fighting anymore."

I turned my head around to glare at him, my eyes full of hatred. "I will keep fighting you, Stoney. I may be a monster, but that won't stop me from kicking your undead ass. If anything, now I have a better chance at killing you. You've leveled the playing field."

His amused expression melted away as he stared back at me. "Defiant 'til the very end, aren't you? I was going to give you time to adjust to your change, but I see now that any generosity I provide you will be thrown right back in my face. If you want to do this the hard way, Lina, that's fine with me!" Stoney growled, grabbing me by the neck. He forced my head towards the man's frail arm, and he held me there, his strength keeping.

"Drink," the vampire commanded.

"No," I whispered, my mouth nearly touching the human's skin. "I won't do it, Stoney."

"Drink from him, Lina," Stoney instructed again.

"I said no!" I shouted, now struggling against his tight grip. Stoney was not pleased by my response, and he quickly turned me towards him, his hand now wrapped around my throat. Once I was facing him again, he raised his free hand and struck me across the jaw. I cried out from the action; my fists clenched from anger.

"You will drink, Lina, even if I have to cut open his veins and pour the blood into your damned mouth," Stoney told me icily. "Is that what you want me to do?"

"I despise you!" I cried, my cheek burning.

"That's enough! I won't tolerate another outburst!" He snapped. "Now, where were we?"

With a huff, he forced me back towards the man, but this time Stoney made a slight cut in the man's forearm with his nail, causing a line of blood to pour from the wound. My eyes were glued to the blood that was now flowing freely, and as much as I tried to, I found I couldn't look away. The sight of the blood was mesmerizing, irresistible even, and I had never wanted anything more in my entire life. I tried to fight the urge to drink, but the desire was much too strong, and as I leaned my mouth down to the man's arm, my eyes zoned in on his pulsing veins.

My mouth was only inches away from the blood when I realized I could hold back no longer. I had lost the battle. My reservations fell away and I leaned into the liquid, my tongue lapping at the man's arm. The blood tasted unreal—unlike anything I had ever tasted before. It still held the same metallic aftertaste, but there was a sense of sweetness about it now that I couldn't get enough of.

I began to drink faster, my eyes closing as I relished in the delicious and refreshing taste of the blood. The smell was almost as appealing as the taste was, and both mixed together was too much for me to withdraw from. As I drank more and more, I lost all awareness of my surroundings. I forgot where I was and whom I was with, and that's when my amazing experienced turned frightening.

My eyes snapped open, and I glanced over at the man, noticing he had awoken. The mixed expression of fear and disgust on his face was too much to bear, and it cut into me like a knife, but no matter how hard I tried to withdraw, I found that I couldn't stop feeding. It was as if my animalistic side had taken over, and all rationality was now lost. Then, before I even knew it was happening, my fangs released into his flesh, and a rush of intoxicating pleasure passed over my body. The man cried out from the pain as I bit deeper into his arm, but I couldn't stop now, not when I had experienced such sweet pleasure. However, Stoney had different ideas.

"That's enough, Lina" he said, and grabbed me by the shoulder. Stoney tried prying me off of the man, but my strength was doubled as I continued to feed. My nails now dug into the human's arm, and I bared my teeth at him when he touched me again.

Stoney growled and commanded me to stop, but I ignored him. I was taken over by the pleasure, and it was a truly unique and freeing experience. I felt like I resided on another plane of existence, and there was no other feeling like it in the world. Not even sex had made me feel this free before, and I wanted nothing more than to bask in the lustful sensations for all eternity.

However, it was when the man was nearing death that I snapped back to reality. I could feel his pulse begin to slow and his breathing turn shallow, causing my fangs to withdraw from his skin. He was begging me to stop, expressing his love for life, and it caused me to twitch. The man didn't want to die, but I could already see in his weathered and pale face that he was nearing his end. He was at death's door now, and it was all because of me.

With a gasp, I scooted backwards, away from the man and on the verge of spilling tears. I stared down at my hands, which were now covered in blood, and I could feel the wet stain of blood on my lips and chin as well. I used the crook of my arm to wipe my mouth, hoping it would make me feel clean. Unfortunately, it only smeared the blood more.

"What have I done?" I whispered, my voice shaking from fear and disgust.

"Disobeyed, for starters," Stoney remarked. "Now there's barely any blood left for me to drink."

"You can't! He'll die!"

Stoney raised a brow at my disapproval. "You're concerned about this mortal's life now, after you drained him of nearly all of his blood?"

"No, I didn't," I murmured. "I—I didn't know what I was doing."

"Sure you did," Stoney replied. "You can't tell me that you didn't feel a rush of profound power mixed with absolute bliss coursing through your entire body while you fed."

I bowed my head, trying to hide my shame under my hair. "It wasn't my fault. I was in a daze."

"That may be, but you can't deny the fact that you enjoyed feeding, Lina."

I said nothing, only continued to sit still as the guilt began to rise up in my throat. Although I would never openly admit to it,

Stoney was right. I did enjoy feeding, and if I hadn't been bothered by the man's slowing heartbeat, I would have continued to drink from him until his heart had beat no more.

"Now, let me just take care of this human, and we'll continue with the preparations." Stoney circled around me and over towards the man, where he bent down near his neck. He lowered his own head until his mouth was almost touching skin, but before he unleashed his fangs, he sent me grin and said, "I think I'm going to enjoy killing with you."

"No, stop!" I shouted, and I jumped to my feet. I lunged at Stoney, shoving him away from the man. We tumbled to the ground, and I tried my best to keep him restrained, but he was far too strong for me to detain. Stoney growled and struck me in the dead center of the chest, knocking me off guard. He now had me pinned me down onto my back and was straddling me, his black eyes wide and furious.

"I am your maker, Lina, and you will do as I say!" He snarled. "You will obey!"

"I would rather die than obey you, Stoney!" I snapped back, trying to free my arms from his grasp.

Stoney's angered expression vanished as he replied, "We'll see about that. You're forgetting that I still have your loved ones in my custody, Ms. Holiday."

"But you're going to let them go," I said, now trembling as I stared up at the impassive look on his face. "You gave me your word."

He grinned, flashing his long fangs. "I lied."

"You promised!" I screamed. With a loud cry, I shoved Stoney off of me and rolled onto all fours. I took to a stand before the vampire could retaliate, and I leapt at him again, this time with my nails outstretched. I slashed at his face, leaving three fresh scratches along his cheek.

Stoney gaped at me, stunned by the action. He touched his face, and after tracing the wounds, he brought his hand before his eyes. When he noticed that his fingers were stained with blood, he frowned and clenched his teeth. "You little bitch. You're going to regret this moment, I can assure you of that."

I smiled with triumph and licked the blood off of my fingertips, finding that his blood had a weird tangy flavor. It wasn't as sweet tasting as a human's, and though I didn't care for the taste, I swallowed it nonetheless.

Once I had cleaned my hand of Stoney's blood, I moved into a fighting stance and motioned for him to attack me. "Come on then," I urged him. "Give me your best shot."

Stoney stared back at me in disbelief. "You can't be serious?"

"Oh, I most definitely am."

He smirked then, obviously amused by my request for a brawl. However, Stoney would not give me the satisfaction of a one-on-one. Instead, he motioned to two vampires that were standing near the entrance doors. I hadn't noticed them before, and I figured they had slipped inside the room when I was arguing with Stoney. They did as he commanded, and were now standing a few feet away. "Take her back to her room," he instructed. "And this time, make sure her restraints are silver-plated."

"No!" I growled. "Face me!"

"Sorry, dear. Not today."

"Coward!" I shot back.

He shook his dark head at my insult. "On the contrary. I would love to teach you a lesson, but unfortunately I don't have the time. World domination takes a lot of planning."

At the snap of Stoney's boney fingers, the vampires crowded around us, but I anticipated their movements. When one made the attempt to grab me, I backed away and ran in the direction of the doors that were no longer guarded. I flung it open with haste, but only to reveal a pair of vampires standing by. They had been waiting on the other side of the door. Before I had a chance to retreat, the two vampires grabbed my arms, keeping me locked in between them. I yelled and hollered, but I ceased when Stoney approached me.

Stoney's minions held me in place while Stoney smacked me across the jaw, from left to right, each blow more powerful than the next. I snarled at him once he was finished, the pain he'd just inflicted on me easing away in a matter of seconds. My new powers frightened me, but I was also starting to see them in a new light. If I had been human and he had struck me with the same force, I would not have been able to sustain the blow. Perhaps I could match him in battle now, if only I could get him alone.

Stoney smirked once he realized he had pissed me off, and with a crude kiss to my forehead, he sent the vampires away, with me struggling in their tow. "Don't fret, my love. We'll see each other very soon."

I scowled as his minions towed me out of the room and down the depressing hall, back to the room where I was forced into solitude once again. To my surprise, the crowd of vampires had lessened into a duo, and I had the feeling I could easily overcome them, but I waited for the right moment to retaliate. So when they commanded me to take a seat in the chair I did as I was told, but when they attempted to shackle me I finally made my move.

Before they could wrap the silver shackles around my wrists, I kicked out my legs, striking both vampires in their stomachs. They staggered backward, surprised by the action. I vaulted to my feet, and I wrapped my hands around one of their necks. I twisted it cruelly, and once I heard it crack, I wasted no time. I picked up the metal chair and shoved one of the back legs through the vampire's torso. His chest swelled until it burst, and I watched him die with satisfaction. The remaining vampire backed away from me in fear, but I refused to let him get away. If he did, he would surely fetch Stoney, and I couldn't take that chance.

I tossed the chair to the side and lunged at the vampire, grabbing him by his legs. He lost his balance and fell to the ground, snarling at me while I attacked him with my nails. I scratched at his

170

face as I kept him pinned on the ground, and he was unable to shake me off. As we struggled on the cold cement floor, the vampire swiped at my head, and his large hand struck me hard across the side of my skull.

I growled at him, and before I could get control of my anger, I began to bite at his neck. The vampire wriggled underneath me, but I kept him there, my thighs squeezing tight up against his torso. Rage was building up within in me, and I was relentless in my intent to kill him. I bit deeper, ignoring the tangy, unsavory taste of his blood as I chewed through dead flesh, tendons and veins. Then, suddenly, there was nothing left to bite through, and I lifted my head.

As I rose to my feet, my anger washed away as I watched the vampire shudder on the floor below, his head twitching as blood poured from the open wound. I raised my foot and brought the pointed heel of my boot straight down through the center of the vampire's chest. With his black eyes gazing up at me, full of shock, he turned into a pile of blood and guts.

Instead of feeling relieved that I had destroyed my assailant, a sick feeling settled in the pit of my stomach. I raised my hands to my face, touching the cool skin softly. I was frightened by how quickly my fury had taken over. My actions had been vicious, to the point that I had actually torn a gaping hole in the vampire's neck with my mouth. The reflection on my actions almost caused me to vomit.

However, I didn't have any time to waste feeling sorry for myself. I had to find Harvey, Leland, and Switch before Stoney became aware of my escape. With one last glance at the bloody mess on the floor, I turned and ran, hurrying down the hall at full speed. I prayed Stoney hadn't moved my family—that I would be able to find them in the same room as before. The warehouse was massive, and the more time I spent wandering, the chances of me having a successful escape diminished. When I came upon the packing room again, I breathed a sigh of relief at the sight of the large cage, and my family still within it. As I approached them, however, I was frustrated to find that Leland was gone.

I ran towards the metal cage, sprinting up the concrete steps, my eyes wild as I looked between Switch and Harvey. The young woman lay huddled in the corner alone, a vacant expression still on her face. As soon as I made my presence known to my friends, they gasped at the sight of me drenched in blood.

"Shit, Lina. What the hell happened to you?" Harvey asked as he looked me over. "Are you okay? You're covered in blood."

I was confused by his question at first, and so I glanced down at my bloodstained clothes. "Oh, that. Don't worry about it," I told him. "I'm fine."

"So that's not your blood then?" Switch asked.

"No." I looked between the two of them, worried over the fact that Leland was gone. "Where's Leland?"

Neither of them responded to my question, which caused alarms to go off in my head. After a quiet moment passed, Harvey sighed and reached out his hand to me through the bars.

"Lina …" he began, but I refused to grab his outstretched hand. Instead, I stared at the solemn expression on his face, which said more than he knew. My stomach dropped as I assume the worst.

"Where is he, Harvey?" I asked again, my voice breaking.

"I'm sorry, Lina," he whispered, and I realized then that his brown eyes were cloudy. "Leland's gone."

I leaned up against the cage, now gripping the bars as tightly as I could. "What do you mean he's gone? He has to be somewhere inside this warehouse, Johnson. Stoney wouldn't have the time to hide him somewhere else."

"No, that's not what he means," Switch finally spoke up, and he too looked just as forlorn as Harvey did.

"Okay?" I replied with a frown, still not understanding their meaning.

With a heavy sigh, Harvey finally said, "He's dead, Lina."

Chapter Sixteen

As soon as the words left Harvey's mouth, I froze, my jaw dropping as I scrambled to breathe. The news of Leland's death made me dizzy, and I leaned up against the cage for support. "No," I murmured. "That can't be true."

"Lina—" Harvey began.

"No!" I shouted. "I won't believe it! I can't believe it!"

"I know this is hard for you to hear—"

"He's not dead! I would know if he was dead!"

"We watched Stoney drain his blood, Lina," Switch explained. He pointed down the steps, in the direction of the empty platform. "Right over there."

I turned my head to examine the platform Switch was pointing to, and once I did, I noticed the large and faded red stain in the center of the concrete pad. I had overlooked the stain when I first entered the room as I was preoccupied with rescuing my team, but it was obvious that someone had bled to death there.

"Oh my God …" I moaned, my hands balling into tight fists. "Not Leland," I whispered, and I could not bear the despair I felt.

I was now a member of the undead and my heart no longer possessed the power to beat, but I still managed to feel the agony of it splitting in half. I leaned against the cage and closed my heavy eyes, allowing emotions to take ahold of me. Not too long ago I had worried about my team seeing me in despair, but now I realized there was no point in putting on a brave face in front of them.

Stoney had taken away my mortality, I had failed at rescuing my Leland, and now the rest of my family was trapped

173

inside a warehouse full of ruthless vampires. I wasn't sure why, but I thought of Gabriel at that moment, recalling how he had told me to have faith. What a joke.

"Lina," Harvey spoke softly, startling me out of my emotional coma. "It's going to be okay."

My eyes snapped open in anger, and I glared daggers at him.. "No, Johnson. It's not going to be okay! I failed him. I failed everyone, including myself!"

"Don't say that. It isn't over yet. Stoney hasn't won."

"If you haven't noticed, Harvey, he's already won! Stoney's taken away everything that I used to cherish. Soon, he'll come for you too." My voice fell as I stared at my pale hands still wrapped around the bars. "There's nothing left to stop me now," I whispered.

"What do you mean, Lina?"

"Stoney killed Leland, when he knew using him as leverage against me was the only way to force me along with whatever he pleased. If my father truly is dead, then there's nothing left preventing me from ripping out his black heart!"

"You couldn't be more wrong, Lina," a familiar voice said, and it echoed around the large room, startling the three of us. The woman sitting on the floor of the cage didn't move an inch. I had a feeling that she was off somewhere in her mind. I didn't blame her.

I surveyed the room with frantic eyes, until suddenly, Stoney leapt down from the rafters above. He landed gracefully in the dead center of the cement platform. His black boots treaded on the bloodstains, and his disrespectful behavior only infuriated me more. I ran towards him, bounding down the cement steps with my fangs unsheathed. My hatred for him had reached a very dangerous level.

"You son of a bitch!" I screamed, my tone shrill. "I'm going to make you pay for killing my Leland!"

174

Stoney grinned and shook his head. "You silly girl. Do you really think I would kill Leland, the wisest, most adept vampire hunter in all of the country? Come now. I'm not that dense."

"We saw you kill him, Stoney!" Harvey shouted, banging his fist on the metal bars of the cage. "I watched you tear open his throat and feed! You can't deny it!"

"He's right," Stoney replied, as he advanced up the steps towards us. "I did drain your father. However, it was a necessary step. I had to make him weak in order for him to fall prey to my ... persuasive suggestions. You know what I mean, don't you, Lina?"

I was overcome with grief, as I understood the meaning behind his remark. I staggered backwards, feeling lightheaded once again. "No ..." I moaned, my eyes filling with tears. "Please tell me you didn't!"

Harvey and Switch seemed confused, and they looked to me for answers. "What's he talking about, Lina?" Harvey inquired. "What has he done?"

I barely heard him ask the question. My mind was going to a dark place, and I fell onto my knees, my face hidden in my hands as I sobbed. I couldn't bear to answer Harvey's question as the truth was too cruel to say. Stoney had stripped me of my humanity, and now Leland's was lost as well. He was a creature of the night, and to Leland, that was a fate far worse than death. He would not be able to deal with his new identity, and it broke my heart. Turning him into a vampire was as sure as killing him.

"How could you do this?" I asked him after a moment. "More importantly, why?"

He approached me with a loud sigh, and once at my side, he knelt down beside me. When I didn't respond to his presence, Stoney took my head in his hands, forcing me to face him as he whispered, "Because I need you both on my side. You're stronger than you ever could have been as humans. Don't you see that? You've been gifted with eternal life, and powers far beyond your understanding."

175

"This isn't a gift," I spat, my brows narrowing as I gazed up at him. "This is a damned curse!"

"Lina!" Harvey shouted. "Don't believe a word he says! You can't let him manipulate you!"

I glanced back at Harvey, and as I stared into his grief-filled eyes, I realized he still didn't know what I was. I was unsure if I had the guts to tell him what happened—to explain what Stoney had done. He had transformed me into a monster, and I was afraid that my friends would not accept me with open arms. Could they turn a blind eye to my immortality, or would they try to drive a stake through my heart the first chance they had? Either way, I was positive it was not something I could keep secret for long, especially with Stoney holding it over my head.

"Harvey, Switch …" My voice was shaking, but that they deserved to know the truth. "Something has happened, to both me and Leland."

"What?" he asked, his tone darkening. "What's happened?"

When I made the attempt to spill my secret, Stoney intervened. "Let's not spoil the surprise, darling!" he said, and slapped his hand over my mouth. "Besides, wouldn't it be more fun to demonstrate your new abilities instead? How about we show your comrades your newfound taste for blood?" he whispered into my ear.

I shook my head violently back and forth. "You're hungry, Lina," he teased. "I can see it in your eyes."

He let go of my mouth and I glared at him. "Don't you dare hurt them!"

He shook his head and replied, "Oh, don't be silly, Lina. I won't be hurting them. You will."

Before I even could beg him to reconsider, Stoney was at the cage. He unlocked it and grabbed Harvey by his left arm, dragging him out of his prison, leaving Switch and the woman behind. With a slur of obscenities, Switch slammed his hands on the bars and hollered at the vampire to let Harvey go. Stoney

176

ignored his protests, and they were down the steps in a matter of seconds. Stoney tossed Harvey onto his knees a few feet away from me, and I scrambled over towards him, reaching out my arms to pull him into a tight embrace.

"Jesus, Lina," he whispered into my hair. "You're ice cold."

"I know," I mumbled, hiding my face in the crook of his neck.

Placing my face next to Harvey's bare throat was an awful idea, but it didn't cross my mind until after I began to sense his heartbeat. He radiated heat, and I could hear the faint sound of his heart pumping blood through his veins. Before I even realized it, I nuzzled my head closer against Harvey's warm skin.

My eyes rolled back in my head when that familiar warmth began to spread in the pit of my stomach. I uttered a soft moan, and planted my lips against Harvey's neck, now sucking the skin. The action caught him off guard, and he pulled back to steal a glance at my face.

"Lina, what are you doing?"

I did not respond, but I kept my focus on him, and once Harvey stared into my eyes long enough, he was lost. I had charmed him, even if I hadn't planned on doing so.

"That's it, Lina," Stoney whispered, as he watched the scene unfold. "Just a few seconds more."

However, something prevented me from tasting Harvey's flesh. It was the sound of someone commanding me to stop. The voice was masculine, familiar, and when I lifted my head to glance in the direction it was coming from, I was dumbfounded to see Bill standing there. It was Bill Sects, or it used to be. He was a vampire now, his once bright blue eyes were cloudy and gray, and his skin was a creamy pale. He seemed slimmer than normal too, and as he approached us, I likened his new appearance to that of a skeleton's.

"Bill?" I whispered, dumbfounded at the sight of him. "Is that you?"

"Hello, Lina," he replied with a smile. "It's nice to see you."

"You're … alive?"

He grinned. "Sort of."

Bill stopped just before me and held out his hand, and I took it happily. He pulled me up onto my feet without a word and we shared a sweet embrace. Once we broke away, Bill bent down to help Harvey stand. Harvey was still out of it; my charms took a toll on him. Once Harvey had regained somewhat of his consciousness, he glanced between Bill and I, as if he didn't believe we were truly there.

"Bill, is that really you?" Harvey asked, with a wholehearted smile.

"Yes, it's me."

Harvey stiffened for a moment, then looked back me. "Am I dreaming?"

"No, Harvey. You're not dreaming."

"Am I dead?"

I shook my head and glanced back at Bill, who seemed amused by Harvey's disorientation. "No."

"Well, then why do you two look that way?"

"How do we look, Johnson?" Bill asked, leaning his face closer to him.

"Strange," he mumbled, after a moment. "You look like …" His voice fell, and I had a feeling that the truth finally dawned on him. All of a sudden his eyes grew wide with fear, and he shoved my hands off of him to quickly back away from us. "Oh my god …"

"Harvey, wait—" I began, yearning to explain what had happened, but my voice broke. When I took a step towards him, he held up his hands to keep me at bay.

"Stay back!" He shouted.

I fought the urge to cry as I stared at the frightened expression on my comrade's face. "Harvey, you don't have to be afraid. It's still me."

Harvey looked to Bill then, who had been keeping rather quiet. "You guys are vampires?"

Bill nodded, then placed his hand on my shoulder. "Don't worry, Harvey," he said, with a wink and a smile. "We're not going to hurt you."

Harvey brought his hands up to his head and dragged them through his hair. I could hear his heartbeat was racing. "Shit," Harvey muttered, nervously eyeing us. "I'm going to need some time to get used to this."

"Just take a deep breath, Harvey. You can trust us," Bill told him..

I looked to Bill then, surprised by his calm demeanor. It was at that moment that I began to grow suspicious. I wondered why he wasn't stuck in a cell with the others. It didn't make any sense that he was allowed to roam the coven freely, while the rest of them were caged like animals. Did Stoney actually trust that Bill wasn't a threat now that he was turned? Or perhaps the reason he wasn't in the cage was something far worse. I wasn't sure if I could handle knowing the truth.

"Bill, what's going on here?" I inquired. The tingling sense of fear crawled up the nape of my neck, but I smacked my hand against the bare skin to deter it.

He seemed confused. "What do you mean?"

"Why are you acting so calm about all of this? And why aren't you caged with the rest of them?"

When he didn't answer, my concern intensified, and I was afraid of asking the next question that plagued my mind. Unfortunately, I knew it had to be asked. "Are you working for Stoney, Bill?"

He smiled at me, but it was an eerie, unfamiliar smile that I had never witnessed before. When he opened his mouth to reply, I stiffened at the sight of his two sharp fangs. "Lina, you're worried, and that's understandable. After everything you've been through these past few days, it's no wonder you're having a hard time trusting people. However, you have nothing to fear from me."

"Bill," I began, and I found that my voice had become shaky. "Answer the damn question."

"Am I working for Stoney?" he asked, still smiling. "No, I'm not."

The tension in my shoulders melted away. "Thank God. For a second there, I thought you might have been."

"Actually, Lina, if you would have let me finish, I would have explained that he's actually working for me."

"What?" I exclaimed. "What the hell do you mean, he's working for you?"

Bill's smile finally faded from his gaunt face, and he advanced d towards Stoney, who was now standing off to the side, watching all of us.. Bill motioned for him to hand over something, and the vampire reached into his pocket to retrieve a small vial of blood. After he tossed it to Bill, he swallowed the blood, and I watched an expression of pure bliss passed over his face.

Once Bill was finished with his snack, he walked back towards us. I kept a close eye on him, Harvey did too, and when he advanced in my direction, I backed away, keeping at least ten feet between us. Bill sighed and shook his head, as if annoyed by my sudden retreat.. "Lina, I've already told you that you've got nothing to fear. It's still me … I'm just immortal now. I promise I'm not going to hurt you."

"I need you to tell me what's going on here," I demanded.

"Yeah," Harvey agreed. "We have a right to know!"

"Of course," he said, with a nod.

"Then spit it out, Sects!"

Bill narrowed his eyes at my outburst, but finally began to talk. "I approached Stoney a few months ago, after overhearing a pair of his goons discussing his conquest of Chicago. My initial reaction was to inform Leland, but another thought occurred to me—a dark thought, one that frightened and excited me. I wasn't sure why, but I suddenly felt compelled to join Stoney's cause. I wanted to help him capture Chicago."

"Why?" I replied incredulously. "What the hell would possess you to want to help Stoney, Bill?"

"Technically, Lina, I didn't just want to help him. I wanted to help lead his takeover."

"That's the dumbest thing I've ever heard," I remarked with a snort. "How could you possibly lead Stoney? He's not the type to take orders from anybody."

Bill glanced back at Stoney and grinned at the stern expression now on the vampire overlord's face. "This is very true, and when I finally gained the balls to propose my idea, he nearly killed me. However, Stoney's not stupid. He was already aware of the fact that he needed to get the vampire hunters out of the way beforehand. I made him see that our team would be much more valuable to him if we were alive and fighting on his side. Lina, I saved us."

"Jesus, Bill..." Harvey muttered, bringing his hands up to cup his face. "What have you done?"

I gasped at Bill's confession. He'd betrayed us...his own family. I had known Bill almost his entire life. Out of the three of us, he was the goody-good. He had never disobeyed Leland's rules; he never put himself in dangerous situations, and I wondered what could have caused him to do a complete 180 and act out in such a malevolent manner.

"How could you do this?" I asked him.

"Lina, don't you see? With all of our skills and knowledge in combat, we could protect Stoney and his progeny from the other hunters in the area. Together, we would be unstoppable."

"Bill, do you have any idea how insane you sound right now? All our lives, we've hunted vampires—we've protected those who couldn't protect themselves against them. We took an oath to help people!"

"I know. I was grateful to Leland, and to you, for welcoming me with open arms and making me a part of your team. But things change. Hunting vampires was becoming tiresome, and I was looking for a way off of the team for quite a while."

"Tiresome? How can you say that, Bill? They murdered your parents—"

"Yes, I'm quite aware that vampires killed my parents, Lina!" he interrupted me with a snarl. "I was there, remember? I watched them devour my father!" Bill suddenly dragged a hand through his sandy hair to steady himself.

"Then what would make you want to protect vampires, Bill? Furthermore, why would you think the rest of us would want to?" Harvey asked him.

He drew a deep breath and waited a few moments before carrying on. "Even though my parents met their demise at the hands of vampires, it doesn't mean I should live my entire life loathing their existence, especially not when I know how much strength they possess. They're an elite being, and they surpass humans on almost every level."

"Vampires are beneath humans. They're merciless monsters, and you know it!"

"What's mercy got to do with survival? Compassion is for the weak. I see that now."

"Bill, what the hell has happened to you?" I murmured in disbelief. "This isn't you!"

He shrugged. "I was enlightened by my transformation, and unlike you, I know what is truly important."

"Which is what?"

"Dominance," he grinned, flashing his fangs once more.

I stared back at my old friend, completely dumbfounded. This was not the Bill I remembered growing up with. This thing before me was cold and cruel, and I wanted no part in the scheme he was hatching. He was in league with Stoney, which now made him an enemy, but as I gazed into his dark eyes, I wondered if I had the strength to go up against him. He used to be a part of my family, and the fact that he had deceived me broke my heart.

"I'm sorry that you disagree with me about our new gifts, but surely you can't deny that you feel it."

I narrowed my brows at his question. "Feel what?"

"That newfound power coursing through your body, giving you the strength to accomplish almost anything you desire. Complete invincibility"

"Is that what this is all about, Bill? Fucking power?"

He didn't bat an eye. "Somewhat, yes."

"So you would damn your family and friends, in exchange for a little dose of inhuman strength? You've got to be kidding me!"

"Surely you must feel somewhat relieved, Lina?" He replied with a frown. "You can never grow old—never die. You will be immortal, as will they. Don't you see? We can be together forever."

"I don't want to be immortal," I told him, my voice trembling. "I never wanted this fate, but I was never given the chance to turn it down." I shot Stoney a glare before adding, "I would have chosen death, if I had actually had a choice."

Bill scratched his chin with an impassive look. "I wanted to tell you everything the first day you were brought here, but I know you, Lina. You, with your moral superiority complex, would not have understood until you were made one of us. You would have refused to. It was the only way to get you to join our side."

His response shook me to the core. "Are you saying that all of this was your doing, Bill?"

"Of course. It was my plan from the start. The rooftop, the theater, and the meeting with Stoney at the harbor."

Just like that, it all began to make sense. Bill was the first to lose contact with the group, so he was able to reach the theater before Leland did and ambush him. The mystery of the UV lights had been solved as well. He had to have returned to the vault and shut them off before Stoney's group arrived. It had been Bill all along. He was the one to blame for our predicament, not Stoney.

My jaw dropped and my eyes widened with fury as I stared at him. "You son of a bitch!" I hollered. "You stole my humanity? You stole Leland's?"

"Turning Leland was necessary."

"How the hell was that necessary? You know how he feels about vampires, Bill! He would rather die than be doomed to live life as one of the undead!"

"I couldn't let him perish. He is my mentor after all."

"Then how could you betray him like this?" I shot back. "Furthermore, how could you betray the rest of us?" None of this made any sense to me. Bill's treachery was so out of character; I would have never thought he would be capable of something so wicked. "Bill, this isn't you. Surely there has to be some other reason!"

"There isn't."

"Are you sure about that?" I inquired curiously. "If Stoney manipulated you into this scheme, you can tell me, Bill. I can help you be free of him!"

He laughed and shook his head at my suggestion. "Stoney didn't manipulate me, Lina. I wanted this—I always have."

Bill hadn't divulged the entire truth to me. He was holding back, but I was going to get it out of him, one way or the other. "Why are you doing this, Bill? Are you trying to get back at one of us? Is this some sort of punishment?"

"Don't be absurd!"

I refused to quit probing. There had to have been another motive for turning on us. "I don't believe that this scheme of yours was based solely on a need for world domination. Frankly, it doesn't make sense. You aligned with Stoney for another reason, and I want to know what it is!"

Bill sighed and leaned his head back to gaze up at the high ceiling above his head. "Just let it go, Lina. It's not important."

"It's very fucking important, Bill!" I snapped. "It was important enough for you to side with a cold-blooded killer and plan to turn your family into vampires!"

"I'm asking you nicely to drop it," he told me, through gritted teeth.

"I deserve to know."

"Jesus Christ! You never give up, do you?" He glanced back at Stoney, an expression of pure fury conveyed on his face. "I don't know how you put up with her!" Stoney said nothing, but I noticed that he seemed to be entertained by Bill's exasperation.

Then, with a bogus, charming smile, Bill turned to face me again. "You're right, Lina. As always. It wasn't solely about gaining power. Above all, I wanted equality."

"Equality?"

"Yes, equality!" He snarled, rushing towards me. "You've always been the leader—you've always been Leland's favorite! No matter how hard I tried, or how many vampires I slayed, I never measured up in his eyes. Even compared to Harvey, I was the weak one. I was sick and tired of it! !"

"Bill, we've always appreciated you—"

"Because you had to!" he growled. "You only ever used me as a backup! You never let me be your right hand on a single mission. Harvey was always given that privilege."

Harvey said nothing at first, but after peeking over at me, he replied, "Bill, it wasn't that you didn't measure up—"

"Wasn't it, Harvey? Or maybe there was some other reason why Lina always wanted you by her side."

Bill grinned and looked to me then. "I know how close you two have become, Lina," he whispered.

My cheeks flushed at the remark. "This is ridiculous!" I finally said. "I never intended to make you feel inadequate, Bill."

"Admit it!" Bill shot back.. "You thought I was weak."

I might have entertained the idea of lying to protect his ego, but after finding out that he had put my life, and the rest of my family in jeopardy, I would spare him no generosity. After all, he had spared me none.

"You're right, Bill," I replied. "Out of the three of us, you are the weakest."

He snickered at my admission and said, "Finally some truth from the great Lina Holiday!"

"You want some more truth? You still are the weakest."

"No, not anymore. I'll agree that I may have been before, but that's all been changed. Thanks to our transformations, you and I are equals now, Lina. I'm just as strong as you are, if not stronger, and we are measured in all our abilities. There is nothing that you can do that I can't." Bill looked pleased as he added, "Leland will be proud of me."

I shook my head, stunned by how pathetic he sounded. "No, Bill. We're not equals, and we never will be. You and I may have matched strengths, but you lack the compassion and humanity that Leland fought so hard to instill in us." With a frown, I added, "He will never be proud of what you've done."

I hoped that my statement would open Bill's eyes to the evil he had committed, but it seemed to only anger him. "You don't know that! He has always loved us unconditionally, even with all of our faults! In time, he will grow to understand that I had to make the change, to better us all."

"No, he won't, Bill, and deep down you know I'm right. No matter how you try to spin your betrayal, Leland will only see it as falling prey to your weaknesses."

"I'm not weak!" he hissed, his eyes glowing with rage.

By the fresh look of fury engraved on Bill's face, I knew he was on the verge of cracking. Although I was aware that bashing his ego might result in a physical confrontation, I couldn't allow him to get away with everything he had done. Family or not, he had stolen my mortality, along with Leland's, and he planned to do the same to the rest of my family. I had to protect Harvey and Switch from the same repulsive fate Leland and I now suffered, and it was evident that there was no use in reasoning with Bill in his current delusional state. He had to be stopped, and if I was forced to ram a stake through his heart, so be it.

"I hate to say it, but I've always known you weren't cut out to be a hunter," I confessed. "Leland thought he was doing you a favor by bringing you onto our team, but in my opinion, he should have just left you on the streets the night he found you—left you in that pool of your father's blood. He always knew you were vulnerable, and that you would never measure up to me or to Johnson."

"Shut up!" Bill howled, now flashing his fangs at me.

I wouldn't let up though. I kept digging the knife deeper, hoping it would send him into a downward spiral of uninhibited rage. "Maybe if you hadn't been coddled so much by Leland, you would've grown into a real man instead of the pathetic failure you are today."

Bill could hold back his wrath no longer. He rushed at me with a raised hand, but before he could do any damage, Stoney caught him by his wrist. He shoved Bill in the opposite direction, but kept his hands on his arm, reaching up to grab him by the jaw.

"You will not touch her!" Stoney growled, his eyes blacker than I had ever seen them before. "Or have you already forgotten the terms to our agreement?"

"You didn't seem to care much for our agreement when you were persuading her to eat Harvey!"

Stoney gripped Bill's jaw harder. I heard the bone crack. "Do not argue with me! Now, be a good little boy and promise me that you won't touch her again!"

Bill detached Stoney's hand from his face and held up his hands. "Yes, I fucking swear I won't." He smoothed down his shirt and fixed his hair before he glanced back in my direction. "She isn't worth my time anyway. The bitch is all yours."

Stoney's disapproving gaze held as he replied, "Good. I'm glad you see it my way."

The vampire moved towards me then, and his heated expression melted into a knowing look. "Nice try," he mouthed with a sneer.

I glared at him, angered that he had realized my plan to egg Bill into a skirmish. Stoney had foiled my attempt to subdue his new partner, and I cursed him for his interference. It would have been the perfect opportunity to slay him. Bill was a newborn vampire like me and would have been easy to kill. I had to think of something else fast, before the rest of my family fell prey to the immortal curse.

It may have been too late for me, but Switch and Harvey deserved their mortality, and I wasn't afraid to die while fighting to protect it.

Chapter Seventeen

After Stoney stepped in and dissuaded Bill from attacking me, I was separated from Harvey and ordered to be brought back to my cell once again. I wasted no time arguing it would have solved nothing. While I was in the process of being towed out of the packing room, I kept a close watch on Bill as he placed Harvey back inside the cage. I was pleased to see that they were engaged in an argument, and I observed their dispute as I was dragged through the door.

Without so much as a word, Stoney directed me through the tight halls and back to my room. I was surprisingly calm, up until the moment he blew me a kiss goodbye and locked the door behind him. I was confined in darkness, as I noticed that the lone light bulb in the room had finally gone out.

I slammed my fists against the metal door, hoping my new strength would help break it down. I was a vampire after all, and much stronger now. Surely I could wear down this measly door with my bare hands? Unfortunately, it was unbeknownst to me until after my fists collided with the metal door that it was coated in a thin layer of fresh paint—fresh silver paint.

Even the smallest amount of silver could harm a vampire, and as soon as my hands made contact, they felt as if they were on fire. I howled and rubbed the flat sides of my fists, yearning to soothe the painful sensation. It only took a few moments before the feeling dispersed, but when I examined my hands, I noticed the skin was now covered in burns.

"Shit!" I hissed angrily. "You've got to be fucking kidding me!"

I kicked at the door to release some of my frustration, and wondered if the force of my legs would do the trick instead. Sadly, I was not strong enough to break through the three deadbolts that were securing the door. I accepted defeat, realizing there was no use in stressing myself by trying to get free, and so I wandered over towards the far corner of the room and sat down.

I huddled there for some time, my thoughts turning dark as I reevaluated my current predicament.. Leland had already been turned, and I wondered when Bill and Stoney would force the others to become members of the undead. Now that I was aware of Bill's true scheme, I figured he wouldn't wait too long. After all, Stoney was his partner, and he wasn't known for being patient. They would try to overtake Chicago soon, which was another reason I had to get loose. I had to put a stop to their despicable plan before they slaughtered half of the population.

As I rubbed my burned hands together, I plotted my next attempt at escaping. I didn't have many options, but it suddenly dawned on me that I needed to find a way to lock Stoney inside my cell. With him out of the way, I had a better chance at stopping Bill and rescuing my family. Although it was a rather risky idea, and Stoney would most likely subdue me if I tried to deceive him, I figured it was my best shot. I had to try something.

Quite some time passed while I remained locked in the dark room, but I used the time to come up with a plan of attack. I had relocated towards the corner of my cell that faced the opening of the door. My strategy was to use the element of surprise, and jump the next person that entered. It was all I could do; I was out of options.

I wasn't sure exactly how long I had been left inside my room alone before the hunger emerged. All that I was able to recall was succumbing to sleep, and just as my eyes slipped shut, a harsh pang shot straight through my stomach. The pangs would not quit. Just as I would begin to drift off, a sharp stab would wake me. They suddenly grew more frequent, until they were hitting me every few minutes.

With a cry, I fell onto my side, clutching my stomach as I rolled around in absolute agony. I howled and wailed from the pain, and as I writhed on the grimy cement floor, the craving for blood stung with such a burning intensity that I could scarcely breathe.. The memory of its taste and smell only caused me to ache further, and when I did not satisfy my desire, I began to lose control. I flung my head back and screeched, my fangs releasing as the desire to feed rushed through me. My mouth was dry and stiff, and the heavy feeling of dehydration had started to drive me insane, and that's when realization dawned on me. This was the fate I was doomed to suffer for all eternity. Stoney was right. No matter how hard I tried, I could not shake the thirst.

I lingered on the floor for nearly half an hour, moaning and hissing until the sound of footsteps approaching my cell silenced me. When the footsteps stopped just outside my door, I detected the savory scent of blood, and I grinned, my pale face twisting from eagerness. I figured it was Stoney at the door with my meal, and although I was relieved that the pain would soon cease, I was disgusted by the smile that crept onto my face at the thought of blood.

The door rattled, and I listened closely as the locks clicked and withdrew. Unable to contain myself, I crawled towards the door, my eyes wild and hopeful for the chance to satisfy my needs. However, when the door opened, the person standing before me was not the person I expected to see. The tall figure was shrouded in a brown trench coat, and when he yanked off his hood, Gabriel's striking face stared back at me.

"Lina?" he whispered. Gabriel bent towards me, taken aback by the sight of me lying on the floor. After he surveyed me with a frown, he said, "Are you okay?

I struggled to speak, but as he grew closer, I became mesmerized by the loud sound of his heartbeat. My gaze fell on his neck, and I watched with wide eyes when a vein pulsed. Without thinking, I lunged for him with my nails outstretched, but the werewolf held me at bay. He must've realized there was no use trying to reason with me while I was in such a wild state, and so he kept his mouth shut as he fought me off.

Gabriel muttered a few harsh words to himself, cursing the fact that he was too late in rescuing me. He saw that I had turned— that I was a vampire now, and he seemed put off by the situation. I ceased in my attempt to feed, and was now debating the werewolf's next move. It would be easy for him to slay me while I was weak, but as I looked up at his face, I had a feeling that he would not kill me. At least not yet.

Then, what I figured was out of pity, he took off his coat, and pulled up the sleeve of his black knit shirt to reveal his tanned bare skin. He turned his arm over, veins up, and offered it to me. "Drink," he told me.

I stared dumbly at Gabriel's arm, taken aback by his generosity. He was a werewolf—I was a vampire. Even though he had the opportunity to destroy me, he didn't take it. Oddly enough, he chose to help me instead. I was afraid of taking his blood because I didn't want to risk the chance of harming him, but when another harsh pang erupted in my stomach, I could hold back from feeding no longer.

I grabbed his arm and leaned my face towards it, my fangs releasing just as the scent of his flesh and blood filled my nostrils. I bit into his arm, allowing the blood to pool around my lips before it dripped into my mouth. It was embarrassing to admit, but I drank eagerly, falling prey to the blood's deep and intoxicating spell. My eyes were closed now as I fed, and just like before, it seemed as if time stopped. I wasn't even aware that Gabriel was trying to pry me off of his arm until he struck me hard across the cheek. I hissed at him, relentless to surrender his limb.

"You've had enough, Lina!" he scolded me, and his tone was threatening. "You must stop!"

192

"No," I cooed, my tongue now scraping across his skin. "I want more."

"If you don't release my arm, I will be forced to make you!"

Gabriel emitted a deep growl, and I detected the beast within him on the verge of emerging. However, it was only when his eyes began to change yellow that I finally withdrew my fangs. I wiped at my mouth and licked the blood that stained my hands. Suddenly, the pain in my stomach dispersed and I was free from the trance I had been lost in only moments before. I frowned and stared at the two large holes in Gabriel's forearm, frightened when they began to ooze more blood. Gabriel reached down to rip a strip of fabric from the hem of his shirt. He folded it in half and proceeded to tie it around the wound. I stiffened when I noticed that blood began to seep through the material.

"I'm sorry," I said, once he had pulled his sleeve over his new wound. "I couldn't control myself."

"Most new vampires can't."

I brought my hands to my face, feeling rather embarrassed about the whole situation. It was then that I noticed the burns that had covered them earlier were gone. I figured I had healed once I'd fed, and although I was grateful my burns had disappeared, the fact that I could regenerate so quickly terrified me.

"Does it hurt?" I asked, motioning to his arm.

Gabriel pulled his jacket back on and shook his head. "No. It'll heal in a few hours, so don't worry about it."

"Why didn't you kill me?" I questioned him, after finally gaining the courage to ask. "I was weak and out of my mind with hunger. You could have gotten rid of me easily."

"I know."

"Then why didn't you?"

Gabriel gave me a considerate look before he said, "I don't know. I thought about it, but … I just couldn't."

"You don't owe me any pity, Gabriel. I refused your help, remember?"

"Yes, you did, but that doesn't mean I feel you deserved this curse."

I was taken aback by his kind words. "Thank you."

His concerned expression returned. He frowned as he looked me over. "Can I trust you?"

I faced him with a sigh, wondering if I even knew the answer to his question. Everything had changed—I had changed, but I prayed I would not turn against him. "I hope so."

The wolf nodded and helped me to my feet. "We have to get out of here. I have a boat docked at the pier."

"How did you find me?" I asked, genuinely curious. I was grateful that he had come to rescue me, but I was still a little skeptical of his motives. After Bill's betrayal, I wasn't sure whom I could trust anymore.

Gabriel frowned and replied, "My clan has known of Stoney's whereabouts for some time now."

"Really?" I replied. "And you just let him be? Allowing that monster to keep on killing innocent civilians—your people included?"

Gabriel seemed irritated by my accusation, but he remained calm. "Lina, there are thousands of vampires in Chicago, and not all of them were sired by Stoney. I don't know if you're aware of this, but vampires and werewolves don't like to get involved in each other's affairs. My clan wanted no part in raiding this coven. Truth be told, we wanted to avoid a war waged between Stoney and us. However, when I found out that he had taken you and your father captive, I decided that it was time to deal with him once and for all."

"You didn't come here alone, did you?"

"Of course not," he grunted. "Four of our pack's Epsilons are roaming the warehouse as we speak, and killing any vamps they come across. They were instructed to aid and secure any human survivors they find."

"Thank God," I replied with a smile, relieved. "Actually, I should be thanking you, Gabriel."

He returned the smile. "Don't worry, Lina. Everything is going to be all right. Your team is safe now."

"No, not all of them. Leland was made into a vampire," I told him hastily. "I don't know where Stoney has him hidden, but he's not caged with the others. We have to find him first. I won't leave without him."

Gabriel scowled. "That son of a bitch." His soured expression wavered when he noticed my distress. "Your father was a great man, Lina. Granted, we always had our differences due to his profession, but he was compassionate to my kind when he could be. When I find Stoney, I will make him pay for what he's done."

"No. I will deal with him."

"Lina—"

"He's not alone in this!" I exclaimed. "Bill, my old partner, he turned on us. He's in allegiance with Stoney now…and he's the reason for all of this!"

"One of your own?" he muttered, incredulously.

"If we come across him, Gabriel, he must be dealt with as well. I can't let him get away with what he's done."

Gabriel nodded. "Understood."

"Good." I gazed up at him then, fierce determination etched on my face. "Now, let's go kick some undead ass."

Chapter Eighteen

Thanks to Gabriel I was finally free from my cell, and we traveled the empty halls of the warehouse together, keeping our eyes and ears strained to detect any undead enemies. It was suspiciously quiet, and I expected one of Stoney's cronies to pop out from around the corner at any given moment. However, none appeared before us, which only intensified my reservations. Then, I detected the faint sound of wolves howling, and my fears eased away. Apparently Gabriel's pack had found the vamps first, and I doubted they would let any escape with their lives.

I was too embarrassed to openly admit it, but I knew that I had a better chance at defeating Stoney and Bill with Gabriel's aid. I felt foolish for refusing his help earlier and allowing my pride to get in the way, and I had the sad thought that if only I had accepted his help from the beginning I could have possibly spared my mortality, and Leland's. Sadly, I knew there was no use in relishing in the what-ifs. I made my choice, and I was now forced to live with my decision for all eternity.

On our way towards Stoney's bedroom, Gabriel and I came across streaks of blood and guts covering the floor. We trekked through the mess, and when I spotted large paw prints leaving the scene of the crime, I couldn't help but crack a grin.

Although I had been to Stoney's room only once, I had the route memorized. I could detect his scent growing more piquant, as could Gabriel, and soon we were standing in front of the red door marked with an X.

"Here," I told him with a hiss. "This is Stoney's room."

"I know." Gabriel's brows narrowed as he stared at the red door, and before I could reach my hand out for the doorknob, he kicked it open. We entered the room in a rush, but were both disappointed to find it empty.

"Shit," I grumbled. "He's not here."

"Where do you think he would be?"

"I don't know," I replied, bitter that we hadn't come across him. "He could be anywhere. This place is huge ..."

"We'll just have use our powers to track him," he suggested.

I frowned, unsure by what he meant. "Powers? That's an odd word to use."

"Heightened sense of smell?" he offered, with a slack smirk.

"Yeah, right."

As I surveyed the room, I noticed my father's torn black trench coat draped over one of the armchairs in the room. I rushed towards it, clutching it tight and stiffened. It was drenched in blood; fresh blood. I turned around to face Gabriel, holding it up for him to examine.

"Leland's?" he asked, with a curious look.

"Yes. This is proof that he was here."

"Let me see that."

I offered the jacket to him, and he pressed his nose against the fabric, avoiding the blood when he did, and breathed in deeply. I waited patiently for Gabriel to raise his head. After doing so, I noticed that his iris's had turned yellow and the pupils of his eyes had altered into thin black slits.

"Gabriel?" I was worried by the fierce expression on his face. "What is it?"

"I've got his scent now," he growled. "We will find your father, Lina, but we must hurry."

I nodded in agreement, and Gabriel and I left the room in search of Leland.

****

We tracked Leland's scent to a massive room located at the far end of the building. It appeared to be a storage space, yet unlike the rest of the warehouse, this particular area hadn't been touched in years. Most of the shelves were empty or contained dusty equipment, and the floor was coated in a thick layer of dust. Two giant, broken-down machines sat in the middle of the room, and upon further inspection, they seemed to be inoperable. If it hadn't been for the two fresh sets of footprints leading towards a door at the far end of the room, I would have believed that no one had entered the room in ages.

Gabriel and I followed the footprints towards the opposite side of the empty room, and when we finally came upon the rusty door, we found it bolted shut. A padlock, connected to a thick chain, was also wrapped around the handle of the door and a metal pipe running up the wall as an extra measure.

Without caution, Gabriel wrapped his bare hands around the chain and tugged, but he howled with pain on contact. They were coated in silver. He dropped the chains, and they jingled loudly as they collided with the door.

"Bastards," Gabriel growled as he rubbed his hands together.

"Why would vampires use silver chains when they know they are affected by the substance?"

"To keep us out," he told me. "Stoney must have anticipated us tracking Leland's scent here."

I shook my head, disagreeing with him. "No, I don't think Stoney locked him behind this door. I have a feeling this was Bill's doing."

"Your partner?"

"Ex-partner."

"Well, he's a smart man to use silver."

"Vampire," I corrected again. "And he's not smart. He's an imbecile if he thinks this pathetic little silver chain is going to stop me from reaching my father."

Gabriel sighed and crossed his arms. "I can break the chain, but I need something to wrap around my palms."

I looked at him and frowned, surprised by his request. "You bothered by it that much?" I snorted and then asked, "I thought werewolves had a stronger immunity to silver than vampires, you know, besides getting shot with silver bullets."

"It fucking hurts," he growled. "And we do, but I would prefer for my hands not to be scarred."

"It'll heal."

"Wounds inflicted by silver take a hell of a lot longer to heal than regular wounds, Lina." He scowled and then whispered, "You haven't been a vampire for very long, so trust me when I say that if you have the chance to avoid any contact with silver, you don't come near the stuff."

I gave his serious expression a quick once-over, remembering burning my hands on the silver-painted door of my cell. It had hurt like hell. Maybe I knew more about the dangers of silver than he gave me credit for.

"Fine," I murmured after a moment. "I get it."

With a sigh, I shrugged off my black leather jacket and dropped it onto the dusty floor. Before Gabriel could question the action, I reached down and lifted the hem of my black shirt, pulling it over my head. I handed him the piece of clothing without a word. Then, after picking up my jacket and tugging it back on, I faced him again.

"Will that do?"

Gabriel's dark brows rose as he studied my unperturbed demeanor; he appeared to be shocked that he had just seen me in my bra, and I found his behavior sort of charming. He said nothing as he continued to stare at me, and I waved my hand in front of his face, hoping to snap him out of his daze.

"Gabriel?"

He cleared his throat and glanced down at the shirt he now held in his hands, but a confused smile crept onto his face. "Why didn't you just give me your jacket?"

I snorted at his question and said, "Are you kidding me? This is my favorite jacket. I've already lost my mortality tonight, I'm not going to lose this too."

"I see." He gestured to my shirt and added, "This will work just fine. Thank you."

I motioned to the door and said, "Have at it then, wolf."

I didn't mind if he tore the shirt, but Gabriel was extra careful with the garment. Once he wrapped both of his hands up in the fabric, he reached for the chains. He clenched his teeth and pulled, the veins in his forehead bulging as he tried to break apart the thick metal, but the bonding was far too strong. When he realized he needed to use just a bit more strength to get the job done, he released a low growl and I knew he was searching for power from his inner wolf.

Gabriel's eyes began transforming; his iris's now glowing and his pupils morphing into long black slits. I stood off to the side, not wanting to interfere. I observed his transformations, growing nervous and hoping he didn't lose his sanity and fully transform. Although I could most definitely take the wolf now that I was a vampire, I didn't want to have to deal with defending myself against him. I had more pressing matters to attend to.

But, Gabriel kept a cool head. After channeling just a bit more strength, he yanked the chain loose. Pieces of the broken silver chain fell down to the floor with a loud clang, and I smiled with relief once the door was free of its bonds. It took Gabriel a minute to compose himself, but it was all he needed to shake the beast away. With a sigh, he unraveled the shirt from his hands and handed it to back to me. I lifted it up into the air, holding back a laugh when I noticed it had been ripped nearly in half.

He frowned at the sight of the ruined shirt. "I'm sorry, Lina. I tried to keep it intact."

I shrugged, not bothered by my shirt's demise. "And that's why I didn't give you the jacket."

After dropping the torn shirt to the ground, I approached the door and opened it without hesitation, revealing a dark and empty stairwell. I turned to glance at Gabriel. He seemed skeptical of the stairwell, and when I made a move to pass through the doorway, he reached out for my arm, squeezing it lightly. I tried to shake him off, but his hand stayed in place.

I twisted my head around to glare at him. "Let go of me, Gabriel."

"Just hold on a second, Lina."

"What for? Leland is waiting for me—"

"How do we even know he's up there?" he asked me. "What if this is just another one of Stoney's ruses?"

I frowned, not wanting to entertain his concerns. "I don't know what's waiting for me up those stairs, Gabriel, but I'm running out of time. I can't let Bill and Stoney get away with what they've done to Leland!"

He sighed then and dragged a hand back across the crown of his head. "I understand your anger and frustration with what has happened to you and your father, but if you're not careful, Lina, and you rush up those stairs in the heat of the moment, you might fall right into another trap." Gabriel offered a weak smile before he concluded, "I know this isn't what you want to hear right now, but how will you help your father if that happens?"

I stared back at him, realizing he was right. I couldn't fall for another one of Bill's ruses, not when there was so much at stake. "Okay. What do you suggest then?"

"Let me go up the stairs first. That way, if there's anything waiting for us up there, I'll be the one blindsided—not you. You'll be safe."

I was skeptical of his generosity. "Why are you doing this?"

"What do you mean?"

"I mean, why are you going to such extreme lengths to help me? Especially when I refused your aid to begin with?"

"Lina—"

"What are you getting out of this, Gabriel?"

He frowned, apparently offended by my question. "Perhaps I should have just left you and your family to rot here instead?"

"Please don't misunderstand. I appreciate everything you've done for me up until now, but it was enough. I can't ask you to put your life at risk for me any longer."

"I'm sorry, Lina, but I'm not going anywhere," he replied. "I'm helping you because I want to. No matter what you may believe, I have no ulterior motive. You just need to trust me."

"Trust does not come easy for me, Gabriel. You know that."

"Yes, I know, but this time you don't really have a choice but to trust me. Like I said before, I'm sticking by your side, whether you want me to or not."

I didn't respond at first; I was still unsure about our current involvement, but after some mental deliberation, I ultimately decided to leave the matter alone and allow him to take the lead. After all, if someone was waiting for us at the top of the steps, surely Gabriel could handle whoever it was. If not, he could count on me to back him up.

"Okay, Gabriel. You lead the way."

He released his grip on my arm, and with a determined look on his face, sidestepped me and passed through the doorway. We were cautious as we ascended the stairs, keeping our eyes and ears trained for any sound or movement, but the only sound that could be heard in the dark stairwell was our faint footsteps as we climbed.

Once Gabriel and I reached the top of the staircase, we came face to face with a metal door. It was the end of the line—we had no choice but to investigate what was on the other side. I was bursting with anticipation at this point, but Gabriel held me back when I made a move to pounce on the door.

"Let me," he said, and reached for the door handle.

To our surprise, the door was unlocked. Gabriel pushed it open to reveal a dark and narrow room, and in its center, was Leland. He was sitting in a metal chair positioned directly underneath a hanging lamp—the only source of light in the room. His bare hands and feet were bound with silver chains, and the clothes he was wearing were torn and dirty. Leland's head was bowed, and it appeared he was asleep.

He had no idea that we had entered the room until we stood only three feet away, and his head shot up at the sound of our approach. I gasped when I noticed his eyes were white and glazed over, and his once shoulder-length gray hair was now sparse and matted down against his pale skull. He looked sickly, unlike any vampire I'd ever seen before, and I wondered if something had gone wrong during his transformation.

"Leland?" I called out to him, and before Gabriel could hold me back, I rushed in his direction. I may have been frightened by his ghastly appearance, but I was more infuriated with the persons responsible for his evident torture. As I looked over his miserable face, I vowed to put Bill and Stoney's heads on stakes.

Leland's chapped lips curled up into a smile once I reached his side and wrapped my arms around his frail body. Realizing his hands were still bound, I broke the chains around his wrists, welcoming the burning pain that came with touching the silver. I leaned my head against his shoulder then, crying when he kissed the top of my head.

"Lina …" he whispered my name, the smile melting off of his face when he touched my cold skin. "Oh god, they've turned you as well. My poor girl, I did not want you to suffer this fate."

"I'm so sorry," I whispered, hanging my head in shame. It pained me that he had to see me this way. "I tried, but I couldn't save you in time. I failed."

"I told you to escape this place when you had the chance. Why didn't you go?"

"Did you honestly think I would leave you here?"

"You should have," he mumbled. "I'm a lost cause now."

"Don't say that!" I cried. "I'm going to get you out of here. Harvey, Switch ... they're both safe, and soon you will be too."

Leland sighed and shook his head. "No, Lina. I won't be."

I studied him, concerned by his tone. "I'm sorry, but I don't understand ..."

"I can't go with you now. I won't go."

"What?" I exclaimed, and I realized that my hands were shaking. "Why not?"

"I cannot go on living this way, Lina. Despite Bill's efforts to force me to see the benefits of this foul change, I have renounced my transformation. I refuse to succumb to the temptations and frailties of this curse!" He gestured to his face and whispered, "This is what happens when you don't consume blood within twenty four hours of being turned."

"Leland ..." I began, now gripping his arm. "I know it seems like all hope is lost, but it isn't. I promise! It may take some getting used to, but we can come to grips with this, together."

"You must understand—"

"No, you need to understand!" I interrupted. "I need you. I can't live without you."

He cupped my face and replied, "Yes, you can, and you will. You're a strong, independent woman, Lina, and I'm touched by your unwavering devotion, but you don't need to worry over me anymore. I've lived my life, and now I'm ready to die."

"But to just give up this way—it's not like you! Where's the man I've followed into battle all my life? The man who's always told me to never surrender?"

"I'm an old man...at least, I was. I wasn't planning on living for all eternity, nor do I want to, especially not as a monster I devoted my entire life to ridding the world of."

"You can get past it..."

"No, I can't."

I stiffened and whispered, "Not even for me?"

"Oh, Lina," he sighed, and bowed his head. "I knew that I was dying months ago." I withdrew from him then. "What are you talking about?"

Leland's bottom lip wavered as he matched eyes with me. "I was diagnosed with leukemia six months ago, Lina. I had already come to terms with it, actually. I had finally welcomed the idea of death, and then Bill turned me." In a bitter tone, he added, "I don't want to live forever.

"What?" I was unable to process this new information. "You had cancer?" I didn't know how to react, but my stomach suddenly flared with anger at the thought of his betrayal. He had been lying to me for months, and I doubted that he had ever planned to tell me the truth.

"Why didn't you tell me?" I asked him after a moment of silence had passed between us.

"I knew how much this news would hurt you, and I didn't want to break your heart."

"Bullshit."

"Lina, please—"

"No!" I shouted. "You didn't tell me because you knew I would have urged you to get medical help. I would not have stood by and allowed cancer to take your life without you even putting up a fight."

He shook his head at my remark. "There was no fight to be had. The cancer had been present for far too long before it was found. I met with four different specialists before I came to the realization that there was nothing that could be done."

"How could you hide something like this from me?" I fell silent then, my eyes watering. "I can't believe you were never going to tell me about this."

"It hardly matters now."

"The hell it does! You were dying and you didn't tell me! I can't believe you would lie about something as gravely important as this."

"I'm sorry."

A sudden thought crossed my mind then, and my eyes grew wide with realization. "Did Bill know about this?"

Leland sighed and glanced off, unable to meet my knowing gaze. "Yes, he found out about a month or so ago."

"It all makes sense now. I could hardly believe that he concocted this entire ordeal simply out of his jealousy for me." My voice softened as I murmured, "He wanted to save you from death."

Leland was angered by my comment. "No matter his intentions, what Bill has done to our family is unforgivable. He's not the same man we knew and loved. He must be stopped, Lina."

"I agree," I said, with a nod. "I just can't believe the lengths he went to prove his worth."

"Lina, do you smell that?" Gabriel spoke up, and his voice startled me. I had forgotten he was even in the room. He stepped towards me, and I noticed that his eyes had changed once again, causing me to grow concerned. Then, he growled, his gaze now fixating on the metal door.

"Someone's coming," he remarked.

I took to a stand just as the door was opened. It was knocked brutally off of its hinges, falling forward to the dusty floor with a loud swoosh, and my brows narrowed with fury as I came face to face with Bill. He had two vampires at his heels, and the pale, grotesque creatures glanced around the room before they looked to each other and snickered.

Bill's gaze landed on Leland, who refused to meet his stare. Leland's eyes remained fixed on the floor beneath his feet, and he made no effort to acknowledge his presence. Bill seemed furious to find me standing there, next to Leland, but his angered expression shifted into an arrogant smirk.

"I see you've finally found him," he said, still smiling. "I had no doubt that you would."

I stepped in front of Leland protectively. "You're damn right I did," I replied. "You and Stoney couldn't keep him from me, Bill!"

Bill laughed and took a short step in my direction. "Don't be overdramatic, Lina."

"Overdramatic?" I repeated the word with disdain. "Are you fucking serious, Bill? How do you expect me to act after all you've put him through?"

"Why must both of you see your transformations so negatively?" he inquired, with a sharp sigh. "Leland is much stronger now—more than he ever was as a human." He looked us both over before he asked, "I suppose by now he's told you of his previous ailment?"

"Yes he did. I now know the real reason why you turned him, but he never wanted this, Bill!"

He chuckled at my response. "Oh please. You and I both know that you would have never accepted his death. You would have found some way to save him, just as I have, except I did it first."

"That may be true, but I would have never thought to do it this way, Bill. Never this way."

"Why not? As vampires we can accomplish anything that we want." He clapped his hands together and asked, "Don't you see how much we've advanced?"

"You call this an advancement?" Leland spoke up, his quiet voice startling everyone in the room.

I glanced over my shoulder to find that Leland was in the process of standing, and I was on the verge of rushing to his side. As soon as he successfully rose to his feet, his left leg gave away and he stumbled forward, tripping over his own feet. When I finally made the effort to catch him, he shoved my hands away and hissed. With a low moan, Leland regained his balance and began limping towards Bill. His legs were shaking as he went, but he paid them no mind and kept moving. He was weak from loss of sustenance, and although I wanted to help him, I knew the gesture would only further damage his pride.

He stood a few feet away from Bill now, and after taking a deep breath, he shouted, "Look at me, Bill! Look at what you've done to me!"

Bill and Leland exchanged a long glance, and I had a feeling that he was finally coming to the realization that Leland was not proud of what he had done.

Instead of apologizing, Bill shrugged and whispered, "You did this to yourself, old man. You refused to eat. Stoney told you what would happen if you did not feed."

"I never asked for this!" he growled at him, his fangs unsheathing from pure rage. "This is not the path I wanted to lead! I was a hunter all my life! I wanted to rid the world of vampires, not become one of them!" Leland's expression softened as he looked over Bill's blank face. "Bill, I taught you better than this. To succumb to such evil…I would have never thought you would be so easily led astray."

"Good, evil…those are silly notions of a superstitious man. I see that now. You taught us to have useless morals, Leland. And for what? In this world, there are those who are weak and those who are strong. That is all. Unlike you and Lina, I knew I was weak, but I wasn't ashamed to admit it."

Bill sidestepped Leland and moved towards me, and I had to fight the urge to sink my teeth into his face. I watched as Leland lumbered over towards the adjacent wall and leaned up against it. I could tell that he was running out of strength.

"Once I realized how beneficial the strengths of the undead were, I not only wanted them for myself, but I wanted to share them with my family. Tell me, where's the harm in wanting to bestow this power in the name of love?"

"Only a complete lunatic would want to subject the people he cares about to this type of sick lifestyle," I frowned. "Especially when doing it by force."

Bill grinned, amused by my comment. "You think I'm insane?"

"Oh, I know you are, but it doesn't matter what I think. Leland and I have already transformed—we have no choice but to suffer through these changes now. I'm just glad Harvey and Switch were able to escape with their morality before it was too late."

"Yes," he sighed. "Lucky for those two, they were rescued by a pack of wolves." Bill turned to glance at Gabriel, scowling as he looked him over. "I suppose I have you to blame for that?"

Gabriel grunted with pride. "You do."

"I find it very interesting that your clan would risk their treaty with Stoney just to save a few human lives, especially if those lives belonged to hunters."

My jaw dropped in surprise, and I looked to Gabriel for answers. He had never mention anything about a treaty with the vampires. "Your clan has a truce with these bastards?"

Gabriel ignored my question and kept his focus on Bill. He stepped towards him with haste, and the look on his face was dangerous as he stared the vampire down. "That contract is bullshit!" he growled. "Did you and Stoney honestly think that our clan would stand by and allow you fucking vamps to take over our city without any consequences?"

Bill, however, was not intimidated by Gabriel's beastly stature. "Does Brulan know you're here, Beta? Or have you come to my coven without the protection of your clan leader?"

Gabriel's intense gaze weakened at the mention of his pack master. "Brulan knows nothing of my interference tonight. I, and a few of the Epsilons, came to rescue Lina and her teammates on our own accord. The rest of the pack has nothing to do with this."

"I see …" Bill responded, a mischievous smile now on his face. He glanced over his shoulder at the two vampires that had followed him into the room and said, "Go pay a visit to Brulan's clan. Let him know of Gabriel's interference in Stoney's matters." His black eyes darkened as he turned to glance back at Gabriel. "And once you've informed the Alpha of his son's betrayal, kill him and every last wolf you come across. Leave no survivors."

The group of vampires nodded, and once they fled the room, Gabriel rushed towards Bill in a rage. He grabbed him by his throat and propelled him towards the wall. "You fucking bastard!" he screeched, squeezing his throat tighter and tighter, until finally, Bill reached up and dragged his nails across Gabriel's face. The wolf released him and reached up to place pressure on his fresh wounds. While Gabriel was distracted by the blood that began to drip into his eyes, it was Bill's turn to pin him against the concrete wall.

The vampire kept one hand around his throat, while the other dropped down and suddenly pierced into the flesh directly above his left hip. Gabriel howled with pain as Bill dug his nails deeper into his body, stabbing through flesh and tissue. He tried to shake the vampire off, but his strength kept, and he was forced to remain against the wall as Bill twisted his hands around Gabriel's torn flesh.

"Let go of him, Bill!" I shouted, and charged towards him. Sadly, I was too slow. As I attempted to attack, Bill released his hand from around Gabriel's throat and struck me across the jaw. I was knocked backwards by the blow, and landed on the floor just a few feet away from where Leland sat.

Bill bared his fangs at me and said, "Interfere again, Lina, and I'll have your head." He turned around to face Gabriel again. "You honestly thought you were stronger than me, wolf? Don't make me laugh!" He licked his lips and murmured, "I've never tasted werewolf blood before, but I heard it has a highly robust flavor."

As he lowered his mouth down towards Gabriel's neck, I jumped to my feet and lunged at him. I managed to shove Bill off of Gabriel, knocking him clear across the room. I stood in front of Gabriel now, shielding him from Bill's reach. Bill sneered and licked the blood off of the nails that had been inside the wolf's body as he rose to his feet. He must've found the sight of me protecting Gabriel amusing, because he chuckled.

"I warned you, Lina," he told me with a sneer. "Get out of the way!"

"Not going to happen."

"I don't want to hurt you," Bill explained, his tone rising with each syllable. "But if you don't get out of my way and let me dine on this filthy wolf's blood, I'll be forced to subdue you!"

"I'd like to see you try and move me from this spot, Bill."

"Is that a challenge?"

I didn't bat an eye. "Maybe."

He threw up his hands and cried, "Are you serious, Lina? You're choosing to protect a werewolf over siding with me, your partner?"

"You're no partner of mine," I shot back. "You made that quite clear tonight."

"Fine," he retorted. "If you won't willingly obey, then I'm just going to have to make you."

He took a step towards me, but was caught off guard by Leland, who had jumped him from behind. Before Bill could evade his attack, Leland restrained him by wrapping the silver chain that he had been shackled with around Bill's neck. Leland yanked Bill backward, directing him away from us. He tugged on the chain again, this time almost causing Bill's eyes to pop out of their sockets. Bill struggled against the silver chain, but Leland's grip was too strong, even if the silver was burning through the skin of his palms, and Bill couldn't get free. Bill finally fell to his knees, his flesh beneath the chain charred.

"Release me!" he cried, his eyes glowing with rage.

"Sorry, Bill. I can't have you harming Lina or Gabriel. You've done enough damage already, don't you think?"

Bill growled at his reply and lurched forward, fighting against the silver chain. Now on all fours, he lifted his head to stare up at me as I watched him with a smug expression. "Lina, please make him stop. Surely you don't want to see me suffer?"

I put on a thoughtful expression before my mouth twisted into an evil grin. "Actually, there's nothing more I would rather watch than your suffering, Bill."

Gabriel stepped around me and said, "I second that."

I noticed that Gabriel was clutching at his side, and before he could dissuade me, I bent down to inspect his wound. There was some tearing of the skin where Bill's nails had torn through, but he hadn't gotten far enough to cause any real damage. I knew stitches wouldn't be necessary; by tomorrow, the wounds would be fully healed.

"Are you all right?"

He looked to me and nodded. "I'll be fine."

Bill glared at us, his face now turning black as well. "When I get free, I'm going to make all of you pay!"

"Here's the thing, Bill … you aren't going to get free," I told him. "I won't allow you to hurt anyone else." I held out my hand to Gabriel, who stared at it with a blank look. When I realized he had no idea what I was requesting, I huffed and pointed over towards the metal chair.

"Stake," I muttered.

Gabriel walked over towards the fallen chair and picked it up. He broke off one of the legs with ease then returned to stand dutifully to my side.

"Here," he said as he handed it to me.

"Thanks."

I approached Bill, but I watched Leland as I moved, and I was disturbed by the profound depressed look on his face. I realized, at that exact moment, just how much he must have been suffering. For Bill to turn on him like he did, after Leland had brought him under his wing and treated him like a son … I was sadly aware that his betrayal undoubtedly cut him deep.

It was then that Leland locked eyes with me and shook his head, causing me to halt. "Wait," he told me.

"Why?" I was confused by his request, but I obeyed and waited patiently for his response.

Leland glanced down at Bill, his eyes crinkling from despair as they wept over his charred face. "I'm sorry, Bill," he began, his soft words startling everyone in the room. "I never noticed your desire for my approval, or your withholding jealousy of my relationship with Lina. Perhaps if I had paid more attention, I would have noticed your cries for attention and none of us would have ended up here in this horrible place."

"Don't blame yourself! Bill knew what he was doing from the start! He's not the victim, here."

"Lina, please!" Leland growled, his face twisting with anger. "Bill was pushed to this because of my negligence. If I had only took notice of what was going on, I could have prevented this sordid experience for all of us."

I gaped at him, shocked by his admittance. "You can't be serious! He's killed countless people—he just commanded a group of vampires to murder all of Gabriel's clan members. He's not innocent! No matter what you would have done, his malice would have shone though eventually. He's pure evil, and that's not something you can change."

"Yes, I know what he's responsible for, and I'm not condoning his behavior. Bill must be punished for the crimes he committed, but he ought to know of my guilt before he dies."

"Dies?" Bill glanced up at Leland in fear. "Leland, please! Don't do this!"

"I know you're scared, Bill," he replied. "Jealously and rage will make us do foolish things, but there must always be compensation for our actions." Leland looked to me and nodded, "Do it."

Bill growled and started to back away from me, eyeing the sleek piece of metal in my right hand with apprehension. However, unfortunately for the shell-shocked vampire, the chains around his neck held him in place. "No, Lina! Stop! Just wait a second and hear me out! I can make things better, I swear. You don't have to do this!"

"Sorry, Bill, but unlike Leland, I'm not so understanding. You might as well just save your breath, because there is nothing you could possibly say to atone for what you've done."

"Bitch!" he screamed. As he glared up at me, I noticed the charred skin along his jaw was now flaking off and falling to the ground. "You won't get out of here alive! Once he finds out I'm gone, Stoney will rip you to fucking shreds—all of you! You and your precious wolf, and Leland, are dead meat! The three of you will suffer—"

"Goodbye, Bill," I said, interrupting his rant. Then, without hesitation, I shoved the leg of the chair straight through his chest.

Bill's black eyes grew wide from panic just before he perished, and erupted into an enormous bloody mess. I cringed from disgust when I realized that his blood had splashed up on my face. Leland dropped the silver chain once he realized that the vampire had been exterminated, and was rubbing his palms together furiously. I knew he was trying to soothe the searing pain of his burnt skin.

After clearing the spots of blood from my jaw and cheeks, I stepped over the large pile of blood and guts that once was Bill, to get to get to Leland. I stole a closer look at his hands, frightened by the severe burns on the palms. The burns looked painful, and I knew they would not heal unless he fed.

"Are you all right?"

He nodded, but did not meet my gaze. "I'm fine," he lied.

"Those burns on your hands look serious. We have to find you some blood. I'm sure Stoney has a stash somewhere in this warehouse."

"No, Lina. I said I'm fine."

"But they won't heal if you don't feed!"

"Will you just leave it alone?" he snapped.

I didn't respond; I was taken aback by his crude tone. I was unsure how to handle the situation, but decided to simply obey his demand and stop pestering. After all, he had just witnessed the staking of one of his progeny, and I did not want to cause him any more stress.

I looked to Gabriel then, who had a tense expression on his face; I noticed his brow had begun to sweat. His amber eyes met mine, and I knew where his thoughts lay. His family and friends were in danger, but there was still time to save them. He could successfully intercept the vampires before they found his clan if he left the coven as soon as possible.

"Gabriel, you need to get out of here and stop those vamps while there's still time."

He nodded, relief washing over his face. "You'll be all right if I go?"

There was genuine concern in Gabriel's voice, and it was a pleasant surprise. I wasn't sure how to respond at first, but I finally said, "Yes, of course. Your family needs you …"

I searched his eyes, wanting to offer my help in defending his clan, but there was still one more vampire I had to take care. I couldn't leave this coven until I knew he was dead.

Somehow, Gabriel knew exactly what I was thinking, because he asked, "Are you going to be okay facing Stoney on your own?"

"I don't know, but I have to try and stop him."

Gabriel smiled at me then, his bright eyes holding a hint of gratitude within them. "Thank you, Ms. Holiday."

"No, thank you. I know that without your help, I would have never gotten this far. You saved my family's lives, Gabriel, and for that I am eternally grateful."

Gabriel said nothing, only gave me a slight nod of his head before making his way towards the stairwell. Then, to my surprise, he paused in the threshold. "I hope we'll be forced to team up again in the future."

I wanted to tell him how much his bravery meant to me, but I knew that now was not the time or place. His pack's existence was hanging in the balance, and I couldn't keep him from saving them. As I stared back at Gabriel, I felt that familiar warming sensation pool in the pit of my stomach. I had feared this would happen again, but as our eyes remained locked on one another, I decided I was starting to welcome the feeling.

"Me too."

With one last smile, he was gone.

Chapter Nineteen

After Gabriel left, I found myself staring at the empty doorway before turning to face Leland. He was a million miles away now, and the thought that I was losing him pushed me to get moving. "I have to get you out of here," I explained. "Stoney could be lurking anywhere."

"Lina …"

Knowing he was going to try to talk me out of rescuing him, I held up my hand to silence his protest. We were not going to negotiate his survival. "I don't want to hear it.. No matter what you say, you're coming with me. I'll carry you over my shoulders if I have to. I won't leave you here to die. Not in this place."

Leland said nothing; I had a feeling he was coming to terms with the fact that he would not win this battle, and it thrilled me to no end. He allowed me to wrap my arm around his shoulders, and I led him towards the door to the stairwell.

I knew that by refusing to feed, Leland's body lacked the necessary energy it needed to function, and it would eventually shut down. I wasn't sure what fate vampires suffered when they did not feed, but by the gruesome look of Leland's weakened state, I knew it could not be good. I feared it would not be long before he died.

We finally reached the bottom of the staircase, but when we walked out into the empty storage room, Leland's legs gave out from under him and he collapsed onto all fours. He began convulsing and he released an agonizing groan, refusing to look me in the eye as he trembled on the grimy floor. I didn't know what to do, and so I just stood there, terrified.

Once the panic had finally worn away, I crouched down beside him. "Leland?"

"I can't go on. My chest ... it hurts." He was clutching at the center of his torso, balling his ripped cotton shirt in his palm. "No more, Lina. I just can't endure anymore."

I watched him shake and cringe with tear-filled eyes. "Please tell me what I can do to help you!"

He was staring off into space now, and clouds of dust were rising up from the floor and filling his eyes, but he didn't seem to care. Leland was lost in another world now, and the flash of rage that suddenly passed over his face took me aback. His jaw dropped low, and his fangs protruded from his gums. He had a fierce expression on his face, one that reminded me of a rabid animal. He stared up at me then, his eyes clouded over and void of any rationality.

"My God," I whispered, biting my bottom lip to keep from sobbing. "Leland, what is happening to you?"

"I can't take much more of this...I'm forgetting who I am." His face went blank for a split second, before he reached out to stroke my cheek. "I love you, Lina."

I closed my eyes with a sigh, relishing in the comfort of his endearing touch. "I love you too."

He forced a smile, but I could tell that it pained him to do so. We stared at each other for what seemed like an eternity before he leaned his head closer towards me and whispered, "Kill me."

His comment startled me. I was speechless as I stared down at my convulsing guardian, his dark eyes crinkling with grief. He wanted me to kill him? How could I possibly do such a thing? He was the one person I would walk into Hell itself for, and I had proven it too.. But, I had no concept of the suffering Leland was enduring; I could not be selfish and allow him to withstand such agony.

"Please, Lina," he urged. With a loud cry, he snapped his eyes shut, his torso twisting and contorting. Leland looked as if he was experiencing a severe amount of pain, and although I wanted to end his suffering, I wasn't sure if I had it in me to end his life.

"It's the only way," he continued, hoping to persuade me. "You can't save me, Lina. It's too late. My body is shutting down, and there's a terrible rage dwelling inside of me that's on the verge of taking control. Once it does, I know I won't be able to control it. I'm a danger to you!"

"I can't kill you, Leland."

"Yes, you can—you just don't want to. But you don't have a choice now. Kill me now or kill me later, either way, I'm not walking out of this coven with you."

"No, I won't do it!" I shouted, latching onto him.

He seethed and shook me off. "Damn it, Lina! There's not much time left. Do it now!"

"If you die, I'll die along with you."

"You're stronger than this!"

I rose to my feet steadily, refusing to look him in the eye. The memory of my birth parents' deaths filled my head, and I felt my heart breaking in two when I realized I was about to lose Leland too. "You're all I have left."

Leland cringed and bawled his hands into fists and I watched as another jolt of pain coursed through his body. "That's not true," he whispered, now struggling to breathe. "You have Switch and Harvey. They're your family just as much as I am, and they need you—they need your guidance. No matter how desperate you're feeling right now, you can't abandon them."

The thought of Harvey and Switch—and how brave they had been throughout the entire ordeal—caused my heart to twinge with guilt. How could I have forgotten about them? I recalled how willingly my allies had followed me into battle with Stoney—how they had been on my side every step of the way, and it was at that moment that I realized that Leland was right. It wasn't fair to forgo my team. Besides, due to Harvey's track record at consistently making poor choices, I knew they wouldn't last ten seconds without me.

"You're right," I admitted with a sigh. "Harvey and Switch do need me."

"They truly do, Lina."

With a low growl, Leland fell back on his knees, his arms hanging loosely by his sides. He wheezed, now clutching at his chest again. Without a word, he leaned his head back and closed his eyes as he focused on his breathing. I hoped the exercise would help keep his grip on reality. Unfortunately, it seemed to do little to calm him.

It was then that his facial features began to change. His eyebrows had descended and were now only centimeters above his eyes, which had sunk deeper into his skull. His lips were withered and pale, and his fangs stuck out over his bottom lip. His skin was ashen and peeling, and almost translucent. I gasped when Leland took on a maddening look. It was at that moment that I realized that I didn't recognize the person I was holding onto. My father had died.

"Okay. I'll do it," I whispered.

I turned my face away, hoping to hide the tears that were threatening to spill. I did not want my tear-streaked face to be the last sight Leland saw before he died. Once I had gained control over my emotions again, I faced my father and moved to approach him. Although I had agreed to kill him, I was unsure of how I would end his life. I didn't have a stake or a gun on my person, but when I made the effort to search for something to use as a stake, Leland grabbed my hand and kept me still.

"Just do it," he said, his voice raspy.

I was confused by what he meant, until he puffed out his chest and placed my right palm directly above his heart. I stiffened and drew back, frightened by the prospect of ramming my hand through his chest cavity like an animal. Sure, I had performed the same action only hours earlier, but this was Leland, not some random vamp.

I swallowed the lump in my throat and repositioned my hand over the spot he desired. My hand was shaking as I stared at Leland's face, memorizing every last inch. "I will never forget you," I whispered. His lips twitched upwards in an almost smile, his breathing shallow.

Then, with one sharp inhale, I shoved my hand into his chest, wrapped my hand around his heart, and ripped it from his body. I studied the red organ in the palm of my hand, surprised to find that it was ice cold. I crushed it, not shaken by the thick blood that poured down my wrist and forearm. Leland's face relaxed, a sense of contentment settling over him, before he dissolved at my feet. I wanted to cry over losing him, but I knew he wouldn't want that. After all, this was a happy moment; he was finally at peace.

I stood there for what seemed like hours, staring at the bloody mess on the floor, before I dropped the pulped heart directly on top of the mass that now was my surrogate father. To my surprise, I kept strong, but I did allow one tear to roll down my cheek and under my chin. It was the only tear I would shed for him. Leland's passing had been swift and merciful, and I was glad that I had been the one to deliver it.

When I finally made the effort to turn and leave the room, I found Stoney waiting for me in the doorway. He was leaning against the frame, with his arms crossed, watching me with raised brows. A minute or so passed and we both said nothing, only continued to watch each other. As usual, Stoney was the first to break the silence.

"I see the old man didn't make it. What a pity," he snorted. "And you killed my protégé? Oh well. We're not all cut out to be vampires, are we, Lina?"

I don't have the vaguest recollection of attacking him. I only recall a surge of fury rising up the nape of my neck and the back of my skull, until the hatred finally consumed me and we were at each other's throats. There was an amused grin on Stoney's face as he dodged my attacks, but I ignored his arrogant sneer. Our fight was being carried out at an extraordinarily fast speed, one I was not accustomed to, and had I not been overwhelmed by my emotions, I may not have been able to keep up with him.

I was in a fiery rage, and I grinned with triumph when I dealt two blows to Stoney's face. Unfortunately, my victory was short lived when he grabbed me by my arm and flipped me over his shoulder. Stoney sent me crashing to the ground, and he made a move to hold me down onto the floor, but I managed to get loose and slide out from under his arms and climb onto his back. Once I wrapped my arms and legs around his body, I sank my fangs into his neck.

Stoney was doing his best to refrain from harming me. It was obvious he was keeping his strength to a bare minimum. I had a feeling he could sense my ebbing hatred for him, because it was radiating off of my body like sour fumes. No matter how much he desired me, he would have to fight back. I would not give myself to him willingly. He had nothing to hold over my head anymore. There could only be one of us walking away from this fight, and he had to face that fact sooner or later.

"You truly want to face off with me, Lina? You think that's wise?" Stoney growled, his deep tone catching me off guard. "Perhaps it's fitting that I end your existence. I gifted you with your immortality, after all, and since you never appreciated it, I may as well take it back."

With a hiss, he whipped his head backward, and the back of his skull collided with my forehead. I growled and sank my teeth further into his flesh as I tried to hold on, tearing a deep hole in his neck in the process. Blood poured from his wound, staining his pale skin and black coat. Stoney howled with pain and reached his hand around, seizing my left calf. Once he had a firm grip on my leg, he yanked me off of his back and sent me flying across the room.

I fell against one of the large metal shelves that contained dusty equipment and tools, and my head collided with one of the metal edges. The entire row of shelves shook from the abrupt impact, until finally they all came crashing down. I covered my head with my arms, bracing myself for contact. Heavy pieces of metal descended dangerously all around me, and I stiffened with surprise when a wrench struck me hard in the shoulder.

When the sky stopped raining metal, I assumed I had experienced the worst of it. I took to a stand, but as I did, a jagged metal rod that had been hanging off of the ledge on the top shelf finally rolled off of the lip and fell, heading straight for me. I tried to dodge it but I didn't make it in time. It was only angled slightly, but it was just enough to pierce my flesh. My jaw dropped as the rod cut clean through my body, and I shrieked. The burning sensation was unlike anything I had ever experienced before.

I glanced down to see that the tip of the rod was now poking out of my torso, and I subconsciously reached down to graze it with my fingertips. Still shocked by what had happened, I barely registered it as my legs gave out beneath me. I was on my knees now and gaping down at the rod in my chest.

Stoney stalked towards me, slowly, dissatisfaction oozing from him. He crouched down cautiously by my side and swept the hair out of my eyes. "I had such high hopes for you, Lina." Then, with a grunt, he cupped my chin and forced my mouth against his. Stoney's thin lips were ice cold, and I stiffened when he forced his tongue into my mouth. I wanted to fight him off, but I was in no position to do so.

He caressed the inside of my mouth with his slimy tongue, wrapped his hand around a fist full of my hair, and yanked my head backward. His black eyes glaring down at me, he finally said, "You could have ruled by my side forever, and I would have given you anything you desired."

With a sharp sigh, he released his hold and finally took a stand. "But you spat on my generosity, and now you will die for it."

Stoney crossed to the other side of the room, but he did not exit. Instead, he glanced over his shoulder to add, "It will only be another moment or so before you die, Ms. Holiday. Since you no longer have a soul, you will be sent straight to hell. Send Leland my regards."

I watched Stoney retreat with tears in my eyes. It wasn't supposed to end this way—he wasn't supposed to get away with all he had done! After everything that had happened, he should've been the one on his knees, seconds of away from death. Instead, it was I. But as I sat there, cursing at my failure, I realized that this was not my end. I glanced back down at the rod, finding that it hadn't gone straight through the center of my chest. It had fallen at an angle, and was positioned slightly to the left, barely missing my heart.

Stoney was still withdrawing, and I only had a few moments before he realized that I had not yet expired. With haste, I reached down and gripped the front of the rod and pulled. I bit down on my tongue to keep from making a sound while I removed the thick piece of metal from my body.

Now holding the blood-drenched rod in my hand, I slowly rose to a careful stand. Stoney had almost passed through the door when he stopped and froze mid-step. He turned his head around to glance back at me, but he was too late. I was already upon him. Before he could defend my attack, I drove the rod deep into his neck. Stoney gasped, his eyes on the verge of popping out of his head. I watched with triumph as blood dripped down the sides of his mouth and from the wound in his throat.

While he was still surprised by my attack, I yanked the rod from his throat and stabbed it into his back, holding it near to his heart. I made damn sure I would not miss it. I kept both hands on him, and when the vampire realized he could not break free from my stronghold, he began to panic.

This was it, the moment that I had been waiting for all my life—the moment when I finally destroy the monster who had taken away all of my reasons to live. I thought of my parents first; their brutal deaths coming to mind. Then, I thought of Leland, and how Stoney and Bill had tortured him up until his death. Finally, I thought of myself and how he taken away my mortality. An uncontrollable bloodlust swept over me, I wanted to kill him instantly, but I kept my hands still. I sought to savor the moment instead. After all, I could only stake him once.

"First you murdered my parents, then you forced me to become a bloodsucking parasite, and now, because of you, the only person I've ever truly loved is dead. You've taken away everything from me, you son of a bitch, and now I think it's about time that I take something back!"

He glared up at me. "I should have killed you that day in the kitchen," he gargled. "I should have never let you escape me!"

"Yes, you should have. Bad move."

With a quick thrust of my hand, I shoved the rod into his heart. "Rot in hell, asshole," I said, and twisted the makeshift stake deeper through his now punctured heart.

Stoney's black eyes widened with rage, and he opened his mouth to make one last resonating scream before he burst into bright red, gory slime. My face broke into a relieved wide smile when I realized Stoney's blood and guts covered almost every inch of my body. I had finally done it. Stoney was dead.

I made my way toward the open doorway, still holding onto the jagged rod tightly. I had decided to keep it as a souvenir; it would be a great reminder of everything I lost, and I had a feeling that somehow holding onto it would keep me going.

Chapter Twenty

The warehouse was nearly cleared out, but there were still a few werewolves left scavenging around, slaughtering the remaining bloodsuckers. The fierce cries of the vampires echoed through the halls as the wolves tore into them. Gabriel's clan would leave no survivors, and I was glad. I wanted each and every vampire that had assisted Stoney to suffer, but I avoided helping finish the rest of the vampires off. All I wanted now was to find Switch and Harvey and get the hell out of the creepy coven.

The air was heavy and laced with the aroma of death, and as I continued to wander the empty halls, I rubbed at my temples, lightheaded. The track lights above seemed to shine brighter than they ever had before, and I shielded my eyes from their intensity. I wondered if the odd sensations were on account of my hunger, but I dismissed the issue and trudged on.

Although I was pleased that Stoney was dead, I was not able to truly celebrate his passing. All I could think about was my father. Losing him left a giant hole in my heart, but I knew I couldn't give up. I had to carry on for my team, just as he had wanted me to.

After a few minutes of wandering aimlessly through the darkened halls, I finally spotted an exit. It was a side door that had been torn open from the middle, the metal looked to be slashed, and I figured that it had been a werewolf's doing. Relieved that I was finally free from the industrial prison, I wasted no time. I climbed through the exit door carefully as to not cut myself on the jagged metal, and hurried out into the night. I closed my eyes for a brief moment when the cool air swept over me, and I found the smell of fresh air intoxicating.

I trekked to the front of the building and found Harvey and Switch waiting for me near the warehouse entrance. A large man was standing off to the side, and I eyed the stranger with apprehension as I approached my friends. When I realized he was a werewolf, I relaxed. I assumed he had been requested by Gabriel to protect my team, and I was honored by the lengths the werewolves had gone to keep them safe.

Upon my approach, the man went on the offensive once he realized I was a vampire, but he did not attack me. I figured Gabriel must have spread the word to the others about my transformation and that I was off limits. I was thankful for that, as I was in no position to fend off a werewolf.

"Oh, thank god!" Harvey exclaimed, rushing toward me. "You made it out alive! Switch and I were so worried." There was joy in his eyes as he wrapped me up in his arms. I happily returned the gesture, but I grimaced as a sharp pain suddenly shot through me. I had forgotten about the fresh wound in my chest, and I knew it would not begin to heal until I fed.

Harvey quickly ended the embrace and examined me. When he noticed the gaping hole in my torso, his bright eyes narrowed with concern. "Lina, you're hurt?"

"I'm fine, Harvey."

"Are you sure? That looks terrible."

"I'm okay," I replied with a forced smile, hoping to convince him. "You don't need to worry about me."

He frowned as he continued to stare at my bare chest. "What happened to your shirt?"

"Don't ask."

"Lina, Harvey's right. That doesn't look good," Switch spoke up, gesturing to my wound. "We should get you to back to the vault as soon as possible."

"It's nothing, guys, really. I'm just glad to see that you two are safe."

"You don't know how relieved we are that you made it out of there," Switch replied. Then, he peeked over my shoulder. I knew who he was looking for.

"Leland...didn't make it."

I knew Harvey and Switch were devastated by the news, but they held their own. After a moment of silence, Harvey asked, "Did Stoney kill him?"

I shook my head, my bottom lip trembling at the memory of ripping out Leland's heart. "No."

Switch seemed confused by my reply. "Then who? Bill?"

"It was me," I confessed. "I killed him."

Harvey jaw dropped; he was taken aback by my admission. "Why?"

"Because he asked me to."

I knew I was on the verge of breaking down, but I managed to remain calm. I had to be strong for the both of them no matter how low I was feeling. I was their leader now—I was in charge, and I had to keep my head up and carry on. It was what Leland would have wanted.

"I'm sorry," I told them. "I tried my best to save him, but it was too late. He was deteriorating too rapidly. He knew he wasn't going to make it."

"Lina, it's okay," Harvey said, reaching his hands up to stroke my arms. "You did the best you could. You were brave and fearless throughout this entire ordeal. Leland was proud of you up until the very end. I know he was."

I said nothing, unable to agree with Harvey's reasoning. A part of me would always hold myself responsible for Leland's death, and nothing could change that. I had a lifetime to deal with my failure; an eternity. It was at that moment that I realized that the young woman I had rescued was not among us, and I questioned Switch and Harvey on her whereabouts.

"She was in need of a blood transfusion, remember?" Switch replied. "I did all I could before the vampires broke into the base, but she was still in pretty bad shape. One of the werewolves took her to a hospital."

"That was very kind of them. I hope she makes it."

Harvey nodded. "She didn't talk much while inside the cage. I know she was more traumatized by what was happening than anything else."

"I was right there with her," Switch agreed

"Yeah," Harvey agreed. "I was surprised she survived."

"She's been through a lot. I just hope she can put this terrible ordeal behind her a lead a normal, happy life,"

"I'm sure she will, Lina."

"We should go," I suggested, after a long look at our surroundings. "There's nothing left for us here. Besides, it will be dawn soon."

I watched Harvey and Switch exchange glances. It seemed they had forgotten all about my new identity, and I decided right then and there that I would not blame them if they wanted out. I would understand if they could not stand by my side now that I was a member of the undead. After all, they had spent their entire lives fighting against vampires.

With a heavy heart, I gave Harvey and Switch the option to leave the team. I explained that in his final moments, Leland had wanted us to stick together, but I told them that they were not obligated to stay under the circumstances.

As usual, Harvey responded first. "Lina, I know these past few days have been difficult on you, but I want you to know that no matter what has transpired—even though you're a vampire now, I will still fight these bloodsuckers right alongside of you."

Switch nodded his head in agreement. "As will I."

"You're sure you both can handle following a vampire's lead?"

"You're still the same ole' Lina Holiday I've always known," Harvey told me. "Becoming a vampire hasn't changed that."

"Besides, we've got a large stock pile of blood back at base," Switch offered. "So I don't think we have to worry about you feeding off of us."

I couldn't help but crack a grin, as I felt overwhelmed with appreciation. For the first time in what seemed like ages, I let go of my anger and frustrations and allowed myself to feel happiness. I could count on Switch and Harvey to always be there for me. Just now, they had proven their loyalty. Leland had been right when he'd said that they needed my guidance, but what I hadn't realized at the time was that I needed their companionship just as much.

"I don't know what I would do without you two."

"You don't have to worry about that, Lina. We aren't going anywhere," Harvey told me with a smile. "No matter what happens, we will always be a family."

Once I thanked the werewolf on standby, my team and I walked off towards the marina in the distance, where Stoney's boat was docked. Déjà vu swept over me at the sight of the old boat, and for a second I expected Stoney to emerge from the cabin. Although I knew my feud with Stoney was finally over, it was still going to take some time getting used to.

The three of us climbed aboard the empty boat; Harvey cast off the lines, I pulled up the fenders, leaving Switch at the wheel to set our course for Chicago. As the boat departed from the dock, I watched the vampire coven retreat into the distance, finding great solace when it finally receded from sight.

Finally feeling safe for the first time in days, I reclined on the bench seat near the stern and leaned my head back to gaze up at the starry night sky. As I stared up at the beautifully darkened atmosphere, I came to a rather depressing realization. Night was my future; I would never see another sunrise again.

But I would still carry on my mission—Leland's mission.

Now that I possessed superhuman abilities, I would be a much stronger force. My enemies would no longer have the upper hand. I was faster, stronger, and my senses were much more acute than they ever had been. With Harvey and Switch at my side, our team would be unstoppable. Vampires would ravage cities forever, and as long as they threatened the innocent, I would be hiding in the same shadows, waiting for them.

As the boat cut through the black waves and we headed home, my determination only grew deeper. My vow to defend humans had been strengthened, and I now promised to do so in my late mentor's name. Stoney may have thought that transforming me into a vampire would have changed who I was, but Harvey was right. It hadn't. I was still Lina Holiday, badass hunter, and ridding the world of vampires would continue to be my sole purpose in life.

For eternity.

About the Author

Chelsea Lynn Charters was raised in Bay City, Michigan, before she moved to Florida at the age of ten. Chelsea is 26 years old and currently lives in Orlando, Florida. She had a passion for writing at a young age and knew that she wanted to pursue a career as a writer when she graduated from high school. Her favorite genres to write are paranormal, horror, and romance. Chelsea has self-published two young adult novels, and has had one short horror story published in an anthology. You can follow Chelsea online at www.chelsealynncharters.blogspot.com.